DAWN THAT BREAKS

A MYNART MYSTERY THRILLER
BOOK 4

ADDISON MICHAEL

PAGES & PIE PUBLISHING
Author Services

2022 Pages & Pie Publishing

Print ISBN: 979-8-9862920-0-7

Library of Congress Cataloguing-in-Publication Data

Michael, Addison.

Dawn that breaks: a mynart mystery thriller/Addison Michael

Cover Design by Art by Karri

Editing by Tiffany Avery

www.addisonmichael.com

For my Dad who always said I could be anything I wanted to be as long as I worked hard to make the dream come true

DAWN THAT BREAKS

PROLOGUE
TWO DAYS AGO

Two bodies seated in the navy-blue Toyota Corolla were trapped as the car rolled uncontrollably down an Arkansas hill. After a short free fall, the car nose-dived into the ground. Loose articles of clothing flew out the open windows, littering the hillside, dangling from trees. Upon closer inspection, investigators would determine they were small articles of clothing. Clothes belonging to a two-year-old girl.

Far too many inexperienced drivers in this particular region had missed a turn, driven off the road, and over the edge. It wasn't uncommon. The Corolla followed suit and continued tumbling down the mountain. It fell until it smashed into the steep incline, then it flipped end over end picking up speed as it fell, careening towards its final destination.

The car caught on fire about halfway down the mountain. Flames lit up the night with promises of a bigger bang at the end. Like the grand finale of a fireworks show, the car hit the ground with one final blast. It was an explosion with breaking glass, crunching metal, and flaming embers.

The crash had been spectacular. No one had been around to witness the out-of-control Corolla. Even as the smoke rose high into the air, it somehow went unnoticed as the subtle light of dawn emerged. It was miles from civilization.

By morning, the smoke still rising into the sky had begun to subside. There was nothing more than a whisp of gray-black barely acknowledgeable by the occasional car that passed on the road above. A faint odor of acrid smoke tinged the early morning air.

If someone could see the smoldering car, they would be able to read the five words on the barely visible bumper sticker. Those five words identified the owner's abrasive personality.

…then back the f*** off.

There was no question. The car belonged to Carley Smith.

No one could have survived a crash like that. Nor had they. The real question would become was this merely an accident?

1

PAIGE

DAY ONE GONE

"We found Carley's car," Lieutenant Roger Higgins announced when we arrived. He had no more than shut his office door when the words were out of his mouth. It struck me that time must be of the essence here.

The sun was barely dawning when we walked into the police station in Arkansas. This was Stephen's turf. It was his home away from home. These were his people, not my people. They were the very officers who'd tried to pin my mother's murder on me from the beginning.

I sank down in a chair in front of Lieutenant Higgins' desk. Stephen and I sat in the chairs across from his desk, but the lieutenant didn't sit. Not at first. He leaned against the wall for a few seconds of silence. I immediately knew the truth. Whatever else he had to tell us was bad and my life would never be the same. My stomach knotted with dread. Finally, he sat on the edge of his desk. His face was drawn and a little pale. Were his eyes puffy?

Stephen followed my lead and began to sit but paused upon hearing the news. "That's great!" He stood back up as if to go to the car.

3

I said nothing. I waited. Call it mother's intuition, but I knew what would come next.

"There was an accident," Lieutenant Higgins said. "Her car went over the hill on Scenic Seven—"

"That's not a hill!" Stephen interrupted, sounding horrified.

"No," Lieutenant Higgins agreed. "It's more of a mountain. From what we can see, the car went over the edge and rolled several times down the hill into the ravine where it exploded."

"No!" Stephen exclaimed. "But they made it out, right?" Denial. It was the first step in the cycle of grief.

Lieutenant Higgins stroked his unshaven face as if trying to decide how much to say.

"No one could have survived that crash," Stephen said, realization dawning. I watched as the color drained from his face. Then his face crumpled, scrunching up as tears immediately began to stream from his eyes.

I looked from him to the lieutenant and back.

"This isn't actually happening, right?" I interrupted the silence. "After all we've been through, there's no way this ends with us losing our daughter in a random car accident. No way!" My own denial spewed out of me and crowded into my brain, pushing away the emotion I knew would undo me.

"No one could have survived that crash," Lieutenant Higgins answered both me and Stephen with those words. "We found Anna's clothes all over the mountainside," he added.

I stared at a spot out the window just past his left shoulder. He might have thought I wasn't listening when he told us this, but I heard everything. My mind vividly imagined Anna's loose clothes flying out the open windows as the car tumbled down the ravine. I tried to shut down those thoughts.

"I want to see her remains!" Stephen demanded. Disbelief was evident in his voice.

"Stephen! Stop, please," I gasped. "I think I'm gonna be sick." I ran out of the cramped office and into the restroom. I barely made it. I was sick alright. Multiple times. I wretched the remains of the last meal I'd eaten into the toilet.

Then I sank down onto the cold tile floor, my back against the equally cold wall. A sound erupted from me like a gasp. It turned into a loud sob. My mouth opened to breathe in the air that seemed to have left my lungs. No sound came out, but tears streamed from my eyes.

I closed my eyes but let the tears fall. Here, there was no one to judge me or my reaction. I pictured Anna on the day she was born. I had been all alone in the world until the doctor placed her squalling naked body on mine.

It's just you and me, kiddo, I had whispered. She'd stopped crying then and her body lie still. It was like she'd recognized my voice. It made sense. I'd spent months reading children's books to her during my pregnancy. They say unborn babies can hear you. So, I talked to her. It's true I was lonely, and I didn't have anyone else to talk to. But I imagined it formed this bond that would be unbreakable. Unbreakable until death.

As I'd laid there in the delivery room with Anna in my arms, I could feel her skin with its extra folds of baby fat. Then after I took her home, I'd feed her and stay up with her until all hours of the night. She'd never just wanted to sleep. It had taken a long time to sleep train her. I had been exhausted for the first three months, but it had all been worth it every morning when I saw her happy face smiling up at me from her crib.

In my mind, I could still hear her giggle for the first time. I remembered making the same silly face repeatedly just to get her to make that magical sound again.

Then there was the first time she'd given me a wet, slobbery kiss. She'd pulled my face to hers and smacked her lips against mine. Then she'd cuddled into my chest. There was nothing better than the feeling of a baby's unconditional love.

Now, I cried while sitting on that bathroom floor until there were no tears left to cry. Then I got up and made my way to the sink. After I rinsed my mouth and washed my face, I stared at myself in the mirror. I didn't even see myself. I didn't see the limp, stringy hair that hung from my head. I didn't see how bloodshot my eyes were from tears that violently erupted from them. I didn't see my pale reflection.

I felt in my heart what no one had confirmed. Anna was dead.

I tried to picture my life moving forward without my daughter. It was bleak and dark. It was a life without purpose, family, or connection. Without Anna, who was I? I could no longer call myself a mom. I had lost that privilege the night Carley ripped Anna from my life. While I was selfishly off trying to protect myself, who was protecting my child? How would I ever look at myself in the mirror again?

I made a fist and hit the mirror. I expected it to shatter. It didn't but pain exploded in my hand. That felt better. It felt deserved. I deserved to feel the pain. Bad people deserve to feel pain.

Finally, I summoned all my courage to walk out of the bathroom. I smoothed my rumpled t-shirt as I exited the comfort of my temporary isolation. It was the same t-shirt I had worn yesterday while traveling. Same jeans and under-clothes too. My Converse tennis shoes felt too tight on my feet.

"Paige Mynart?" an official-looking man in an ugly brown suit that was about two sizes too big addressed me. Either this was evidence that he recently lost weight, or he just didn't have enough money to buy a suit that fit his short, petite frame. His brown shoes didn't quite match his suit and I wasn't sure why that bothered me. I'd never seen him before. He wore small, John Lennon-style glasses and stood a full head shorter than me.

"Yes?" I asked, feeling more confused than curious.

He hesitated. "Were you married to James Friesen?" he asked.

"I am. I am married to James Friesen," I declared. *Dear God, don't tell me he's dead too*, I thought. I tightened my stomach and prepared myself for the worst.

The man handed me a manilla envelope. I took it without thinking.

"You've been served. I'll need your signature on the marked pages to take back with me," he commanded.

"Served?" I asked blankly. As I clutched the envelope, pain shot through my hand. With great concentration, I ignored the pain and pulled out the documents inside.

Original Petition for Divorce

My name is: James Edward Friesen
I am the **Petitioner**, the person asking for divorce.

My spouse's name is: Paige Erin Mynart
My spouse is the **Respondent.**

"Oh." I looked up at the small, pretentious man who appeared to be waiting for my answer. My eyes wandered to the parking lot. I stared into the distance for half a second.

"I'm going to need your signature," he said again. He was holding a pen in his hand and offered it to me. His tone was emotionless. From my vantage point standing taller than him, I could see a bald spot on the back of his head that he tried in vain to cover up with the rest of his hair.

I saw the empty line at the bottom of the page. I should have felt defeat and sorrow or grief over the finality of this news, but I didn't. I felt relief. James was alive. If he was serving me divorce papers, it meant he was alive. At the moment, that's all that mattered to me.

The pain in my hand overwhelmed me as I took the pen and bent down on a table to sign the divorce papers. My hand shook and I noticed it was swelling. Finally, I was able to clutch the pen between my thumb and first finger and sign a shaky signature. I straightened after the first two tears hit the paper and hastily swiped at my face.

If James wanted a divorce, there was a good reason. I had a feeling it had more to do with him and his mental state than me and mine. Although, hiding the fact that you might be a murderer from your husband is a pretty strong reason for a divorce. Granted, they had not found me guilty.

Still, I deserved this. I deserved all of this. Who did I think I was to believe I could be happily married and have a daughter of my own to love? My only goal once I was safe was to reunite with my daughter and live happily ever after. It was a fairytale for someone else. That would never be my life again.

"Paige?" I heard Stephen's voice behind me as I put the last swoop on *Mynart*.

Because I had used the last name *Mynart* on my passport, it was the name I had used to sign our marriage license.

"You okay?" he asked. Stephen's voice grated against what nerves I had left. I didn't want to talk to him. Not now.

I quickly picked up the envelope and shoved the papers inside. I thrust them at the man. "I don't need a copy."

"Are you sure?" The man fished a business card out of his pocket and extended it to me. He made up for his lack of height in the superior attitude he wore. "Why don't you take this in case you change your mind?"

I snatched the card and turned back to Stephen. "Fine. I'm fine," I'd lied. I found Lieutenant Higgins across the room and made eye contact with him as I walked his direction. He was talking to Detective Brandt and both went quiet when I approached.

"Do you know who owns the car for sale in the parking

lot?" I had noticed it when I'd walked in the building earlier today and again when my eyes had wandered out the window.

"The burnt orange Subaru?" Detective Brandt asked. "It's mine—well, it's my wife's—you interested?"

I nodded. I didn't care what the car was, I just needed one that ran right now.

"Tell ya what," Detective Brandt reached into a desk close by and produced a set of car keys. "Test drive it. If you like it, you can buy it."

"I'm going for quite a drive," I protested gently.

"I know where to find you." He shrugged. "Besides, I probably owe this guy a favor or two." Detective Brandt gave Stephen a half smile. I'd forgotten Stephen was there.

"Thank you." I nodded, accepted the keys, and quickly turned around. I desperately needed to be alone before my emotions welled up in me again. I started walking as fast as I could to get out of the building.

Stephen followed me quick on my heels. "Who was that?" he asked, pointing out the window to the lawyer who was walking slowly in the parking lot.

"No one who concerns you, Stephen," I snapped. Stephen was the last person I'd planned to cry to about my divorce. In the elevator, I quickly hid my swelling fist behind my back.

"Hey," Stephen said.

I watched the elevator doors shut and reluctantly turned to look at him.

"Don't do this, Paige," he said.

"Do what?" I asked.

"Don't shut down your emotions. You're not a bad person. This isn't what you deserve."

I flinched. It annoyed me the way Stephen seemed to get in my head at the most inconvenient times. There was just one thing. Stephen was wrong. This was exactly what I deserved.

"What do we do now?" I asked him, eager to change the subject.

"About what?" Stephen stared at me without comprehension.

"What are the next steps with Anna? What do we need to do?" I could hear the cold tone in my voice. I hated that Stephen was right. It was a thing I did. If I shut down my emotions, I could function. Still, I felt a little bad for my coldness. *Sorry, Stephen, it's self-preservation*, I thought. If I let down my guard with him, I would never recover from all the shared grief. We might bond over our sorrow. The sweat on my forehead betrayed my emotion.

"I'm going to investigate the crash site. Do you want to go?" he asked.

"God, no!" I said emphatically. What I wanted was to fade away someplace where no one would ever find me. "I'm surprised they're letting you investigate the accident. But then, this station never enforces boundaries when it comes to your personal investigations, do they?"

Stephen flinched at my bitter tone. "They don't know I'm going. They can't stop me, Paige. I won't believe it until I see it for myself."

I wasn't surprised. Stephen didn't obey orders when it affected his personal life. When the elevator opened, I marched quickly to the parking lot.

"Okay, where will you be when I get back?" he asked as he followed me. His eyes were soft.

I took a deep breath and blew it out, battling my impatience. His sympathy was the last thing I wanted. Nor could I give him mine. It didn't occur to me that no one would understand my grief more than he would. He and I understood the unspeakable pain of utter loss. We had both lost everything.

"I don't know, Stephen. I might take a drive. You can text or call when you have answers." I waved my phone at him weakly.

"Paige," Stephen lowered his voice. "Take care of yourself. The last thing I need is for something to happen to you, too." He put his hand on my shoulders and looked caringly into my eyes.

My stomach revolted again. It was all too much. I stepped to the other side of my car and emptied bile onto the gravel parking lot.

No, what Stephen wanted, or needed, would always be the opposite of what I wanted or needed. He seemed to need me, but what I needed, with everything in me, was to be alone.

2

PAIGE

DAY ONE GONE

I had arrived home to the Mynart Murder House. Only it didn't feel like my home anymore. It didn't smell like my home. Gone was the overpowering odor of dust and smell of cedar closet that had hit me so hard when I'd first broken into this tiny log-cabin-looking home. Gone was the sweltering heat of the summer that had gotten trapped inside when the windows wouldn't open. Gone was the air mattress where Stephen and I had made love for the first time and quite possibly conceived Anna.

I found myself looking out the back window. Gone was my target where I'd practiced shooting a gun for hours to learn how to protect myself. Gone were the days when I had never shot and killed another human being before.

I walked back through the house, taking inventory of what I needed to change to make this my home again. The smell of cinnamon roll that lingered in the air could not be from a year of baking them every single day. I didn't have to search long to find a Scentsy wall plug-in.

"Carley," I spoke through gritted teeth. I yanked the electric glass wax warmer out of its socket and slammed it to the ground. The glass broke with a loud, satisfying crunch and twinkle. For a fleeting moment, I felt a little bit better. I made quick work of locating all the matching wax warmers and slamming them to the ground the same satisfying way.

"That was fun," I said, feeling a little disappointed when I could not find any more. As the adrenaline wore off, I felt pain throbbing in my hand from where I'd hit the mirror after I'd heard the news about Anna.

I shook my hand, trying to ignore the pain. I took inventory in the living room. The new Italian leather couch that wrapped around the room had to go. The big screen TV mounted on the wall was fine. Carley was tacky and the way my home was decorated reflected it. Stephen must have given her full control. I rolled my eyes.

"Note to self, sell all things leather."

The dining room had a nice sturdy square dining table with four matching chairs.

"Keep," I noted with a nod.

The kitchen was fully stocked with neutral white and black dishes and a nice assortment of pans.

"Convenient," I commented. "Keep."

I turned toward the bedroom with dread. I reached out a hand to turn the doorknob. I opened the door a crack but stopped suddenly. Not only was my hand swollen to the size of a small baseball, but an unexpected surge of emotions flooded over me the minute I stepped two feet from the door that would lead me into the room. Like a movie with detail my brain must have blocked, the memory played.

I gasped, quickly moving my feet backwards because I could suddenly see the vivid memory of a stream of the brown-red viscous blood running toward my feet as I approached the bedroom doorway. It had been Stephen's blood. I had managed to step over Stephen's body and through the door to bend and check his pulse. I stood in that spot right now at this moment.

There was no trace of the blood on the floor now, not even one drop of evidence from that memory.

As I stood looking at that bloodless spot, I felt the hair on the back of my neck stand up. I grabbed the doorknob, shut the bedroom door, and walked away. Instant pain shot through my hand.

"Not today," I took several steps backwards. I turned to the kitchen, found a Ziplock bag in the cabinets, and went to the freezer. I put ice in the bag and put it on my hand.

The last room in the house to explore caught me off guard. It was clearly Anna's room. Immediately, tears sprang to my eyes. I paused at the door, taking in the blue and yellow twin comforter and matching curtains in the small room. The room was a disaster of toys and stuffed animals all over the floor. There was a board game sitting open with some pieces still on the board and others laying scattered on the carpet.

There were no memories here for me. A deep sense of sadness washed over me. I'd lost the last year and a half with my daughter. Time I could never get back. This room showed me who she was at that time. I swallowed hard, trying to get past the lump in my throat. A sob erupted out of me so power-ful, I collapsed on Anna's floor. For minutes, I allowed the tears to fall while my body shook with pent up emotion. I would never see Anna again. She had to be gone. The evidence was too real.

I was beyond exhausted. I took my shoes off and crawled into Anna's bed. Then I realized if my daughter was dead and gone, wouldn't she come visit me? Why would my mom, Darby, and Brittany come visit me after they were gone but not Anna?

Then I knew why. I didn't deserve Anna. I didn't deserve

happiness or joy in my life. I was destined for sorrow. *Bad people deserve the bad things that happen to them. I deserve this.*

I breathed in her fresh child-scent still etched into her pillow and cried myself to sleep. Until I woke suddenly.

Bang!

3

STEPHEN
DAY ONE GONE

Stephen couldn't sleep. He lay with a pillow over his head. At first it was because he thought the emotion that threatened to overcome him would burst in a loud torrent once his tears began and he wanted to muffle the sound. Then he kept the pillow there, pressing it hard against his eyes trying to erase the horror he saw earlier in the day when he'd investigated the crash.

After Paige had run out of the room, Stephen turned back to Lieutenant Higgins with intensity.

I wasn't kidding. I want to see what's left of the car. I don't believe it. I won't believe it until I see it, Stephen had said.

No, replied Lieutenant Higgins. *You're not going anywhere near that car, Stephen. I went out there myself so you wouldn't have to. No one survived. Anna's car seat was in the back. Her teddy bear and various articles of clothing littered that hillside. No parent should have to see that. As an officer in my precinct, I forbid you.*

Stephen felt himself slipping from the denial stage. But it didn't make sense. If Carley wanted a family, why hadn't she stayed with him? The answer came just as swiftly as his question and slapped him hard in the face. Because Carley hadn't wanted him. She had only wanted Anna.

She wasn't from around here, Stephen, Lieutenant Higgins was saying. *She didn't know those roads and curves like we do. It could have happened to anyone.*

His words were unhelpful. They dug a pit of horror and rejection and deep loss within Stephen's heart.

Where did they find the car? Stephen had finally asked.

A Park Ranger in Ouachita National Forest found it.

I'm going out there, Stephen had restated.

It wouldn't be the first time you disobeyed a direct order from me, but it would be your last. I'm putting my foot down, Stephen. Lieutenant Higgins made his final declaration.

Stephen hesitated as he thought through the consequences of Lieutenant Higgins' ultimatum. He'd made mistakes in his life. Most of them could be traced back to the women he'd desperately loved and his attempts to get them to love him back. He'd like to say he'd learned from them and moved forward, but his lapses in judgement only continued.

Evidence of this was a rumpled piece of paper he'd pocketed the other day. He could see it now sitting on the dresser along with his pocket change and cell phone. He had found the paper laying on the floor the day he and Paige had learned about Anna's death while they were still at the police station.

Stephen had noticed a small man in a suit approach Paige just as she was exiting the bathroom that day. Stephen stood back as the man served Paige papers. Stephen had seen it before and even had accompanied visits where papers had been served. He assumed they were from James. Who else?

He had already decided to go to the crash site and was getting ready to leave. Stephen needed to check on Paige before he left, but she was already doing what Paige did best. Retreating.

He saw the small piece of paper flutter to the floor from a

folder the man had been holding. Stephen had picked it up before she left the building and read it.

Dear Paige,

I guess neither of us is who we thought we were. I've made such a mess of my life. I can't drag you into that anymore. I'm the reason they found you. You could be dead now for all I know. All because of me. I'm sorry I doubted you. I don't deserve you. I'm going to get my shit together. Maybe the universe will bring us back together some day. Until then, please know that I love you. I have since the first time we met, and I always will.
~James

This handwritten note that had originally been in the stack of the marriage dissolution papers confirmed to Stephen the little man had indeed served Paige divorce papers. *James has impeccable timing*, Stephen had thought angrily, feeling mad at James. Of all days she could have been served. Did it really have to be the day she'd learned about Anna's death? *Way to kick her while she's down*, Stephen had inwardly chastised James' timing though there was no way for James to know what had happened.

He'd quickened his steps and caught up with her. He'd stepped in the elevator behind her.

Hey, he'd said to her as the elevator doors shut.

Paige had turned and looked blankly at him.

Don't do this, Paige, he'd said.

Do what? she'd asked.

Don't shut down your emotions. You are not a bad person. This is not what you deserve.

Paige had flinched. Stephen could tell he'd struck a nerve. He knew her so well. *It's the reason we should be together*, Stephen thought as he stared into her eyes. He had felt so much frustration. James would never know Paige the way Stephen did. Why should James get to explain his part in this? This was the last thing Paige needed to deal with. Angrily, Stephen shoved the note into his pocket.

Though clear evidence of her tear-stained cheeks and her puffy eyes gave her away, Paige had looked at Stephen void of emotion. It was scary when she got like that. She dissociated from her emotions, letting no one in. She had shaken her head at him. She asked him to call her when he had answers, turned and walked quickly to the parking lot. After that, Stephen didn't hear from her.

He tossed around, then settled on his back and stared up at the ceiling of his parent's guest room. His mind turned to what came next. It was what his mind returned to obsessively. Lieutenant Higgins had been right. Once he saw it, he couldn't stop thinking about the accident site. Stephen didn't regret investigating. Now he knew they were gone. He had to see it with his own eyes before he would allow the devastating loss to settle in his heart. The problem was, he couldn't *unsee* it now.

When Stephen drove out to the site, it didn't take long for him to figure out Detective Brandt was following him. He had been Stephen's friend since the day he joined the force. Right now, Stephen was sure he was there to inform Lieutenant Higgins of Stephen's actions. Stephen didn't care. He welcomed his friend's presence.

As he looked at the remains of the fiery crash, Brandt stood back as a silent observer. Lieutenant Higgins was right. No one survived this crash. When Stephen saw the car, he was convinced. Carley and Anna were both dead. He felt numb to his own pain as he stood considering the pain they must have experienced. The thought took his breath away.

He didn't view Carley's actions the same way Paige did. Stephen knew Carley didn't ever accept the word *no*. If she wanted something, she figured out a way to get it, without thinking about the consequences. Carley loved Anna and without Stephen, she had no legal right to see her. Carley lived in the moment. If Carley wanted to see Anna, she'd see her, and she wouldn't let anyone get in her way. Not him, not his parents, and certainly not Paige.

Paige was right about one thing. Stephen should have known better. Carley was impulsive and wild. He should have known he wouldn't tame her. But he never thought her capable of something like this.

When Stephen saw the car, all hope that it was a case of mistaken identity was dashed. Stephen and Detective Brandt made it to the crash site after parking the car and hiking half a mile down the steep hill. It was definitely Carley's blue Toyota Corolla. The snarky bumper sticker that was permanently affixed to the back was partially visible in the wreckage. He knew even though he could only see the words *then back the f*** off*. It was the only identifying feature visible on the car. That was Carley for you—always saying exactly what she thought without thinking about who it might offend. His heart stopped, and for a moment time stopped as well. His vision blurred. He shook his head and looked away.

Stephen gazed up the ravine to gauge the distance the car had fallen. If Carley had been going fast, the car would've flown off the road and fell straight down until it hit the ground. That's not what happened here.

How high up do you think that is? Stephen had asked Brandt, pointing to the top of the mountain. Stephen's throat had constricted with a lump that made it hard to swallow. He had cleared his throat in effort to hold his emotions at bay.

A fall from up there along Scenic Seven highway? I think I've heard eight hundred feet, Brandt had said, following Stephen's gaze up. *Truth is, they wouldn't have found the car at all had it not been for a park ranger. I hear the car was still smoking as the sun was rising. The ranger was doing the rounds. He called it in and discovered the BOLO. It was a match.*

Stephen had nodded, trying to keep perspective. *So, her car went off the road, but she must have just missed her turn and rolled the car down the hill—*

Mountain, Brandt had corrected.

Look how many trees are all over this mountain, Stephen had mused. *It's like the car found the one path with few trees and fell straight through it.*

Brandt had followed Stephen's gaze. His eyebrows pinched together. *That* is *strange.*

Then at some point, the car caught on fire, Stephen had said looking a little confused.

Brandt had nodded with concern evident on his face. *Listen man, are you up for this? You've been through so much. Why don't you leave the investigation to us?*

It just doesn't make sense, you know? Stephen had ignored Brandt's concerns. *Why was she here? She knew the way back home. She'd driven it several times. This wasn't the way home.*

She wasn't going home, Wilton, Brandt had stated directly.

Stephen had said nothing but nodded, acknowledging his point. He looked at the car with deep dread. Up until this moment, he had stood several feet away as if afraid to breach some invisible field. Once he crossed the line, he would have his answers. There would be no going back.

Look, I'm your friend, right? Brandt had asked in a low voice.

Right, Stephen had agreed, staring at the car, trying to get up his nerve to approach.

And friends need to be honest.

Right, Stephen had agreed again.

She left you, man. She took your kid and she attempted to disappear. No clue where she was going but she was driving fast enough to miss a turn and go off the road. Around here, a mistake like that is fatal. She was trying to get as many miles as possible between you and her before you found out and came after her.

Stephen had grunted his agreement and turned to the car.

The damage was extensive. The roof was crunched flat against the car and had trapped both of them inside. He tried to quelch the nausea. The window glass appeared to have been blown out. The metal was crunched like an accordion in the front. There was half an inch of space where the window glass would have been. The damage from the blast had tinged and tarnished the blue paint on the metal.

Stephen had moved forward, touched the car, and gasped. It was still warm. He bent and tried to peer into the cab. One window frame was bent up enough to get a peek inside. The stench of incinerated human flesh smacked him in the face. It was so overwhelming, he gagged and staggered back.

We're going to get those bones out of there to test for DNA, Brandt had said as if he was trying to find something useful to say. *It won't be easy, but I won't rest until we do.*

Why haven't they started the process? Stephen had asked. He tried to wedge one of the doors open but it was no use.

There was another accident in town where they dispatched the unit with the jaws of life. We put in an order for them to come here as soon as they're done. They should be here anytime, Brandt had answered.

Thank you, Stephen had acknowledged. *Then we should have a definite answer within—*

Twenty-four to seventy-two hours, yeah.

He could see bones in the passenger seat that Brandt had pointed out, but he couldn't see into the back seat. He walked around to the space where Anna would have been sitting. The metal was crunched too completely to see into the car.

Pain filled his blue eyes and sudden tears fell down his face. On the ground a few feet from the car lay a single shoe. It must have flown out the window when the blast occurred. It was Anna's shoe. Then Stephen's gaze fell on a small article of clothing. He recognized it. It was one of Anna's favorite t-shirts. Then he saw multiple items of Anna's clothes strewn everywhere. It was exactly as the lieutenant had said. Anna's clothes seemed to have gone right out the window as the car fell. Which meant—

These windows weren't blown out. They were rolled down. Stephen had tried to confirm but the car was too collapsed to tell.

Why would that matter? Brandt had asked, looking confused.

Because Carley didn't ever roll the windows down. She thought the country fresh air was overrated and she preferred the air conditioning. We had a whole argument about it once.

Not to mention, it's November, Brandt had said. *It would get pretty chilly driving around here with the windows down. So, this glass on the ground here must be from—*

The front windshield, Stephen had interrupted.

Right, Brandt had said, surveying the ground.

Suddenly, Stephen felt a deep desperation and heard a loud wail that came out of the deepest, darkest place in his soul. He had spotted an object on the ground that had been special not only to Anna but to him. They had been out shopping one day when Anna had wanted to rescue this poor stuffed bear. The button eye had come undone and was hanging by a thread. Stephen allowed her first animal rescue. Anna had named him "Eyeball."

Brandt walked away in the opposite direction as Stephen stalked over, picked up the bear, and sank to the ground. He clutched the teddy bear to his chest and sobbed in devastated acceptance.

Lying in bed now, Stephen remembered Paige's reaction when he tried to tell her what he saw. He'd only gotten as far as telling her about Anna's clothes all over the mountainside when Paige had interrupted.

She's gone, Stephen, Paige had said.

They're going to get the bones out of the car to test for DNA—

Stop! Paige had hissed. *I can't prolong what I already know. I don't want to wait around with false hopes. I don't want to play detective. Anna's gone. I feel it. In my bones.*

At the thought of bones, Stephen turned his thoughts to the process for extracting the bones from the crushed car and sending them off for DNA. It was more complicated than he would have guessed.

Not counting the amount of time it would take for them to extract the bones from the car, there was the process of sending them off to the crime lab. Once at the lab, Stephen knew it would take a total of twenty-four to seventy-two hours to complete the actual task. They couldn't hold a funeral until they had confirmation. They needed confirmation to issue a death warrant.

It didn't matter. Stephen knew what the results would be. That thought brought on a whole new wave of emotions. Stephen had grown up thinking tears were weak. But for the first time in his life, he could not hold back his tears.

When Stephen finally fell asleep, his dreams were tortured. He felt the chaos and fear of driving over a cliff. He felt himself plummeting toward the ground. Then his whole body jerked as the car hit a tree and flipped end over end. The effect was nauseating. Then he felt his whole body heat up until his discomfort level was unbearable. He was burning alive. And then there was nothing but a black abyss.

He jerked awake then. He was sweating and breathing heavy. If the DNA tests confirmed Anna and Carley were really dead, Stephen would also mourn the fact that this had been a wretched way for them to go.

4

CARLEY

DAY ONE GONE

Carley sat in her new mini mansion in Greenfield Village, a ritzy, upscale neighborhood in Kansas City, Missouri. It was a posh community full of wealthy citizens who like to mind their own business. At the moment, she was stalking obituaries in Little Rock, Arkansas, and Brighton, Missouri.

"Shit!" she swore to herself as she found no signs of funeral proceedings for herself or Anna Wilton. This was only going to work if everyone believed they were dead. She chewed on a nail and sat back, admitting defeat.

Carley had a pretty good life until she found herself in the last place she ever wanted to be. Domestic hell. Those days when she looked in the mirror, she didn't see her own reflection, she saw the reflection of her mother. She despised her mother. Which was another perk to disappearing. No more bothersome, obligatory conversations with family members who didn't add to her life.

There had been one complication—Anna. Carley thought she'd be able to break up with Stephen Wilton and never even think twice about Anna. But something about that little girl had gotten under Carley's skin. There was something so sad and vulnerable about her. No matter how much her dad tried to make her happy, she just missed her mom.

What if Carley could make Anna forget her mom? Or better yet, what if she became Anna's mom? Anna reminded Carley of a three-year-old version of herself. Sure, Anna was only two and a half, but she was far advanced for her age. Anna was sassy and smart. She was already speaking in complete sentences. She was strong-willed and energetic. She knew how to defend herself. Like the time she'd punched a kid in preschool when he bullied her. Anna had told Carley all about it when Carley had picked her up that night from her grandparent's house.

With a mom like Carley, Anna might thrive. Her own mother had shut Carley down as a child and "molded" the pieces of her that made Carley a unique and carefree, albeit *wild*, child in attempt to tame Carley. Carley hadn't needed to be tamed. She'd needed to be set free. Just like Anna. So, she paid a visit to her Uncle Scott.

Her Uncle Scott was the head of the Kansas City crime syndicate. Or as he cleverly like to call it, *The Milternett Family Organization*. For years, he'd been begging Carley to come take a job working for him. She was an accountant by trade. Numbers were the only detailed thing about her. Scott's organization had a constant opening in that department. It paid well.

Not only would Anna be safe with Fria, the nanny, but she would also be under twenty-four-hour surveillance from cameras around the home. There was a bodyguard on property every day. Not to mention, Carley's office was on the ground level of her new home. No one would ever take her little girl from her. They wouldn't even get close enough to try.

Carley had no desire to live under any man's thumb. Which is why she'd been denying her uncle's free gifts of cash recently. It would appear she had contradicted the passionate stand she'd taken to live on her own.

This is different, she justified. She would do a job and get paid. There was nothing demeaning about that. She would have a nice paycheck and a beautiful home where she would live comfortably and make a nice life for her daughter.

She thought back to the conversation she'd had with Uncle Scott, who was not really her uncle at all. He had been one of her mother's many revolving boyfriends who'd continued to take care of her and her sister long after the break-up. She had come up with a plan that involved taking Anna and disappearing. Who better to make someone disappear than a crime boss?

With a determined resolution in her heart, Carley had phoned Scott Milternett.

Uncle Scott? she had tried to summon the sweetest, most southern charm voice she could muster when he answered. She knew he would still be miffed at her for refusing his last several cash gifts.

Uncle Scott? he had asked. *It was just "Scott" the last time we talked but if you would like to talk about that money, I'm still in town. Just released from the hospital. We should meet. Phone conversations aren't safe.*

Carley had agreed. She'd drove to where he'd been released from a hospital after a near-fatal hunting accident, surviving an arrow to his stomach. She had met him in his private hotel suite. Conversations such as these were not to be had in public.

I need you to help me disappear, Carley had walked right into his suite, barely letting the door shut behind her, and announced her news to him.

Why would you want to do that? Scott had asked in a low voice. He'd gotten up from the table where he had been eating room service. He kissed her cheek in greeting and motioned for her to sit down.

I think my relationship with Stephen put me in danger. It would be best for everyone if I just disappeared.

Okay, so come on up to Kansas City and we'll keep you hidden and protected, he promised.

I need more than that, Carley had insisted. *I need people to think I'm dead.*

Your mom will go crazy! Scott had protested.

No, she won't. She'll be fine. We never even talk. And if we do this, you must never tell her the truth. I mean it, Scott. Never.

If I agree to help you, and I'm not convinced I should, I need to know the whole truth. It seems so extreme. What else is going on? You're not afraid of anything.

Fine, Carley had dropped the sweet act. *I've got an ex-boyfriend who won't let me go. You know the sentimental type who believes in marriage? I haven't seen the last of him. I considered sticking around because he has this daughter, Anna. She deserves someone who will love her and pay attention to her as she's growing up. I'm the best thing that ever happened to her—*

You want to be a mom? Scott had interrupted her with astonishment in his voice and perhaps a little respect.

Yes. I'm more her mom than her own mom has ever been. And I'm damn good at it, too. Carley had pounded the table for emphasis.

So, it's not just you who needs to disappear? Scott had asked slowly, putting together the big picture and the full scope of the request. *You want me to help both of you fake your deaths?*

Carley had nodded with relief. Finally, he was getting it.

If we do this, you need to do something for me, Scott had requested.

What's that? Carley had felt instant dread over his words. She had known this would be a negotiation.

We need a new accountant. You need a new place to stay. Let me put you up in a house and pay you to do our books. Scott had issued his demand. Carley knew better than to argue. She had known there would be a price if he helped her and Anna disappear.

Scott, if this accounting is illegal, and I get caught, my cover will be blown, and I'll lose everything. I'll lose Anna. I'm going to be a mom now.

Scott had waved his hand dismissively. *It'll be your job to keep us legal.*

Okay, Carley had agreed and shook his hand, sealing the verbal contract. She felt relieved until the night she had to stage her and Anna's death.

Carley thought the plan was brilliant. She wanted to keep it simple. They would drive Carley's car off a cliff and Carley would disappear within The Milternett Family Organization, leaving everyone to believe both she and Anna were dead. Carley had told Scott the less she knew about details, the better. She still held hope that she could someday plead plausible deniability.

Right on target, Scott had pinged her phone with the location. Carley was there on time as was Scott. The steep hills around the Scenic Seven highway would be the best place to drive a car off a ravine. Carley had given Anna cough syrup, so she would sleep as she transferred from her from her own car to a new car seat Scott had bought and installed in his BMW X7. Carley was about to hop in the driver's side to drive the car to the starting point and put it in neutral. The downhill incline would take care of the rest.

But then Scott stopped her. He'd popped his trunk and Carley immediately smelled a rank odor that she had never quite smelled before.

Help me out here, Scott had commanded.

Ew, what's that smell? she had asked, but she put it together before she walked around to the trunk of the car. Uncle Scott had shown up with two decaying bodies and Carley could not look the other way.

What the hell, Scott? Carley had hissed while gagging.

Trust me, lack of bones will make this suspicious. The fire will burn everything but the bones.

What about dental records, Scott? Jesus, I thought you did this for a living! Carley's tone had been sharp. *And those are adult bodies. They aren't the same size as Anna!*

You ever been to the dentist? Scott peered at her.

Well, no, actually, Carley admitted. She ran her tongue over her teeth. She was blessed with very nice teeth and didn't like going to the doctor for any reason.

Has she? he asked nodding his head toward the car where Anna slept soundly.

No, Carley answered.

Then don't worry… I pulled a few of their teeth so their dental records won't match anything. Trust me, after the car flips so many times, it'll crunch up like an accordion. No one will even be able to get into the car to access the bones. Just knowing bones are there will be enough to prove there were incinerated bodies. Believe me, police only see what they need to see to close a case. I've seen it time and time again.

You better be right about this, Carley said through gritted teeth. Reluctantly, she had assisted Scott with transporting the bodies. So much for plausible deniability.

Then Scott had planted an explosive device under the hood of her navy-blue Toyota Corolla. They had put the car in neutral and let it roll from the top of the road that led into a hill. The car had picked up enough speed and continued straight when the road had curved, driving over the edge of the road as planned. It was late at night and this stretch of highway was empty. There were no other witnesses. After the car rolled a few times down the hill and hit the ravine below, they had blown the bomb. They had timed it perfectly to explode at the same time the car hit the bottom.

See, Scott chuckled, his eyes twinkling with excitement at the sound of the explosion. *There's not a lot left down there to investigate. This isn't my first rodeo.*

Carley knew Scott had never been to a rodeo in his life, but she got his point. He did appear to have thought through her objections. Anyway, even if they did discover her treachery, Carley would be long gone and fully immersed in her new life.

She wasn't naïve. She knew this new life would come with some pretty steep consequences. One, Stephen would kill her if he ever found her. Two, Scott would kill her if she ever betrayed him. It was a good thing she was smarter than both of those men put together. Her new life plan was to stay one step ahead of both of them at all times.

"Carley!" Anna's excited voice shrieked loudly as her little feet ran down the stairs. "It's a Barbie mansion!" Anna must have opened the present Carley had left in her room. She came running in, her blond curls bouncing. Fria followed slowly behind her.

Carley smiled as Anna tackled her in a hug. The Barbie mansion was only the beginning. She'd provide Anna with everything her mother had not provided for her growing up. This new lifestyle was part of the bigger picture. Carley was going to give Anna the life she deserved.

Still, as Carley turned her focus from the computer to Anna, she couldn't shake the feeling that this might be her last hurrah.

5

PAIGE

DAY ONE GONE

Bang!

I awoke with a neck cramp and my body contorted in a weird position on a twin bed. The room was unfamiliar to me. Then it all came flooding back to me. I must have fallen asleep on Anna's bed.

Bang!

I jumped with a start and covered my mouth to keep from screaming. I half thought this was some strange dream and I was still sleeping. My foggy mind was not fully awake, so I didn't realize I was now standing and walking through the darkness.

I was outside the door to the master bedroom. Only the door wasn't closed anymore. Someone or something had thrown the door open. My body began to shake involuntarily.

I peered through the darkness into the Mynart Murder Room. I took a step forward, moving my body reluctantly each step. I looked down at my feet. My toes were over the threshold. As if I was in a trance and I could not control my actions, I stepped into the room. Not wanting to look, but unable to fight the intense desire to know what was in the room, my eyes searched the wall. They found heavy red blood dripping down the wall. It was the place where I had brutally shot Ray and killed him. Because Ray's blood had poured from six holes in his body, I was surprised there wasn't more blood stained on the wall. Still, the vision of the blood didn't help my shaking body.

"Hello, Paige."

I knew that voice. I'd know it anywhere. The hair on my neck stood up. It was Ray.

"We have unfinished business," he said. "You were supposed to die and take your bloodline with you."

I screamed as I spun around. I fell against the dresser. I felt instant pain, but I couldn't look away from Ray Lennon. He was the man who had tried to murder me. The man who was my biological father. He was sitting in the exact chair where he'd sat the last night I'd spent in this house before I'd fled to Canada. He was holding a revolver in his hand. He sat as calmly as I'd ever seen him. It was the exact one he'd held the night he'd tried to kill me.

He's not real, I told myself. *You know this is a projection of your guilt*, I tried to reason with myself. Still, I couldn't move. My fear left me frozen.

"I killed you," I said when I found my voice. My body was shaking so hard my teeth were chattering. I clenched my jaw shut, trying to still my body.

"How did that work out for you?" Ray asked, his tone mocking.

"I shot you at least five times. There was blood everywhere. You are dead."

"The name of the game is Russian roulette," Ray said as he pointed the gun to his head and pulled the trigger.

"No, no, no, no," I moaned. I couldn't do this again. I could not relive that night. I was frozen in my position. Unable to move, to blink, or to breathe.

Ray laughed that deep, sinister laugh then pointed the gun at me and pulled the trigger.

I turned and ran out of the room. I grabbed my coat, which I had haphazardly discarded on the washing machine. I slipped my feet into a pair of slippers before I opened the back door. I put the coat on as I ran. I was running through the dark woods alone. My feet on the ground were the only sound for miles. Leafless branches smacked me in the face. I ducked at the last minute and narrowly missed a thick branch that might have knocked me out.

Up ahead, I could see a light. I ran toward that light until my lungs burned. I was unaware of the scratches on my face and small trails of blood they produced. I ran until I found myself in a clearing. Then I stopped. I stared at the view, gasping for breath.

In the distance, I could see a little white house with forest green shutters. The single light on in the house illuminated the otherwise dark, open field surrounding the house. I was looking at the back of the house and what seemed like a mile of open field. Convinced no one was behind me, I walked forward, not thinking, just moving. It was as if I was drawn to the light.

Beep. The sound of my phone reminded me it was there, in my coat pocket. I hadn't seen it all day. But it was right where I had left it. I put my hand in my pocket and looked at it. That light was the only thing I could see in the darkness. The battery was low but that didn't concern me. There were messages from Stephen. That didn't surprise me.

Stephen: *You ok? Just checking on you. Let me know if you need anything.*

Stephen: *Hey, haven't heard back from you. Assuming you made it to the Mynart House?*

Stephen: *Paige, the outdoor cams just triggered. Saw you running. It's 2 a.m. You ok?*

I stifled my irritation. He was trying to be helpful. He had sent the messages all this afternoon. I dialed Stephen's number. I knew he'd be up since he'd just texted me.

"Hey," I said. I was still walking toward the white house.

"Paige? Oh, thank God. Are you okay?" Stephen asked.

"I'm not okay and I might never be okay again," I spoke honestly, my voice cracked, and I felt tears threaten to fall yet again.

"I know. I understand," his voice betrayed his emotions. "I saw you running on the cams. Are you in danger? It's really late. What are you doing?"

"I'm in an empty field walking toward a white house."

There was a beat of silence. "That was Carley's house," Stephen said with intense sadness in his tone.

I had no love for Carley. She was the reason Anna was gone. But I hadn't considered that Stephen had lost two people he'd loved at once. Carley was the second woman he'd bought an engagement ring for.

"I'm sorry for your loss, Stephen," I said quietly.

"It was Ray's house before Carley lived there," Stephen bypassed what I'd said.

"What?" I stopped walking abruptly.

"That's how Carley and I met. I thought the house was vacant. She caught me trying to break in to search Ray's house. It's how I found the piece of evidence that put your mom's murderer behind bars," Stephen explained.

"Wow, I didn't know," I said.

I was now at the house. I walked around to the front porch. I assumed the house was vacant.

"You still there?" Stephen asked. "Listen, Paige, I need to tell you about the accident site."

I took a deep breath. I didn't want to hear about the accident. I wanted to put my finger in my ears and hum loudly to block it all out. But I couldn't block the way life was unfolding right now.

"What about the accident?" I asked. "Please, Stephen, I don't want any horrible details, just tell me what I need to know."

"It was definitely Carley's car. Anna's clothes were all over that mountain side. I found her favorite—" Stephen's voice cracked.

I waited quietly.

"Her favorite teddy bear. It was them, Paige. They're running the DNA and we'll have confirmation in the next few days." He was crying now. Soft, muffled sniffles came across the phone.

I covered my mouth and began to cry as well. "I can't believe this is happening."

"I know." Stephen took a ragged breath.

"Listen, Stephen, I gotta go. My phone is dying."

"Promise me you'll be okay, Paige," Stephen pleaded.

"I'll be okay, Stephen." I hung up before he could answer and shoved the phone in my pocket. I had reached the house. I hesitated at the door. I wiped my eyes and worked to shove down the emotion that threatened to undo me. For a moment, I had forgotten what I'd been running from. No matter where I ran, I couldn't outrun this loss. The realization was momentarily staggering.

I put my hand to the doorknob. I thought it would be hard to get in the house but to my surprise, the door was unlocked. I walked right in. I immediately noticed the similarities between Carley's house and the one she had been occupying with Stephen—mine. Her home also smelled like cinnamon rolls. Her furniture and home décor was practically the same. One single light from a back room in the house cast eerie shadows. I squinted a little as I looked around.

"She was a much better mom than you," Ray's deep cynical voice sounded behind me. I whirled around.

"Are you following me?" I gasped. I couldn't see him anywhere.

Ray laughed again. "You didn't know any better. Your mom was a terrible human who cared only about herself."

"Go away!" I yelled. "You have no business here!"

"But it's my house. I have more business here than you." Now the outline of Ray's human form illuminated in the dark house.

"What do you want from me? Did you think we should reconcile and be a family?" I snarked, using the words I so clearly remembered him saying as he pointed the gun at me that fateful day years ago.

"Admit it. You wish now I would've killed you. You wish that bullet would've hit you not your boyfriend. What do you have to live for? I mean, really? How many people are dead because of you? Killing me only set off a chain of events that led to the death of your only daughter. The daughter you never deserved in the first place. Just like your mom."

"Stop it!" I screamed, but I started crying. I couldn't deny anything he said. I had shot Ray and killed him. He had been my father and I had killed him. The legal system would say it was self-defense. He was in my home, trying to kill me. Those circumstances didn't leave me any less damaged.

I'd killed someone else too. A man in Georgia. His name was Johnny Jenkins. He had broken into my safe house. He was waiting there for my return. All hell had broken loose, and I shot him in the head too. He was a corrupt ex-prison guard doing the bidding for my corrupt ex-boss, the lieutenant turned serial killer who I'd also had a hand in killing.

Other people had died as a direct result of my actions. I

thought of my best friend from Canada, Brittany Garbo. At the thought of Brittany, I felt sick and tears fell harder. I hadn't killed her, but she was dead because of me.

Then there was Joe. Joe was a dedicated US Marshal who had been my guard for over a year. He didn't have a family. He'd committed his life to reside with me and keep me safe from the deranged ex-lieutenant. Joe was patient and kind. He put up with a lot from me. He taught me to fight, to meditate, and find peace within. He, too, was dead because of me. He'd died protecting me.

"Why has there been so much death?" I whispered.

"Because you're a bad person, Paige." Ray's deep unmistakable voice answered my question. I could clearly see him now. I could see his dark hair and his green eyes. Eyes that were like mine. Blood poured from a hole in the center of Ray's forehead. If I didn't feel such horror at the gruesome sight, I might have felt proud. My shot was typically off but I had managed to hit him dead on. His chest was soaked with blood. This was extra evidence of where I'd hit him in the chest.

I closed my eyes and screamed.

Ray laughed.

I took three deep breaths and opened my eyes. I knew what I needed to do. I'd done it with my mom. I'd told her *goodbye*. I released her. I needed to tell Ray *goodbye* as well.

The words stuck in my throat when Ray pointed to a drawer. Tears flowed freely from my eyes, down my face so strongly, I had to blink hard to see. I remember a time when the tears wouldn't come. Now, they wouldn't stop. I walked toward the drawer and opened it. I gasped and staggered backward.

It was a gun. A revolver that looked just like the one Ray used the night he'd died. I stared at it, fighting the darkness. My emotions overwhelmed me. I impulsively grabbed the gun. I would take it.

But only for protection, I reasoned with myself. I put the gun in one pocket of my coat.

I reached deep and found my courage and my voice. "I'm leaving. Do not follow me. Stay in your house. You have no business in mine!"

I walked out the front door.

Good riddance, Ray Lennon.

6

JAMES
DAY ONE GONE

James lay in the darkness staring at the ceiling. He felt in his gut that something was wrong—the kind of wrong that wasn't easily fixed. He couldn't describe it exactly. It was just this intense anxiety that settled over his chest and held him down, making it difficult for him to breath.

Breathing was something he had learned a lot about since arriving at rehab. They called it *returning to the basics*. He took a deep breath in, held it as long as he could, and let it out slowly. A few more times and he felt his anxiety subside a bit. Sometimes, this breathing exercise put him back to sleep. No such luck tonight.

Breathing wasn't the only thing James was learning about. As it turned out, James was quite a runner. The first day he ran, he understood, for the first time in his life, how freeing the exercise was. When he ran, he felt alive. Upstate New York was as cold as Canada. The thought of running out in the cold was not appealing.

But if James was honest, nothing was appealing when he'd first arrived at the men's treatment facility. That was less than two weeks ago. He realized he had a lot of work ahead of him.

It was during a long stretch of free time on that second day that he'd become a runner. From that point on, when he found himself with an hour between classes and meetings, he would run. He couldn't stand the quiet time. Time alone with his thoughts was unbearable. It always had been.

In the quiet time, his thoughts harassed him. He'd deeply loved two women in his life. Both women had deceived him for their own purposes. Therefore, James determined, he must be unlovable. Unworthy of their honesty. He'd tried so much harder the second time he was married, though it had been a very short time. He vowed to love Paige harder than she loved him. It had been working too.

It would have worked forever had that stupid ex-boyfriend of hers not shown up more alive than she'd remembered him being. Anger boiled inside him every time he thought about Stephen Wilton, and he just wanted to punch something. Instead, James ran, punishing himself for the darkness of his thoughts.

Some days he ran hard and fast as if trying to outrun his mind. On other more peaceful days, he ran at a nice, even pace. He'd even started to enjoy running.

Then there was the view. A beautiful lake practically surrounded the facility, making him feel like he was on an island. He could see the water from his room. He'd moved his bed so that the first thing he could see every morning was the sun coming up, reflecting over the lake. In the afternoons, he'd find a place outside to watch the sun cast a glow as it set. When he went to bed at night, he stared at the moon and thought about Paige.

He couldn't help it. He loved her. Maybe he always had. Can you find your first love in kindergarten? James didn't know the answer to that, but he guessed he was just a hopeless romantic. Someday, he would meet his long-lost soulmate. Thing is, he already did. But then he'd blown it.

Thoughts of Paige caused sleep to elude him for hours every night. He had only slept well when he'd been with Paige. He had been happy when he was with her. That she had a child only made Paige more appealing as a life partner to him. He'd always wanted children. He knew he was still young, but he feared he wouldn't have any of his own now. Anna had become the precious little beam of sunlight he'd always imagined he'd see when he had a child. His new family had cast a happy glow in his life.

Wherever they were, he hoped Paige and Anna were happy. He no longer wondered if Paige was alive. His lawyer had communicated via email that she'd signed his divorce papers without a fight. He hoped he'd done right by her in the end by releasing her from this sham of a marriage.

She knew the truth about him now. As did he. He'd had to get real and admit it to himself. As it turned out, he really was an addict. The incurable type. The unlovable type. He would see Paige again someday. But not to get back together. He owed her amends. Making amends for the wrong he'd caused was part of the step process he was learning. He had to admit to a higher power, himself, and another person what he'd done wrong. After he'd asked his higher power to remove his short-comings, then he needed to make a list of who he'd harmed and ask for forgiveness.

If he'd learned anything in his short time here, it was not that he had mommy and daddy issues or abandonment issues. His issues were more about lack of purpose. James got bored easily. When he got bored, he thought too much. His mind was a dark mine of trouble.

That's why he'd taken up running. There was nothing more freeing than pushing his body physically. When he exercised, it helped him stay ahead of his demons. His thoughts weren't as dark. After a week, he didn't mind being alone with his thoughts as much.

The first day of rehab had been terrifying. In addition to those dark, torturous thoughts, he blamed and shamed himself into wanting to take his own life.

"You're in the right place," counselors told him.

"You aren't alone," they said. "Others here feel the same way." The counselors were speaking from experience. They had similar pasts. They had found the path of recovery and now wanted nothing more than to give back. He had started working through this with the help of Dr. Burkshaw.

You're an empath, James. Do you know what that means? Dr. Burkshaw had asked him.

No, James had felt stupid even admitting he didn't.

It's such a powerful thing if you can find a way to harness it. Without work, it means you take on the emotions and feelings of other people around you. If they feel pain, you feel pain. If they feel anger, you feel anger. Only it's not yours, it's theirs.

That sounds about right but I don't want it, James had acknowledged. *Can you help me get rid of it?*

No, it's a gift. Many human beings these days lack the love, compassion, and empathy for others. They have tunnel vision and are on a quest to conquer life. When you encounter those people on a mission, they tend to run you over. They don't see you. You might have even mistaken their emotions as your own. Have you ever noticed your mood shift suddenly? Dr. Burkshaw had asked.

James had thought about it for a minute. Several instances popped into his head. He nodded slowly. *Yeah, I can be having a great day and walk into a place and suddenly feel anger and hostility,* James had recalled the instance when Paige and Stephen had crime scene photos spread out across his dining room table when he'd come home one night. In that moment, he didn't know if he was offended by the violence they'd brought home, or by their close proximity to each other as they discussed the case.

The answer was both. He had felt their outrage over the

senseless violence and the driving desire for vengeance in the name of the law. But he'd also felt their closeness and love in mutual respect for each other.

The counselor had explained it might have just been a moment. But James didn't believe that. After that night, he decided if he took himself out of the picture, it might give them a chance to finish what they had started. Before Paige believed Stephen had died, they had made a beautiful child together. James thought they might actually make great parents if he stepped aside and gave them the chance.

That brought him to the hardest topic of all. Anna. His beautiful little daughter by marriage. His first marriage had failed after his wife had terminated a pregnancy during a time when they had agreed to try to have kids.

Somewhere in his childhood, James had been taught it wasn't manly to want children. Yet, the desire to have them was stronger than anything else he wanted in life. He adored his niece and nephew and couldn't wait to have his own. He'd loved Anna like she was his own. He also believed he and Paige would have a few of their own to add to the family.

Then he learned Paige was wanted for murder. The day she'd been taken in, he'd bolted. They had arrested her under suspicion of murdering her own mother. He didn't give Anna a second glance, he had just run. Now he knew there was a term for that. Abandonment. He had abandoned her. Only, Anna was young enough, she might never remember him. She had her real dad now. She didn't need James. What James hadn't counted on was how much *he* needed Anna and Paige.

They had been a family. Family stood together like a pack. When one family member separates, you go find her and bring her back. He should never have left Paige. He should have given her a chance to explain. He could have at least heard her side of the story.

When James arrived in rehab, he knew Paige would never

forgive him for leaving. He wouldn't blame her. Then Dr. Burkshaw had asked him a question he knew he needed to think about before coming to a conclusion. It was a question that would take some work to answer in a healthy way.

Can you forgive yourself?

7

STEPHEN

DAY TWO GONE

Stephen came to work a little earlier than usual to find Lieutenant Higgins in his office with the door shut. Stephen sat at his desk. He told himself he needed to get a jump start on a few reports he was behind on. Not that he could focus on anything right now, let alone reports. But the truth was, he couldn't sleep. He was sick of lying in the darkness.

"Stephen, come in here a sec," Lieutenant Higgins requested. He stood in the doorway of his office, leaning out. Stephen jumped a little at the intrusion into his thoughts. He didn't know anyone was here yet.

"What's up?" Stephen asked as he walked into his superior's office.

"Swing that door shut behind you, would you?" Lieutenant Higgins commanded as he sat at his desk.

Stephen knew there was no one else in the office but he did as he was instructed.

"I hear you went out to the site of the accident yesterday," Lieutenant Higgins said.

Stephen nodded. He hadn't made any secret about his intention.

"This isn't the first time you directly disobeyed an order that came from me."

"I know. I can't just—" Stephen attempted to defend himself but the look on the lieutenant's face stopped his words.

Lieutenant Higgins held up his hand. "It occurred to me that I've let that slide far too many times. I rationalized it when you were investigating Krysta Mynart's murder. It was a gray area given your relationship—well breakup, with Paige. This is different. This accident involves your daughter. And when I told you not to go, I meant it. I feel I should have earned your respect by now."

Stephen said nothing as he observed the man who had been his boss and mentor for roughly ten years now. He'd never seen him so serious. The lieutenant's neck was red, and it was creeping into his face.

Lieutenant Higgins stared at Stephen without blinking. He pushed a manilla envelope across the table at Stephen.

"What's this?" Stephen reached forward to pick it up but didn't open it.

"It's a severance package."

Stephen felt breathless, like he'd taken a punch to the gut. "You're firing me?"

"You could call it *fired*. I call it promoting you to your next career opportunity. Not only will you find severance papers, you'll find a letter of recommendation and a job description for a position that just opened up. It's up to you if you want to apply. I won't stand in your way. Like I said, there's a letter of recommendation from me in there. But you can't work here anymore. I can't tolerate your blatant disobedience. Fellow officers are starting to notice, and I can't start a trend of people walking all over me."

Stephen's mouth hung open. He couldn't think of one thing to say.

Lieutenant Higgins' eyes softened. He leaned back in his

chair. "Truth is, Wilton, I consider you a friend. An equal. It's damn hard to manage you so I'm not gonna try anymore. If you leave quietly and accept the severance, we'll throw you a going away party. You can leave with dignity and go on to a different career. One you might even be better suited for."

"What's the position?" Stephen asked, finally finding his voice.

"US Marshal."

8

PAIGE

DAY TWO GONE

In the log cabin house surrounded by darkness, in my daughter's room, under her yellow and blue comforter, I lay wide awake. I was shaking uncontrollably. I couldn't sleep. This little bed in this little room was my only connection to Anna. I didn't belong in any other room in my own home anymore. The constant, torturous reminder that Anna was gone was where I belonged. There was nowhere else I fit in this world. In fact, I was certain I'd slept all day here. I couldn't seem to wake for anything. Nor did I have a reason to. Until now.

I had heard something. That *something* was in my house. I felt the sweat trickle off my forehead and onto the bedsheets. I lay as still as my shaking body would allow. I listened, lowering my comforter and peering into the darkness. It took a minute for my eyes to adjust to the dark night.

When did you become such a coward, Paige? I shamed myself. My inner voice was harsh and critical.

I quietly reached for the bedstand. I felt for the gun I was sure I had left there. There was nothing on the stand but Anna's bedside lamp.

Shit! I swore silently at myself. *Why would you not put the gun on the nightstand?* I rolled out of bed. I moved myself forward on all fours. I slowly crawled into the dining room.

"Looking for your gun?" Ray's deep voice broke the silence.

I screamed and jumped defensively into a crouched fighting position.

"I'm not here to fight you. I'm just here to help you finish what I started. The gun is on that table, Paige. It's ready for you to use," Ray's voice was clear and strong.

"I told you not to follow me here," I hissed angrily. "You don't belong here."

"Neither do you," Ray laughed. "How about a new game?"

"No more games," I insisted. "The last one didn't end so well for you." Still, I stood upright and looked on the table. The gun was, indeed, there. I knew without looking that there were bullets loaded in the chamber. I knew because I had checked it myself earlier.

"What do you really have to live for, Paige?" Ray's coaxing voice simply mirrored my own thoughts. "Your daughter is dead. Your husband is gone. Your mother was murdered. You have no family and no purpose. Play a game with me."

I didn't feel fear anymore. I felt resigned to my fate. I could see the outline of the silver revolver on the table. It was pointed away from me at the back wall. He was right. I had tried to get out of bed when the sun came up. It hadn't lasted. Without Anna, I had no direction. There was nothing left for me. I'd gone back to bed to escape the nightmare that was my reality.

"Spin it," Ray commanded quietly.

I stood frozen, staring at the gun. My mind replayed his words. *Your daughter is dead. Your husband is gone. Your mother was murdered. You have no family and no purpose.*

"You don't want to be here anymore," Ray said. "Play the game."

I put my hand to the table. I trailed it to the gun. My fingers inched their way closer until I could feel the cold steel laying lifelessly. It called to me to pick it up.

"Uh-uh," Ray said in a sing-song voice. "Don't pick it up, spin it. Let destiny decide."

I did as I was told. I grabbed the gun. I spun it hard. With all the anger and force of my feelings, I sent the gun spinning out of control. It spun toward the corner of the table. Then, it hit the ground. The force from the fall against the floor caused a reaction.

The gun discharged as it hit the floor.

Two things happened instantaneously. I heard the gunshot reverberate loudly in the small dining room. The loud noise echoed in my ear. Then I felt excruciating pain. Pain so intense, I lay writhing on the floor fighting consciousness.

9

CARLEY

DAY TWO GONE

"Read me another one, Carley." Anna yawned and snuggled into Carley.

"Only if you close your eyes," Carley commanded while thumbing through the next book. If she had to read one more story about a princess… ugh! "No peeking and I told you it's okay to call me *mama*."

"Okay, Mama Carley," Anna giggled. She closed her eyes.

"Once upon a time, there lived a little kitty cat—"

"No! A princess!" Anna protested.

"Close those eyes or story time is over," Carley conjured her meanest tone. "Princesses are overrated and unrealistic. It's time for a story about a kitty cat."

"Okay," Anna said with another yawn.

"Anyway, there once was a kitty cat name Anna Banana—"

"Anna Banana? That's me!" Anna sat up excitedly.

"Oh no! I told you to close your eyes or story time was over," Carley leaned over and turned off the light.

"Noooo!" Anna screeched. "I'm closing my eyes. Promise!" Anna said the word *promise* slowly because she had been working on pronouncing her *r*s.

"Okay, but this is your last shot. I'll leave next time. I will."
Carley waited until Anna was quiet and continued. "Once upon
a time, there lived a little kitty cat named Anna Banana. She
was the luckiest kitty in the whole universe. Her parents were
superheroes. Because they were busy fighting crime, Anna
Banana got to choose a new mama to take care of her. No one
gets to choose their parents. We're all stuck with who we get.

"But not Anna Banana. Anna Banana got to pick, and she
picked a new mama who was the coolest, the prettiest, and the
smartest mama in all the land. Anna Banana knew that her
parents would always love her and come see her when they
could. For now, Anna Banana kitty cat would go on a new super
cool adventure every single day. But that's a story for a different
night."

"I choose you, Mama Carley," Anna said sleepily.

"I choose you back, Anna Banana. Now go to sleep." Carley
slipped out of the bedroom. She wrapped her short silky robe
tighter around her as she walked down the stairs. She would be
able to hear Anna on the baby monitor if she needed anything.
But Carley would be up for hours, so she thought she'd get a
peek at the books. She'd just gotten here after all. It made
sense to familiarize herself before she met with Scott in the
morning.

Carley walked down the wide staircase that reminded her of
something she would see in an old movie. She'd always
wondered if sets of old movies made the staircases so wide just
so they could act out scenes easier but now she knew. Older,
Victorian houses like these were just made this way. Regardless, she felt a little regal as she descended.

At the foot of the staircase to the right was a heavy oak door
that was set on a slider. It was the study. Carley easily slid it
open. This was the room Carley loved the most. She paused
and leaned against the doorway as she looked into her new
home office.

When some people said they worked from home, Carley assumed they meant they worked from the kitchen table or the couch. This study was a true working office. The big bay window looked out on a cul-de-sac. The lovely front yard had a small koi pond surrounded by decorative stone. The front of the yard was lined with mature trees. Though right now, there were light billowy curtains blocking Carley's view.

There was a round ivory table in the middle of the room. On the table was a faux bouquet of red roses in a crystal vase. Carley moved into the room and ran her finger over the table. Not a speck of dust in sight.

Her eyes roamed over the black leather couch which lined the wall facing the door to the hallway. It was small enough to be cozy, big enough for Carley to curl up on should she decide to take up reading someday. The thought was laughable. Reading took too much time.

The room had been decorated tastefully. Hardwood floors that appeared centuries old were a bit cold under her feet. The walls were cream colored, and a large Ansel Adams photograph hung on the wall above the leather couch.

But her favorite part of the room was the work desk that sat at the back of the room facing the window. She turned toward the desk. She could see everything in the room from this vantage point behind the desk. The computer sat right in front of her. There was an elegant lamp on the edge of the desk that she turned on as she made her way to sit at this big, substantive table. The table was meant to indicate who was boss in the room. Carley hoped that would always be her.

Carley turned on the computer and found the accounting files with ease. All the passwords Scott had given her got her in quickly. She was familiar with the program Scott used so she clicked it open.

A quick scan told Carley a lot that she had previously left up to her imagination. The Milternett Family Organization, as

Scott had named the business, was a shipping company. There was a nice, clean trail of invoices from vendors with names like Meat Me, Farm Fresh Veggies, Farmer's Original Eggs, Sunny's Side Up, which was not oranges, but a quick search showed it to be an apple orchard with a breakfast café attached. The list went on.

"Charming," Carley mumbled, processing at a quick glance the business Scott was doing. "So Scott picks up large shipments from farmers, they load them in large trucks, and drive them over state lines to the grocery store or farmer's market where the products are sold. Nothing illegal about that." Carley scratched her face as she continued to peruse. From what she was seeing, the business was clean.

Carley knew better. There were rumors about The Milternett Family Organization that circled through the town. Carley had known about Scott Milternett and his business long before her mom started dating Scott. The stories were horrific but likely exaggerated just for her classmates to scare the bejesus out of each other.

It was rumored that a state patrolman had pulled over a truck and found a dead body in one of those freezers they used to transport meat. Another story was about finding pot stashed under a fake bottom on boxes of corn on the cob. All the stories concluded with Scott Milternett getting picked up by the feds and walking out of jail less than a half hour later. Everyone knew he had bought the cops.

Carley shook her head at the fantastic stories. Here now, looking at the books, she could see no evidence of illegal activity though Scott had more or less admitted to some form of it when Carley had known him as a teenager. Not to mention the dead bodies he'd brought to help stage the car accident scene less than a week ago. Scott Milternett was very much in business. He was just very good at hiding it.

Then she caught sight of a large donation to the local police and the US Marshals. Carley snickered. There it was. Scott had indeed found a way to put the cops in his pocket. It was brilliant, really. It was so simple, she wondered why more people didn't try it. Oh yeah, because more people weren't criminals.

Carley was deep in thought in front of the computer when she heard her front door open quickly and shut. Her eyes flicked to the clock. It was after midnight! Her mouth dropped open, and she shook her head in disbelief as she reached for the handgun she kept in her desk drawer. Carley grabbed the cold metal gun securely in her hand and soundlessly crept to the foyer.

She could see the dark shadow of a man in a dark suit coat before she saw him key in the code to disarm the alarm. It worked! Then the man turned to lock the door behind him before resetting the alarm. All actions halted as Carley snuck up behind him and put the cold metal against the base of his skull.

He immediately held his hands up like he was surrendering to the police.

"This ain't your house. Who the hell are you?" Carley's voice was low and menacing. She was near enough to his ear she didn't have to talk loudly to be heard. Why did strange men feel compelled to break into her places like they owned them?

"You're a woman!" his voice had a faint accent that mixed together with his disbelief.

"Why so surprised? You think it takes a penis to know how to handle a gun? I could blow your head off in point two seconds. Who the hell are you?" she repeated slower.

"Demitri Abbott, an associate of Scott Milternett. There's been a mix-up. I pay Scott for this place when I'm in town, like a VRBO. I'm supposed to be here this weekend," his voice was deep and sexy with a decidedly Italian accent to it.

"Not anymore you ain't. This is my house now. Tell you what, let me get Uncle Scott on the phone and he can tell me if you're supposed to be here or if I get to pull this trigger. Deal?" Carley asked him. She had her own accent that came out when she was stressed out.

"Yes, yes, deal," his voice was quiet and shaky.

Good, Carley thought, *that'll teach him to break into houses*.

Scott picked up on the second ring. Carley had the phone on FaceTime.

"Hey, there. Settling in okay?" Scott asked immediately.

"I was until this guy broke into my house," Carley flashed Demitri's face on the camera. "I'm holding a gun to the base of his skull. Do you vouch for him, or do I get to pull the trigger?"

"Please, Scott, tell her I'm here to stay, like VRBO, for the weekend!" Demitri was practically begging and couldn't get his words out fast enough.

"Demitri? Is that you?" Scott started laughing. "Shit, I forgot you were coming. Of course I can vouch for Demitri. Demitri Abbott, this is the new lady of the house. You'll have to go find a new place to stay. Sorry for the mix-up. You can see we had some last-minute changes to the plan. Carla, put the gun away." Scott shook his head, still laughing.

Carley was glad Scott remembered to use the fake name they had both agreed on. Just in case cops got nosey or the true cops with conviction came around. The only name anyone would know her as would be *Carla*. The plan was to slow cops down enough to put time and distance between Carley and the car accident.

Now that Scott had vouched for him, some of Demitri's confidence had returned. He stepped away from the gun and turned around. His eyes roamed obtrusively over Carley's scantily covered body. Carley didn't even try to adjust her short, silk robe to cover the cleavage she knew must be showing. Hearing that Demitri was a friend of the organization, she did her own appraisal of him.

Demitri Abbott was uniquely handsome in a dark and

dangerous sort of way. She could tell standing with him here in the shadows he had dark skin and light eyes. He was tall. She could see from where she stood that his body underneath his suit jacket and jeans was built. She found herself wondering just how built he was under those clothes and what she would find if she removed them.

"Thanks, Scott, I can take it from here." Carley had already put the gun away.

"Night, Carla. Behave yourself."

"Never," Carley said with irritation and abruptly hung up the phone. No man would *ever* tell her what to do. She'd been taking care of herself long enough.

"Well, I guess I'll be going. It'll be hard to find a hotel at this time of night," Demitri said, making moves to leave.

"Hold it right there," Carley commanded. "Why didn't you try to fight back? Someone's got a gun to your head and you just stand there?"

Demitri took a step closer to Carley. He looked her in the eyes. "I'm more of a lover than a fighter. If I would've taken out my gun, your brains would be splashed across the wall right now."

"Is that so?" Carley asked.

"You can thank me any way you'd like," he dropped his voice. They were now standing inches from each other.

"Thank you? I think I'm the one who spared *your* life, so *you* most definitely owe *me*," Carley countered. As she crossed her hands, her breast pushed together, making her cleavage prominent. She noticed Demitri glance down at her chest.

"Well, then, tell me, miss—"

"Carla. My name is Carla." It felt strange to use the name so close to the truth yet so unfamiliar on her tongue. She and Scott had agreed that staying as close to the truth as possible was always the best plan.

"How would you like me to make it up to you, Carla?"

Demitri's eyes continued to roam and his appraisal left her feeling hot under his gaze.

"Well, you can't stay the night, but you don't have to leave just yet." Carley walked into the office assuming he would follow her.

"Can I put my bags down?" he asked.

"Sure, drop them there and come into the study. There's a nice little alcohol bar in here." Carley invited him into the room. "Pick your poison?" She waved toward the alcohol bar that sat on an oak wood cabinet in the corner of the room.

"I pick you." Demitri was suddenly standing so close to Carley that when she turned around, her chest was against his. Demitri put a hand on her elbow and looked into her eyes with question.

"What does that mean?" Carley asked. Her heart rate sped up and she felt a tingle of adrenaline and excitement for what would most definitely come next.

"Let me show you," he said as he traced her scanty robe with one finger from where it lay against her collarbone down along her breast, gently grazing her nipple through the light fabric. Then he cupped his hands under her jaw and kissed her full lips lightly at first, then with more intensity.

Carley tugged off his jacket in response and threw it on the floor.

Demitri's hands found her bottom and he moaned when he felt bare skin and barely-there panties. As he kissed her, he skillfully led her toward the black leather couch.

Carley tugged off his white t-shirt to reveal his well-developed chest and ripped abs. His arms were toned and had the right amount of definition. She felt herself being gently pushed onto the couch. She fell on the cold, soft material but didn't try to cover herself up when her robe fell open showing her lacey panties and long, bare legs.

"Carla, this is the part where I plan to take advantage of

you. But only if you say *yes*." Demitri paused, looking into her eyes seeking approval.

"I'm okay with that," Carley agreed quickly.

Demitri dropped his jeans and knelt on the floor in front of her. His finger traced her lacey panties, finding their way underneath them.

Carley gasped as his fingers entered her, slowly at first, then faster and faster until she cried out in excitement. She untied the tie on her robe and allowed him to see her round bare breasts and flat stomach.

Demitri stood and Carley helped him out of his boxer briefs. She returned the favor by sitting back down and putting her mouth around him. She worked her own magic for minutes until she heard him groan in pleasure.

Carley stood up and kissed Demitri. Demitri picked Carley up, wrapping both of her legs around him. As he fell back on the couch, Carley found herself on top of him. She slowly slid onto his erection and paused to tease him, then she sat down on him, moving more deliberately. She rode him slowly at first, then more urgently. Their bodies made the right amount of friction until Carley gasped in powerful orgasm. Demitri moaned in turn, each of them finding intense satisfaction.

When they were done, Carley stood up and put her robe back on. She threw Demitri's clothes at him.

"It was nice to meet you, Demitri. Now it's time for you to go."

Demitri immediately put his clothes back on. He came close for another kiss.

Carley wagged her finger at him. "Uh-uh, that's all I have for you tonight."

"Well, Carla," Demitri picked up his bags to leave. "I hope to see much more of you this weekend."

Carley shrugged casually. "We'll see."

As Demitri turned to leave, she missed the way his instant anger enlarged his pupils, turning his eyes from brown to pure black.

10

STEPHEN

DAY THREE GONE

Stephen walked into an overcrowded café and scanned the crowd for the two men he was meeting. Lieutenant Higgins had set up a meeting with a US Marshal to answer Stephen's questions. Though Stephen had to turn in his badge and access keys, he felt grateful that Lieutenant Higgins still agreed to help him transition should he choose to train as a US Marshal.

As Stephen spotted the lieutenant and an athletic, dark-skinned man in the corner and walked their direction, he had to acknowledge this conversation wasn't the one he needed to have to make this decision. He'd done his research and knew he was qualified for the US Marshal job.

In the midst of feeling devastated over the loss of his job, and his daughter, Stephen almost felt another misplaced emotion—excitement. Lieutenant Higgins was right. This would be a promotion. He wasn't surprised to find someone was holding him back. Paige. Not to mention, they were still waiting for news of Anna.

"Hi, Stephen. This is US Marshal Brix," Lieutenant Higgins immediately stood up and introduced the man sitting at the table to Stephen.

"Nice to meet you." Stephen put his hand out and firmly grasped the Marshal's hand.

"Brix here is the man who informed me of the position opening with the Marshals."

"Great, thanks for taking time to answer my questions," Stephen said.

"Not to put you on the spot," Marshal Brix said. "But have you ever thought about becoming a Marshal before?"

"I can't say that I have. I mean, I've had a little interaction with a few Marshals over a year ago, but I always felt content in my job as a detective, so I never really thought about it. I did a little research. Doesn't it usually take a good six months to a year to walk through this process? What's the time frame if I qualify?" Stephen wondered.

"You qualify, Stephen," Lieutenant Higgins stated.

"Provided you can pass a physical fitness test, have three years of experience, a bachelor's degree, fall within age parameters, and pass a background check—"

"I have those qualifications and can pass a fit test, Marshal Brix," Stephen nodded.

"Just call me Brix," he corrected. "You're right, it usually takes quite a bit of time to walk through the qualification process. Plus, you probably know there's a training period before you get a job?"

Stephen nodded.

"Well, we had a candidate drop out of training at the last minute, so we have a position to fill. If we can get you through the steps, we can offer you the training position."

Stephen felt doubtful. Answers about Anna had to be his first priority.

"Well," Brix said after they put in an order. "What questions do you have? Fire away."

"Do you know what region this position is for?" Stephen asked.

"Once you finish the training, which is rigorous, by the way, they'll position you wherever they need you," Brix said. "I do happen to know we need a US Marshal positioned in the Midwest region, Kansas City specifically. But once the job assignment is done, you could be reassigned anywhere. You'd need to be able to travel."

"I know that US Marshals aren't bound to a specific jurisdiction necessarily. They're able to move freely across borders, correct?" Stephen paused.

"Correct," Brix answered.

Brix looked at Lieutenant Higgins, then at Stephen with question. "Are you single? Have any kids?"

Stephen inhaled sharply. He hadn't expected such a question to hurt his heart the way it did. But it might be another reason why Brix seemed interested in him. Did he still have a daughter? After seeing that accident, Stephen felt he knew the answer.

"I am unattached," Stephen said. *This position would be a huge promotion*, he thought.

"Tell me about the training," Stephen said, trying to channel some excitement. "You said it was rigorous?"

Brix went on to describe his own training experience and some of his worst fails. The three men laughed heartily at not only his experience but the experience of others around him.

"How long is the training?" Stephen asked.

"Nineteen weeks," Brix answered. "Look, Stephen, we only take the best. This job is not for everybody. It's not easy. The things we see on the job daily make the average person want to quit. I'm talking to you because you've been named as the best at what you do."

Stephen stole a glance at Lieutenant Higgins. Was he firing Stephen to push him into this position, knowing Stephen would never apply on his own? No, Stephen knew his actions deserved the punishment. Still, he felt grateful to Lieutenant Higgins for bringing this opportunity to him.

"Also, I'm going to be transparent with you. We had a death at the Kansas City office, which is why we're short a guy there. We're expediting the process to fit another recruit. That would be you if you decide you're interested. You just need to decide quickly if you're in or out."

"Define quickly," Stephen said.

"Can you let me know at the end of this week?"

By then, they should have the DNA results of Anna's test. Stephen nodded.

It felt like the universe was lining him up and showing him a clear path to what was next in his life. This was a job he could really enjoy. At the same time, it would take him away from the family and people he loved. The people who might need him more than ever before in the days to come.

Another thought surfaced. He'd just gotten fired from a job he'd loved and never considered leaving. He'd never been fired before. What value did he really have to provide in a job bigger than the one he had recently failed at?

He wasn't worried about passing the physical fitness test, not even with his recent lung injury. He was back to running on a treadmill and he'd recently upped his weightlifting regimen. He wasn't even worried about the five written tests Brix mentioned he'd have to commit to. He was a decent test taker.

"So, what do you think? You interested?" Brix asked.

"Maybe. I can let you know by the end of the week. What's the first step?" Stephen asked.

"Physical fitness test. Make sure you pass that and fill out the online application." Brix smiled.

The food arrived and the rest of the time passed with Brix recounting his experience with the US Marshals.

Stephen knew it wouldn't hurt to take a physical fitness test. He knew he was likely due for one anyway.

But his mind was on Paige. He knew he didn't have to run anything in his life by her. But he felt a deep sense of obligation. At the very least, he felt he should let her know what he was considering. Plus, it would give him a chance to check on her.

11

PAIGE
DAY THREE GONE

I woke with a gasp. The room was bright. I blinked a few times and shut my eyes again. I was quiet. I got the impression I was in a hospital room. But why? I dozed off again, feeling cold. I pulled the sheet tighter around me. I couldn't move freely. I peeked out of my eyelids again. This time, my eyes widened in surprise. I was hooked to an IV. There was a clear bag and my veins felt cold.

Other than being cold, I felt comfortable. I felt no pain. I became aware of a rather large bandage that wrapped around my leg just above the knee. I looked under my sheet to confirm there was a large bandage wrapped there.

"Paige, you're awake," a sleepy voice sounded in the corner of the room just far enough back, I hadn't caught her in my peripheral vision. She sounded like she'd been sleeping in her chair.

"Dr. Burnett!" I exclaimed in surprise. For the first time since the news about Anna, I felt like I wasn't alone.

"Paige! Are you okay?" she asked with a look of concern on her face. The concern brought a momentary wrinkle in her otherwise smooth forehead. Her giant glasses sat on her nose.

Her brown hair was pulled back into a ponytail. She wore jeans, a cable knit sweater, and canvas tennis shoes. I'd never seen her look so casual.

"Why were you worried?" I asked.

"Paige, you called me last night. Do you not remember?"

I shook my head.

"You said you were shot," tears sprang to Dr. Burnett's eyes.

"Oh!" It all came back to me. When the gun hit the floor, it discharged, and the bullet hit my leg. I must have gone into shock because I remember the initial pain which dropped me to the floor. Then I got up and limped to the kitchen for a towel. I pressed the towel to my bloody knee and looked at it as if it wasn't my own knee. Then I called Dr. Burnett.

I got shot, I'd told her.

What? she'd gasped. *Did you call nine-one-one? Are you in danger?*

No, I'd said. *I shot myself.*

"Paige, I'm worried about you," Dr. Burnett cut right to the point. "You said you shot yourself. Were you trying to—"

"No, I'm not good." I let the tears come. "But I didn't do this on purpose. It was just an accident. It was my fault the gun went off but I wasn't trying to harm myself."

"Maybe you should explain," she said quietly.

"I saw the ghost of Ray," I began. "He was terrifying. More so than the other ghosts I've seen. I ran out of my house and found Carley's abandoned house a mile away. I walked right in. Ray's ghost showed up there and showed me where there was a gun."

"Ray's ghost told you where a gun was?" Dr. Burnett looked surprised and skeptical. "Was that after you pulled out several drawers and looked around?"

"No," I assured her. "He pointed to the drawer, I opened it, and there was a gun inside."

"Okay," her brow furrowed deeply.

"Then I picked up the gun and took it home with me."

"I still don't understand how you—"

"I slept all day and woke up in the middle of the night. Ray was there and he asked me to play a game with him like the night he was in my house. Only this game was different. He told me to spin the gun on the table and let fate decide if I live. I spun the gun."

"And the gun went off when it hit the floor?" Dr. Burnett asked.

"Yes. Do you know how bad the gun shot is?" I was worried and felt a little embarrassed.

"It's above your knee and the bullet barely nicked your leg. It skimmed over your skin, taking out a good-sized chunk, but it didn't lodge itself or blow off your kneecap. You got very lucky, Paige."

I nodded. What a stupid stunt I had pulled.

"I almost wonder though," Dr. Burnett stopped talking and bit her lip.

"What?" I asked.

"If it wasn't a cry for help."

"Oh," I said processing her words. They made sense. "Well, I didn't plan to shoot myself for attention."

"No, it doesn't sound like you did. But sometimes a person can subconsciously do something that shows others that he or she needs help. Living in that isolated cabin by yourself right now cannot be good for you."

Before I could answer, an attendant came in pushing a cart of food. My stomach rumbled loudly letting me know how hungry I was.

"Who's ready for food?" the woman cheerfully asked.

"I don't know what you have on that tray, but I'll eat anything!" I said, feeling thankful.

"What would you like to drink?" she asked. "Anyone want coffee?"

"Yes, please!" I agreed. "Can you bring a pot and two cups?"
I smiled pleadingly.

"Sure," she agreed. "Be right back."

"Paige, that's another thing," Dr. Burnett lowered her voice.
"They had to give you an IV because you were dehydrated. You
seem so thin. Are you eating?"

I stared blankly at Dr. Burnett. I couldn't remember the last
time I'd eaten.

"Here you go!" the attendant said as she put down a pot of
coffee with creamers and sugars.

"How do you take it?" I asked as if to serve Dr. Burnett,
forgetting the obstacles attached to me that were pinning me to
the bed.

"Two cream, two sugar," came her reply. "But I'll get it and
I'll get yours too.

"Double, double," I said. My eyes got misty.

"What?" she asked.

"It's what they say in Canada," I explained as she handed
me a cup. "James used to take his coffee that way. It's called a
double, double."

"Paige, so much has happened to you, lately. So much loss,"
Dr. Burnett peered at me.

"I know," I admitted. "I've lost everything. When a person
loses everything, how do they find a reason to move forward?"

Dr. Burnett tilted her head. "Good question. You know,
since we first met, your life has been in crisis."

"It's what I deserve," I stated solemnly. I tried to swallow
the hot coffee but struggled to get past the lump in my throat.

"No, it's not. Nobody deserves the things you've been
through. But life happens. Why do you think that?" she held
the coffee mug in her hands like she was trying to warm
them up.

"I am bad—Margaret, my grandmother, used the word

wicked the last time I saw her. She was right. I *am* bad and I deserve the bad things that have happened," I stated it as a fact.

"You believe this don't you?" Her eyes were filled with compassion.

I nodded. "To my core."

"It would be useless for me to tell you otherwise, wouldn't it?"

I nodded again feeling weepy. I didn't trust myself to speak.

"Listen, Paige. The doctor has asked me my professional opinion about if you need to be under watch. I don't think you are well, but I'm not sure you're suicidal."

I nodded slowly, understanding her meaning. I didn't think I was suicidal either. But I didn't know what it was called when a person lacked the ability to get out of the past and move into the future.

12

CARLEY

DAY THREE GONE

Carley drummed her fingers on her desktop. Scott Milternett sat in a nice chair across the desk from Carley as she studied some figures on her computer screen. Scott waited quietly. Finally, Carley looked up and addressed him.

"Who exactly is Demitri Abbott to you?" Carley asked.

Scott shifted uncomfortably in his chair. "Carley, you don't—"

Carley interrupted him. "I'm not asking what kind of work he does for you. I don't want to know any details that could be incriminating or put me in a sensitive situation. I need to keep Anna safe."

"How is Anna these days?" Scott smiled warmly. "Does she love the new preschool?"

"She's great. I appreciate the pull and financial donation you contributed to get her into the school. But don't change the subject. Specifically, I need to know how important Demitri Abbott is to your operations?"

"Very," Scott answered. "He's in a key position, and he has been a powerful alliance. It's vital to keep him."

"And?" Carley asked, knowing there was more.

"The short and clean version is no one knows this business better than Demitri. He used to be my biggest rival, but I hired him to head up operations. He's a very smart businessman. I did a favor for him to get him to trust me and he agreed to work for me. You know the saying about keeping your enemies close?"

Carley nodded. "So, you trust him?"

"Meh," Scott tilted his hand sideways.

"Has anything about his product or service changed in the last quarter that would justify a raise in invoices?" Carley stared intensely at Scott. She didn't care that she'd slept with Demitri. If he was stealing from her family, the guy needed to go.

"No, same service, same price." Scott frowned. "Why do you ask?"

"Then here's what you need to know. He's stealing from you. He has been for a while. Three months ago, his *operations* fee jumped from $12,650 to $16,250. I went back and double checked the invoice. By the way, good job keeping invoices to show money and cash flow… At first glance, I thought maybe he was just dyslexic, and he transposed the numbers. But the next month, the fee went from $16,250 to $18,250. Can you think of any reason why his invoices would go up like that?" Carley asked directly.

Scott's jaw clenched tightly. "No, there's no reason his fees should be going up. That's not part of our arrangement. This is why I need you, Carley. I don't have time to watch these things and he knows this. Have you looked at any other accounts?"

"Yes, I haven't seen any other obvious discrepancies at this point," Carley told him. "What are you going to do about Demitri?"

"I'm going to kill him," Scott said as he looked intently into Carley's eyes.

"You are?" she gasped and leaned forward in surprise.

"Of course not," Scott laughed.

Carley rolled her eyes and sat back.

"Tell you what, why don't you just go back to paying him the original total and if he complains, you have my permission to throw him out, and send him to me."

"Okay," Carley agreed. She smiled. "It's kinda like I'm the boss."

"You are one hundred percent the boss of all family finances, Carley. Trust me, you don't want the job of big boss. It's a dirty job but it's what I signed up for." Scott got up from his chair and put on his jacket. "I'll be happy for Spring when it starts to warm up around here."

"Anna's birthday is in the Spring. She'll be three," Carley announced proudly.

"Three? That's all she is? She is so mature for three! The sentences that come out of that girl's mouth…" Scott shook his head.

"Yes, she's mature alright. And she has this crazy good memory on top of those big sentences." Carley frowned a minute not sure she could take credit for that one. Anna seemed to have this supernatural ability to communicate. She wondered if Paige had been one of those moms who talked to her baby like a little adult. At the thought of Paige, Carley decided to shut down the conversation.

"Good to see you, Uncle Scott." Carley put the computer on sleep mode.

"I ought to throw Anna a big party. It'd be a great chance to meet the family."

Carley shrugged. "Let's think about it. We have plenty of time."

"Well, always a pleasure, Carley." Scott got up out of the chair to leave.

"About my name. I think we need to start calling me *Carla* all the time or one of us is going to slip up at the wrong time. I almost told someone my real name the other day. It's going to get me caught."

"Right you are, *Carla*," Scott winked at her as he got up to leave and disappeared out the front door.

"Right, now what do I do with the rest of this day?" Carley said aloud, feeling bored and restless. The problem with being dead is it created a need to disappear from normal society. Which meant her one option was to keep going through these finances and pay some bills.

It would be three soon enough and Carley's driver would take her to pick up Anna from her ritzy private preschool. She smiled, remembering the conversation she'd had with Anna on her first day.

No punching kids on your first day of school, Anna.

Anna had giggled.

You're not a ninja, even if you think you are.

I know…

This is a nice school, and I can't afford to have you kicked out. And for God sakes, tell everyone I'm your mom. Trust me, it's so much easier than answering the kids' questions.

I don't want to talk about my mom. I punched that boy cause of my mom.

Tell you what, Carley had whispered. *If you do hit someone, just don't get caught.*

Okay, Anna had whispered back like it was their little secret.

Okay, then we're agreed.

I'll call you mommy for now, Anna said shyly.

After they had been quiet for a minute, Anna spoke up again.

What about dad? When is my dad coming back? Anna had looked at Carley with those big blue eyes brimming with tears.

She really was a beautiful child. She reminded Carley of a porcelain doll. She had big, expressive blue eyes, her dad's dimples, and curly blond hair that tended to get frizzy without the right products. Carley had tried to smooth Anna's wild curls, making a note to buy her some more curling hair shampoo.

We never know when he's coming back. He's a superhero, remember. He has an important job to do, catching bad guys and getting them off the street. I'm sure he'll come when it's safe. When the driver stopped the car, Carly had gotten out abruptly, helping Anna out of the car.

Come on, kiddo. Let's get you to school.

13

PAIGE
DAY FOUR GONE

Dr. Burnett had been a godsend. After a day of observation, she recommended to the doctor that my mental state was strong enough for me to go home. It had been a mutual decision for her to stay with me. Mutual in that I was a little afraid to be alone and Dr. Burnett seemed afraid to leave me alone.

Since I'd gotten home, things had been looking up. Dr. Burnett's daily dose of medicine was keeping me busy. As busy as I could be with a chunk missing from my leg and my heart. Though I walked with a limp, a dose of Tylenol kept the pain low. I really had gotten lucky.

"We have lots of work to do," Dr. Burnett stated.

We had barely gotten home from the hospital. It was still morning and truth be told I would have loved to take a nap. But she was only going to be here until I was physically better. I was unaware there was anything to do at all.

"On the house?" I asked doubtfully. In truth, she could have been talking about me.

"For starters. Is any of this yours?" She swept a hand around. I wasn't sure how she figured it out, but she rarely asked questions she didn't already know the answers to.

"No, I feel like a stranger in my own home," I admitted.

"Okay, let's work on that."

I nodded in agreement. Though secretly, I worried. It would be harder to hide my reaction to Ray's ghost when he tortured me in the middle of the night with her staying here.

"There's something I have to tell you," Dr. Burnett said when we took a lunch break.

"What's that?" I asked before I took a big bite of a sandwich.

"I can't be your therapist anymore."

"What? Dr. Burnett, no! Why?" I felt devastated. Instant tears filled my eyes. She was all I had left. The feeling of abandonment instantly threatened to undo me.

"Because I want to be your friend." She reached out and patted my hand. "Please, call me Brandi from now on."

"Is that your name?" I smarted at her with a reluctant smile. I swiped my eye quickly with relief. "I've known you as Dr. Burnett for way too long."

"You'll get used to it," she stated. "Paige, what would you do with this house to make it completely yours?" She got up to put the dishes in the dishwasher.

My sore muscles from sleeping on an uncomfortable twin bed answered that question. Brandi had been brave enough to sleep in the murder room and had lived through the night. I didn't think I'd ever have the courage to do that. Which meant I needed a new bed.

"That's easy," I said. "I took inventory of what I would keep and get rid of. The only thing I want is the dining room furniture and the kitchen plates, cups, utensils, and silverware. The rest of this stuff isn't mine to get rid of though."

"Whose stuff is it? Carley's?" Brandi asked.

I shuddered. "I bet some of it is," I could hear the edge of anger in my voice.

"You blame her for Anna?" Brandi asked. She studied me

like I was a science experiment.

"Yes. She stole my child and drove off a cliff. Who else would I blame?" Some days the bitter edge in my voice sounded like a permanent new tone. "Ray says it's my fault. He says I was probably a terrible mom like my mom."

"Okay, as your *friend*, we should process that." She smiled softly with compassion in her eyes. "Did Ray know your mom when she was a mom? If I remember correctly, he didn't even know about you. You sure didn't know about him."

"Good point," I said, pausing to think about it.

"You knew your mom and you formed an opinion about her parenting, right?" she asked.

"Yes," I whispered, feeling ashamed of my judgment of my mom.

"You and Ray are very different people. Why would *Ray* be thinking the same things you think and torturing you with those thoughts?"

"Because Ray is the personification of my darkest thoughts and deepest, most tortured guilty places?" I asked.

"What do you really think?" she asked.

"I think I've had some pretty dark days, and I can't let myself be okay ever again," I admitted. "But I wasn't a bad mom." I felt this was true. But my guilt over the lack of time I'd spent with Anna still haunted me.

"Good, I'm glad you know that," Brandi encouraged me. "Do me a favor?"

"Sure," I smiled, feeling vulnerable.

"Every time Ray, or a negative, horrible thought pops up, replace it with the opposite thought, a positive one, until you believe it."

"Thank you, I'll try. That's good advice coming from a *friend*." I smiled bigger.

"So, if this stuff isn't Carley's, whose is it?" Brandi asked, changing the subject.

"Stephen's," I admitted. "I bet Carley decorated it, but he bought it."

"Could you text him and ask? If he wants it, he can come get it. If not, we could sell it for him?" she suggested.

"Sure," I picked up my phone but couldn't bring myself to text him. I stared at my phone.

"What is it?" Brandi looked up at me.

"I know that when I pull up his number to text him, I'll see at least ten missed texts from him. I don't even read them. He's been texting me since I got here to make sure I'm okay."

"He cares about you, Paige. He wants to be your friend," she stated logically.

"He wants more than that. I know Stephen. He's still in love with me. He's harboring some fantasy that someday we'll get back together. Like now that we have more in common than we ever did, he probably thinks it makes sense."

"Did he tell you that?" she asked.

I shook my head. "No, but he thought I was sleeping on the plane ride back home and he admitted that he still loves me. He said *I'll love you forever*."

"Is that a bad thing?" Brandi asked.

"I just don't want to get sucked into life with him again. I don't feel the same way about him, and I end up feeling guilty because no matter how much I tell him I don't want a relationship, he gets his hopes up, and I hurt him. It's an endless cycle." I sighed, still fiddling with my phone. "I thought you hated Stephen."

"Hate is a strong word, Paige. In the beginning, I could see the level of control he worked hard to have over you. Controlling people are dangerous for people like you and me. We allow them to dominate us. It reminded me of my controlling ex-husband. Now, from the few short encounters I've had with Stephen recently, I feel like he's grown up a lot."

"Maybe," I was unconvinced.

"He's hurting too, Paige. Maybe someday, the two of you could be friends and he could fill you in on the years you missed with Anna, and you could tell him about the time you spent with her before he came into Anna's life."

I picked up my phone. I was right. There were too many missed texts from Stephen to count. He was predictable if he was nothing else.

"I don't have the energy to go through all of these messages right now."

"Don't. Ignore them. You don't even have to answer them. You aren't obligated to even acknowledge them unless you want to. It's up to you what you decide, but it would be helpful to ask him if he wants his furniture back."

"You're right," I said. I decided to call him.

It took less than a minute for Stephen to answer. When he did, it sounded like he was driving.

"Paige, hello," he answered.

"Hi," I responded.

"How are you?" he asked. His voice was warm.

"I'm okay… I was just calling to ask about the furniture here at the house," I cut past his concern. His voice made me feel emotional and emotions made me feel uncomfortable.

"The furniture?" he sounded confused.

"Yes, I'm redecorating, and I wondered who it belongs to?"

"The furniture is mine, but I don't want it. Would it be too much to ask you to sell it and send the money? Keep what you want, of course…"

"Okay, thank you. Yes, I could do that," I replied.

"But you didn't answer my question. How are you?" he asked again.

I was quiet for a minute then chose honesty. "I've been better."

"I know," he said. "I'm just sad but I suppose that's the same as every other day."

I was quiet for a second. I was so focused on my own feelings, I hadn't considered his. In the silence, memories of the two of us when we were happy paraded through my mind. Dr. Burnett was right. Stephen had grown up a lot. I, on the other hand, was still holding a grudge that didn't serve me. I thought about what Brandi had said about being Stephen's friend.

"Would you like to come for dinner?" I asked

"I would like that," Stephen agreed. "When?"

"I have company now. Dr. Burnett is here. Maybe when she leaves?"

Stephen agreed. Then we said our *goodbyes* and hung up the phone.

Hours passed with Brandi and I moving furniture and posting pictures to sell items online.

"I just called Sandra and she's coming to pick up the leather couch," Brandi announced.

"Sandra Stockman, my lawyer?"

"And my best friend, don't forget," Brandi said. "She can be fun. I invited her to stay for a girl's night. If that's okay?"

"She's coming out here?" I asked astonished. I could not imagine my expensive looking, rather uppity lawyer in this little house. "Brandi, there are only two bedrooms here. I don't think we'll have enough space!"

Brandi waved her hand. "I can sleep on the couch."

"The couch she's coming to get?" I could hear the pitch of my voice going up.

"Heavens, no. On the couch we're going to go buy to replace it. Do you have money?" she asked.

"Some," I acknowledged. "Let's just hit some antique malls and see if we can bargain shop a little."

"Perfect, I'll grab my purse." Brandi disappeared into the master bedroom and came back. She found me in Anna's room lost in thought.

"You don't have to change this room, Paige," her voice was

quiet, as if she didn't want to intrude on my thoughts.

"It's the weirdest thing," I said. "This is the room where I feel most comfortable. I defaulted here because I didn't want to sleep in the murder bedroom—"

"You mean master bedroom," Brandi corrected. We had been talking about the power of positive words and reframing my dark thoughts.

"Yes, but I have no memories of Anna here. It's hard to imagine what she was like. This room is like a little clue into who she was," I told Brandi with tears in my eyes.

Brandi spontaneously hugged me.

"I don't feel nostalgic because I didn't live here with her, but it does feel wrong to change it… I just think I need the spare bedroom."

"What about a compromise then? What if you keep the bright, cheerful colors, the blue and yellow is nice, but get a bigger mattress and a similar but bigger comforter and clean the rest of it up. Maybe you could make a memorial box for Anna and pull it out when you want to feel connected to her."

My eyes filled with tears. "Brandi, that's a beautiful idea!"

When I opened the door for us to leave, we came face to face with a couple of cops who were about to knock on the door.

"Ms. Mynart?" A woman with dark hair pulled back in a bun flashed her badge at me. She was short and on the heavy side. This woman was familiar. "I'm Officer Huntington and this is Sturgis." Then it came back to me. She was the one who showed up to take my statement when Margaret, my grandmother, had taken a sledgehammer to the floors. That seemed like a lifetime ago.

"Yes," I answered finally. The feeling of dread welled up inside me.

"We need to ask you some questions about how you shot your knee."

I invited them in. "Can I get you some coffee?" I asked nervously.

"No, thank you. We just need to ask you some questions so we can wrap up our report." Officer Huntington stood looking uncomfortable where the couch had sat an hour before.

"Such as...?"

"Where did you get the gun that discharged?" Sturgis, who had been silent up until then jumped right in, pulling out a plastic bag with Ray's revolver in it.

My face grew hot. "I found it in an abandoned home," I admitted looking at the floor.

"What home?" Officer Huntington pressed.

I felt embarrassed. "Carley Smith's."

The officers exchanged glances.

"Isn't that where Ray Lennon used to live?" Sturgis asked Officer Huntington.

She nodded.

"Maybe that explains it?" he asked her.

"Explains what?" I asked before she could answer.

"The gun you shot was a gun we have been holding for years in evidence. We collected it the night Ray died here. We have no record of releasing this gun. But what you see here," she pointed to the plastic bag. "Is most definitely Ray's gun."

"Oh," I glanced at Brandi to see her processing the words.

"We picked up the gun and recovered the bullet the night the EMT picked you up. We compared this gun and bullet to the report. This is Ray's gun. We didn't even realize it had gone missing from our evidence locker. Do you know anything about that?"

"I'm sorry," I shrugged. "I don't. I only just got back a few days ago."

The officers exchanged glances as if trying to decide what to do next.

"I can take you to the place where I found it."

"Can you, please?" Officer Huntington looked appreciative.

"Sure. We were just on our way out anyway." I walked them out the door.

Brandi and I drove to Carley's, taking a road I guessed would wind me around to her house. It was guessing since I had walked across the field. The officers followed us. I walked them in and showed them the drawer.

"Where is Carley Smith now?" Officer Huntington asked as she looked around the house.

"Was she kin to Ray?" Sturgis asked then shook his head answering his own question.

"No, I don't think she was." Officer Huntington went deeper into the house.

"Carley is presumed dead. Her car was found after it drove off a mountain. They're waiting for the DNA report to confirm their identities." I pointed to the drawer that had held the gun. "That's where I found it."

"And you were in this house, why?" Sturgis asked.

"Hold on, Paige," Brandi said in a polite but firm voice. "You aren't obligated to answer any other questions. You've already over accommodated these officers. If there's an investigation somewhere in all of this, you can talk to them with a lawyer." She turned to the officers. "Will there be anything else?"

They shook their heads and we all trooped out of the house and into our cars.

"You've seen and heard Ray?" Brandi asked when we'd sat down in the car and buckled ourselves in. The color seemed to have drained from her face.

I nodded. "He told me where the gun was, remember?"

Brandi nodded but didn't say a word. There was no logical explanation for how Ray's gun had gotten out of evidence and into that drawer. It seemed Brandi was beginning to believe in ghosts.

14

PAIGE

DAY FOUR GONE

"Wow," Sandra exclaimed later that afternoon when she arrived. She was looking at the couch I needed to get rid of. "Whoever owned this couch is my kinda people!"

"Really?" I snarked. "The kinda people who kidnaps someone's daughter and drives over a cliff with her?"

"Of course not," Sandra frowned at me while she studied me intensely. "Are you always this snappy?"

"Of course not. Only when my lawyer decides to side with a woman who she would be working to put in jail right now if she'd survived that crash." I crossed my hands over my chest.

Sandra leaned in and lowered her voice. "Sometimes death is the ultimate sentence in life."

I leaned in and closed the space between us. "Not when my daughter went with her."

"At ease, ladies." Brandi breezed back to my side.

It had been a very productive day. We had found everything we'd been looking for—furniture, new mattresses, and sheets. The queen-sized yellow comforter that looked similar to Anna's twin-size comforter was the cherry on top of a successful day. A delivery guy had loaded everything into a truck, followed us home, and helped us unload it.

Until now. Sandra and I stood staring at each other, not blinking.

"Paige, Sandra is not your lawyer today. She's the most loyal friend you could ever have, if you let her be," Brandi said lightly. She turned to Sandra. "Summon your most sympathetic state of mind and remember that Paige is dealing with a huge loss and is still going through a horrific time right now. Be nice."

"Fine," Sandra said, taking a step back. "I'm sorry. Brandi is right. That was insensitive of me. I hate the couch, the person who had it before you has terrible taste, but I'll take it off your hands as a favor."

Against my will, I smiled a little, feeling my defenses come down. "I forgive you. You may stay here tonight after all," I invited her.

"About that…" Sandra started, clearly unimpressed with my little home in the woods.

"You said you'd stay, Sandra," Brandi reprimanded.

Sandra rolled her eyes. "I can change my mind, can't I? Why don't I take you both to dinner and we'll go from there," Sandra negotiated.

"Deal," Brandi said. "Only…"

"What? Is there nowhere to eat in this tiny little town?" Sandra asked curtly.

"There's a quaint little diner." My smile was big now as I tried to imagine her in her designer jeans and high heels sitting in our small-town diner.

Sandra must have caught me looking at her shoes because she quickly defended them. "Honey, I can move quicker in these heels than you can in those tennis shoes. Let's load this thing, ladies."

Between the three of us, we were able to load the couch in

pieces in the U-Haul Sandra had brought. She reached into her Coach wallet and paused, looking expectantly at me for the total. I gave up trying to process how many hundred dollar bills she looked to have in there.

"He wanted seven hundred and fifty dollars for it," I told her.

Sandra peered at me for a minute and counted out seven hundred-dollar bills. "Will he take seven hundred?" she asked. She shrugged and said, "I don't have a fifty."

"Sure," I agreed.

"Now about dinner…" Sandra puzzled aloud.

"They have a great pizza place," I suggested. "We could grab it and come back?"

"Ugh, I haven't eaten carbs in forever," Sandra complained. "If we do this, we need wine. More than one bottle."

"We can make a run," Brandi said.

"We also need—" Sandra rooted around in her purse and produced a deck of cards.

"Sandra!" Brandi cried out dismayed. "I thought you'd quit!"

Sandra waved her hand dismissively. "I did quit. I quit casinos, not cards. Do you play poker, Paige?"

"Never have," I followed Sandra into the room where she kicked off her heels and sat down comfortably at the dining room table. "It's the perfect time to learn."

Brandi clucked her tongue, a clear sign of disapproval. "I guess I'll go get the pizza and wine."

"Thanks, Brandi, you're the best." Sandra was already explaining the rules of poker to me.

By the time Brandi got back, I was having a nice run of beginner's luck.

We devoured the pizza she put on the table. After she had a glass of wine, Brandi reluctantly joined our game.

"Paige, are you not drinking?" Sandra asked bluntly. She had just filled her glass and was looking around for a glass for me.

"I don't think I should..." I trailed off, remembering the last time I drank. It was when James took me on our first date. I was lucky he was a gentleman because it only took a few glasses before I blacked out, at least I think it was a few glasses. I drank enough to miss the end of our date.

"Okay, up to you," Sandra shrugged.

"I'm a lightweight. Two and I'm drunk," I explained.

"Oh, fun!" Sandra's eyes lit up. "In that case..." she poured me a full glass.

"Would you do okay with one, Paige?" Brandi asked to let me know I had a choice.

"Sure," I agreed.

From there, our game got louder and funnier. It seemed my beginner's luck was more than a phenomenon and I kept winning.

Somewhere around game number five, I hit my wine which spilled and soaked the cards. My eyes instantly misted up with tears. *You always have to ruin things, Paige,* my thoughts tormented me.

"I'm sorry," I said with a sniff.

"Don't be, it was Brandi's fault. She's been moving your glass closer to your hand all night. She hates to lose. She was pretty strategic on this one," Sandra blamed her friend.

"I did not!" Brandi protested. "I mean, I do hate to lose, but I wouldn't go to such elaborate schemes to win! Trust me, the more drunk you two get, the more chance I have of winning!"

Gone were my tears, quickly replaced with a smile at their long-time rivalry. They continued to banter while I got up to get paper towels to clean up the mess. As I left the room, I didn't miss the way Brandi winked at Sandra as if to say *thank you.*

They really were here to help me heal and move forward

and I loved them both for their efforts. Most of all, I loved that they were helping me make new, happy memories in this little home of mine.

Maybe the bad things that were happening to me weren't because I was bad. Maybe bad things just happened. Maybe that was life. Somehow, I felt myself clinging to my original belief. Because if I kept my guard up, I could protect myself when more bad things happened.

Because I knew more bad things were going to happen.

15

_____

PAIGE

DAY FIVE GONE

I awoke feeling happy and well-rested. The bed we'd put in Anna's room was warm and comfortable, so I lingered and snuggled into it. I also had fallen in love with the new comforter we'd bought to replace Anna's. I had boxed up all of Anna's toys and put the box on a shelf within arm's reach in the closet.

Brandi was already up, having said good-bye to Sandra who'd explained the night before she had to be off obscenely early the next day to get prepped for court Monday. I assumed I would miss her exit and said my goodbyes last night. Brandi would be leaving today as well.

"Here," Brandi came around the corner with coffee. She had figured out how I liked it. *Sugar in a cup,* James used to tease me. My heart longed for him with sudden intensity.

"Thank you," I remembered to say after taking the coffee and trying it. I had been quiet a beat too long.

"Are you okay?" Brandi asked. "Were we too crazy for you last night?"

I smiled. "Yes, I'm okay. No, not too crazy. It was fun. I was just thinking about James. I miss him."

We sat at the table.

"He just seemed to disappear, huh?" Brandi asked sympathetically.

"Yeah, he had divorce papers served to me and that was it," I pouted.

"Oh no! Really?" She tsked her tongue sadly.

"When I was in hiding, I stole a phone and called him from time to time. He was either drunk or high, I never really knew which, almost every time when he answered. He'd made friends with some low-life people who we assumed were trying to find me. The night I finally told him my location they came after me. I'm sure he blames himself."

"What happens when you call him now?" Brandi asked.

"His phone has been disconnected. I have no clue where he is or if he's okay. I just know we aren't married anymore." I brushed away a tear.

"I'm sorry, Paige. I know you love him," Brandi's voice was soft.

"We didn't really know each other that well."

"Do you think you knew your true self?" she challenged me.

"Ah, good point. The dissociative fugue I battle everyday... I realized the truth. When I was in Canada, I changed my identity complete with a new name, I took a job I wasn't even qualified for, in a country I had fled to. I even changed my hair cut and color," I agreed.

"Well, that last thing isn't so bad. Some of us have no choice but to cut and color," Brandi made a crack about the difference in our ages. "Anyway... what's on your agenda for today, Paige? After I leave?"

I knew she was asking because if I was making plans with my life, it meant I was choosing to move forward. I smiled because I had given this a lot of thought.

"Well, I was thinking about going back to my old routine. I loved it when I first lived here. I went to the gym, to support group, and then shooting at the gun range." I wondered if all my old friends I'd made at each of those places were still around.

"Those things all seem positive to me. I'll be ready in about fifteen minutes. Then, I can get on the road."

"Take your time." I smiled. "There's no hurry. The group doesn't meet until noon." I didn't tell Brandi that Stephen was coming over for dinner. I wasn't sure why. Maybe it had something to do with that declaration that I missed James. Or maybe it was the urgency in his text when he told me he needed to talk to me. Either way, I wasn't in the mood to analyze what that meant.

"Sounds like a great day." Brandi said as she disappeared into the bedroom.

I wandered around my house while finishing my coffee. As I looked around this little home of mine, I started to feel ownership and pride. In the living room, my couch sat facing the TV I'd kept. The couch was a nice, gray, comfortable, overstuffed microfiber material with a matching recliner chair. I still needed to get some paintings to hang on the walls, but I had time for that.

The dining room was the warmest place in the house. We had found white and blue striped seat covers to go on the chairs. The adjoining kitchen was fully stocked with dishes and appliances I would use.

I stopped in Anna's room where I had been staying and dressed quickly. I ran a brush through my hair and put on a quick touch of mascara. I put on a pair of warm, comfortable boots with my jeans and hoodie.

I knocked softly before I peeked into the master bedroom where Brandi had been staying and sleeping. The curtains and the comforter I had bought for the master bedroom were a nice, neutral shade of blue. Someday, maybe I would have the courage to sleep there.

"Come in," Brandi called.

I opened the door. The room still spooked me, but it no longer gave me an eerie feeling. Brandi was pulling on her shoes, looking fresh from a shower with makeup on her face. She packed the last of her clothes in her overnight bag.

"I'm gonna miss you," I said.

Brandi hugged me. "This isn't good-bye, Paige. You're going to be just fine," Brandi said with a smile as we walked through the house and out the front door.

I thought about those words. I believe them. I *am* going to be fine. I felt so much pain and loss when I thought of Anna, and I thought I always would. But maybe, just maybe it could get better in time. I wanted to believe I could even move forward and embrace life. Maybe someday.

I hugged Brandi Burnett goodbye again and thanked her for coming. In truth, she might have saved my life.

"I'm just a phone call away." She held up her phone. "I mean it, Paige. Anytime you need me, please call."

"I will." I smiled.

She walked a few feet then turned back. She looked at me as though contemplating something. "And Paige?"

"Yeah?"

"I was wrong about Stephen. I don't think he's like my ex. You both suffered a tremendous loss together. Maybe you could offer him a truce."

"What do I do if he reads into it though?" I worried.

"Well, assume he will but set strong boundaries," she suggested. "Oh, and one more thing…"

"Anything," I smiled.

"Stephen's mom also suffered this loss. It might be nice to have people who love you in your corner. Don't be afraid to reach out. Adopted families can be more powerful than real ones because you get to pick them."

"Thank you." I waved to her. I repeated her words from earlier. "I'm gonna be just fine."

"I know you will." She smiled and waved, got in her car, and backed out of the driveway. I didn't know if Ray would show up again now that she was leaving, but I did feel like I was stronger and could combat him should he decide to show up.

I limped back inside. My leg was starting to hurt from the last day of activity. I sat down for a half hour to rest. I found myself utterly alone in the Mynart House.

That's when I heard a sound that turned my veins to ice before adrenaline flooded through me. Outside, tires screeched, then there was a loud thump, followed by a long, mournful howl.

16

CARLEY
DAY FIVE GONE

Carley was pouring over the books. It was bill pay day and she wanted to devote all her attention to paying them correctly. She had decided she would pay bills two times a month and she didn't want to get anything wrong her first time. Today, she set her phone to silent, and no one was to disturb her.

That's why she was surprised by a knock on the front door. She paused and listened as Carlos, her bodyguard, answered the door. She had told Uncle Scott, mincing no words, that she was perfectly capable of taking care of herself and didn't need someone as antiquated as a bodyguard. She had lost that fight.

Do it for your daughter, he had demanded.

Now she could almost see the value in Carlos. Who would possibly want to see her at her home today of all days?

She heard a man exchanging sharp words. Then the door to her study opened and Carlos walked in looking irritated. Carley had already risen to her feet in expectation of someone walking through the door.

"I told him you didn't want to be disturbed," Carlos said loudly as Demitri burst through the door to her study behind him.

Demitri Abbott strode angrily into the room. He was more handsome than Carley remembered. Today he was casual, wearing a thick, white, long-sleeved shirt made of a quality material that must have had spandex in it because it hugged Demitri's chest, showing his nice definition. The shoulders of the shirt had about ten folds on either side which drew attention to his broad shoulders. The black jeans he wore showed his slim build. He also wore a pair of static black True natural shoes he might have worn if he were golfing.

It was clear that Demitri wasn't here for a social call. His dark brown eyes shot angry daggers at Carley and his body language was stiff. It was all wrong and he was coming toward her pretty fast.

"Thanks, Carlos." Carley met the men at the door. "Please stand outside the door in case I have to throw this gentleman out on his ass," Carley said defensively, noting Demitri's position of anger. Carley shut the door when Carlos left.

She was rocking her four-inch black Michel Kors heeled boots, which evened the height difference between her and Demitri. She wore skinny jeans and a red long-sleeved shirt that fell off her shoulder in an 80s sort of way while hugging her body and showing off her curves. Her long, wavy hair hung down her back. Gold hoop earrings adorned her ears.

No matter that she worked from home. Carley refused to be one of those frumpy women who rolled out of bed in her pajamas, peering at the computer screen with eyes that had barely opened. She'd dress nice simply because she wanted to. She'd do it for herself.

"You look stunning, Carla," Demitri said, letting his guard down a bit as he put a hand to her waist and leaned in to kiss her cheek.

Carley could feel the heat from his touch, so she moved away quickly.

"There's most likely a reason you're here," Carley stated as she walked back to her desk. She could feel his eyes on her. She assumed he was watching her backside as he followed her further into the room.

"There's been an accounting mistake, Carla," Demitri said angrily as he waved a check in the air and approached her office desk. "I've come so you can fix it for me."

"Sit down, Demitri," Carley commanded. She tried to ignore the way his cologne smelled but it brought her back to the night they had spent together on the black leather sofa in this very room.

Demitri sat on the edge of the seat. She sat in her seat on the other side of the desk.

"The only mistake that's been made is the amount you've been charging my uncle for the past few months." Carley reached in her desk and pulled out a folder labeled *Demitri Abbott*. She also noted the gun she left sitting in the desk just to the side of the folder.

"Big words for someone who just got here," Demitri sneered. His pupils were black and dilated in anger. "Perhaps you need a history lesson so we can catch you up to speed?"

"This is every invoice you've given my uncle for the past year. Three months ago, your invoice jumped up four thousand dollars. I thought you'd made an honest mistake and transposed the numbers. But two months ago, your invoice went up by another two thousand dollars. I'm told your contract is not up for negotiation until the end of the year. Nothing has changed. How can you justify this?" Carley kept her voice dead calm.

Demitri said nothing as the color came into his face. "There are things that go on in your family you would be shocked to know. It gives me certain rights. Such as the right to charge whatever I want for my services. I doubt your uncle will frown on that."

"Scott told me the history I need to know. The rest is not

my concern," Carley cut through his words. "If you have a problem with this, you need to talk to Scott. He has the final authority here."

"He told you that I've spent the last three years of my life hating him? He came to me with the idea of an alliance between our two families. He came at the perfect time. See, I had a problem, make that *two* problems, I needed to get rid of quick. Scott volunteered to make them go away in exchange for an alliance. Only, the alliance wouldn't be with my family, it would be with me. Which is why I now run his operations."

The corpses in the car we sent down the ravine, Carley realized with surprise, connecting pieces of the story she'd just heard with the mystery. Does that mean she was an accomplice to whatever this was?

She wondered if Scott had chosen to do this as a way to bond the two of them to one another. From the smug look on Demitri's face, it seemed like Demitri had the upper hand. He must have some power over Scott. Not only did Scott kill his people and dispose of the bodies, Demitri had knowledge and could tell the cops what he knew.

"Well, I run his money. My concern is that I protect the family finances. The way I see it? You took advantage of the fact that our accounting department was unprotected. You stole money. Scott is willing to let it go because of your working relationship. From now on, we expect to pay you what we owe you. That's the deal."

"This isn't over," Demitri seethed, his displeasure obvious.

"Oh, it's over all right. You walking into my home is over, too. Never again. This is where I live. You won't *ever* come here again without an invitation. And if you do, I'll shoot you myself for trespassing. Get out."

"It doesn't have to be like that, Carla," Demitri said, looking a little stunned at the quick turn of events.

Carley thought she saw something else in his eyes as well—respect.

"Go bitch and cry to someone else. I've got work to do."

Demitri got up to leave but paused after opening the door. He looked over his shoulder at Carley with those large, dark eyes shooting daggers of rage across the room.

Carley never looked up, but she heard Demitri's footsteps fade out into the hallway and then she heard Carlos close the door behind him.

"Carlos," Carley called out.

Carlos appeared at the door.

"Demitri Abbott is not welcome in this house until further notice."

Carlos nodded and left the study, closing the door behind him.

While he was gone for now, Carley knew in her gut this wasn't the last time she would see Demitri Abbott. Carley wasn't sure, given his anger, why she felt more excited than scared.

17

PAIGE

DAY FIVE GONE

I hobbled out the door as quickly as I was able, adrenaline flooding my veins and helping me ignore the pain in my leg. I could see a beautiful golden retriever with red blood matting her fur on her front leg. She was lying on the side of the road in front of my house panting hard. I ran to her side. I looked down the street in time to see an old Chevy pickup racing away.

"Did they hit you or throw you out of the car?" I asked sympathetically. I cautiously put my hand on her head.

The dog whined painfully.

I looked around and realized I'd never seen a dog around here. If she was a neighbor's dog, she was a long way from home. The nearest property was miles down the street.

I was going to have to pick her up and get her to a vet. First, I got in my car and moved it close to where the dog lay. After parking the car, I opened the door to the back seat of the car. Careful not to touch her leg, I squatted and picked up her heavy body. I watched her for signs of aggression. I'd heard some dogs got mean when they are hurt. She just whimpered quietly. I staggered awkwardly to my car and put her in the back seat, ignoring the pain that shot down my leg as I put full weight on it.

"It's okay, girl. I'm gonna get you help."

I looked up the nearest vet and headed in that direction.

"You'll be okay, girl." I watched her in my review mirror. She was still whimpering quietly. I couldn't help but think about Anna and the accident I couldn't save her from. My heart hurt at the thought. At least I could save this girl.

Animal Tales Veterinary Hospital had a lobby full of people when I walked in. I waited patiently until someone spotted me.

"Can I help you?" a kind elderly woman greeted me sounding frazzled.

"Hi, I'm Paige," I introduced myself. "I found a dog on the side of the road. She's in my car right now. I'm not sure if she was hit or fell out of a moving truck but she has a bloody leg and I worry it might be broken. Can you see her?"

"Of course. Do you need help carrying her in?" the woman asked me.

I nodded.

"Bobby?" she called.

A young guy appeared. He readily agreed to help me with the dog.

"Hey, girl!" he said in surprise when he saw the retriever. He checked the name on her collar. "I know you!"

"You know this dog?" I asked as I followed him back into the clinic. He opened a door and waved me in. He put her right on the exam table. Another man, who was quite a bit older, presumably the vet, came into the room.

"What do we have here?" he asked. He immediately began assessing the dog's leg.

"It's Molly, sir."

"Yes, it is. But how did you end up with her?" he asked as he stopped to assess me.

"She was on the side of the road in front of my house. I saw an old Chevy truck drive away as Molly was howling. I couldn't tell if they hit her or if she fell out of the truck."

The doctor and the young apprentice exchanged glances.

"Molly here belongs to a man who they found dead earlier today. That Chevy truck belongs to the man's wife. They're investigating the cause of his death. Kinda looks like Marge was trying to get out of town before they find the cause of her husband's death," the doctor said, giving me a look that explained his underlying meaning.

The apprentice nodded.

"Well, this paw is pretty bad. I'm afraid we need to reset it."

"Can I leave you my number? I would really like to hear how she's doing after surgery."

The doctor looked at me for a long second. Then he nodded. "Yes, I'll do that."

I stopped at the front desk on the way out. "I would like to leave my phone number. For when Molly wakes up from surgery. I want to be sure she makes it out okay."

"Sure!" the woman handed me a piece of paper and pen. I jotted my number on it.

I thought about asking for a job application. Perhaps fate had brought me here. But the thought of working a job right now overwhelmed me so I left it at that for now.

After I left the vet's office I signed up for a gym membership, then headed to a meeting. I barely made it through the door when I heard my name shrieked in a high-pitched, happy tone. My friend, Amy, came flying at me. Same big personality, same big smile, and same warmth, but she had lost a lot of weight.

"Look at you!" I exclaimed. "You look great."

Amy grabbed my hands happily. She was glowing. "I've missed you! Where have you been?"

"That's a long story!" I smiled back at her. "What's this?"

She held up her hand and showed me the beautiful diamond on her finger and giggled. "I got married," she squealed happily.

"That's wonderful, I'm so happy for you!" I answered.

The meeting started shortly after. The warmth and love I felt from those who remembered me, and even the ones who were newer in the group, reminded me of why they had become my people so quickly. We were bonded by a common theme.

When the meeting ended, I headed to the gun shop.

"Paige! Well, I'll be damned! You move back here?" Peter greeted me the minute I walked through the door.

"I did," I admitted with a smile. "But I need to buy a new gun."

"I'll let you," he said. "Let's see, what did I sell you before?"

"A Glock 43x," I reminded him.

"Right. You want another one?" He was looking under the counter to see what he had available.

"Yes, please."

"You know the drill. License and a piece of mail," he requested.

Now I hesitated. I shouldn't have a felony on my record. The charge for murder had been dropped. But I wondered if the faked passport charge had been dropped from my record. I guessed I'd find out the hard way. I handed him my license and a piece of mail.

"Alright, I'll let you know when it goes through," he told me with that big smile.

I thanked him and left.

I stopped to buy a computer and inquired on how to set up Wi-Fi for the house. I had restarted my degree program in Georgia and there was no reason not to finish it.

My background check went through a lot quicker this time

than the last. Peter called me back in. By that afternoon, I was once again carrying a gun.

The last stop was the grocery store. I checked my watched. The afternoon was getting away from me and Stephen would be here before I knew it. I walked into the grocery store and tried not to remember the day I'd met James. I sighed. It would be a very long time before I got over him. If I ever did.

18

PAIGE

DAY FIVE GONE

"I don't know why I took Brandi's advice," I mumbled to myself. "Regardless, Stephen Wilton is on his way here as I speak."

I was extending an olive branch to Stephen. He had something to talk to me about and I had taken Brandi's advice. Brandi was right and I assumed Stephen would understand exactly how I felt without me saying a word. I thought he would be easy to be around.

I wasn't sure why I felt so nervous. Maybe it was because I had made twice baked spaghetti and I wasn't much of a cook. I thought it just looked like overcooked spaghetti in a baking pan. Or maybe it was because it was Stephen, and we had a lot of history.

Before I could decide why, there was a knock at the door. I went to open it.

"Hi, Stephen!" I smiled at him as I opened the door.
Stephen smiled back.

I hugged him tightly before inviting him in. It was nice. Maybe this would be a new beginning.

"I brought French bread," he said, handing it to me.

"I'm gonna go put this in the oven," I said as I walked through the house and into the kitchen. I set the timer for ten minutes.

Stephen followed me into the kitchen. "Can I help with anything?"

"Nope, I'll just warm this up and we'll be ready to eat. Can I get you something to drink?" I asked.

"Water is fine," he said.

He would be on his best behavior because I'd asked him to be. I didn't want him to get the wrong idea. That was perhaps the thing that made me the most nervous of all.

"I found a dog in a ditch today," I said, not sure what else to talk about.

"Really?" Stephen asked.

"Yes," I smiled. "I took her to a veterinary clinic in town and thought about picking up an application. I haven't decided if I want to do that yet."

"I think it would suit you. How's the dog?"

"I haven't heard yet."

The timer on the oven buzzed and I pulled out the French bread. Still wearing oven mitts, I carried the hot pan to the kitchen table and went back for the spaghetti.

"Also, I bought a computer to finish my online classes." I started cutting into the food and scooped spaghetti onto my plate and Stephen's.

"Great news," Stephen said. "I like what you've done to the place," he lied kindly.

"No, you don't," I laughed a little. "You have a tell. I always know when you're lying."

"I do not!" Stephen protested then shrugged. "Fine, I liked it the way it was."

"Really? I thought Carley had decorated this place."

"What made you think that?" he wondered.

"It matches her house." The minute the words were out of my mouth, I clapped my hands over it.

"Paige, you were in Carley's house?" Stephen asked, looking shocked.

"Yes," I had to admit. I knew Stephen could tell when I was lying as well. So I didn't even try.

"Why?"

"I'm not sure what made me go in the house exactly," I said, trying hard to remember. "I was just walking through the woods when I saw the house—"

"Wait, is that the day you tripped the alarm, and it alerted my phone?" he asked.

"Yes."

"So, when you got to Carley's, did someone else live there?" Stephen smirked.

"No, the house was empty."

Stephen looked down at his plate sadly and ate a few bites of his spaghetti. "Can I ask... did you redecorate Anna's room too?" Stephen asked as his voice dropped a notch.

I was about done with my food. I ate the last bite and tilted my hand. "Kinda."

"What do you mean by *kinda*?" Stephen wondered.

"Well, come see for yourself," I invited him.

Stephen followed me in. "Oh, wow, you changed it but only a little. It looks like an older girl version of Anna's room. What a great idea!"

I gave him space because I could tell his mind was playing out memories of their time here.

"Oh, I put her things into a box, just to tidy up a bit," I pointed to the box on the top shelf. "Help yourself."

Stephen grabbed the box down and began rustling around. I could see the raw emotions on his face. Tears sprang to his eyes.

"You know what? I'm gonna give you a minute." I practically choked on my words and left the room in a hurry. Once outside the room, I fell backward against the wall for strength. I covered my mouth and sobbed silently. I didn't know if I'd ever get over this loss. Nor did I know if I was supposed to.

Stephen came out of Anna's room. When he saw my tears, his eyes softened, and he pulled me into his arms. He held me while we cried together for a minute. Then I saw what he had carried out of Anna's room. It was a toy Teenage Mutant Ninja Turtle.

To my surprise, I burst out laughing. "From that whole box, that's what you're taking?"

Stephen smiled too, reluctantly.

"Oh, I have chocolate cake," I said, remembering suddenly. "Do you want coffee with it?"

"Normally, I'd say no, not so late, but I do need to drive back tonight."

I cut two pieces of cake and started the Keurig. I set the cake in front of him.

"What's the story with the Ninja Turtle?" I had to ask.

Stephen smiled. "After you went away Anna missed you so much. She tortured Carley by saying things like *you're not my mom*. Then Anna started hiding from her. When Carley would find her, Anna would say she'd only come out for daddy."

I smirked to myself thinking, *Good, that's my girl.*

"Anna just missed you so much. I made sure to show her pictures, so she didn't forget you… Anyway, one time she hid so well, she fell asleep in a laundry basket and Carley, not knowing she was there, piled towels on top of her. We couldn't find her for hours. We had the neighborhood come and search the property. Finally, Anna woke up. When I picked her up and asked her what she was thinking, she said, *I'm a ninja, daddy.* She said she was the *best hider in the world.*"

I laughed in delight. My heart hurt over this loss, but laughter was a wonderful way to honor her memory.

"Tell me another story about her," I requested.

Stephen chuckled. "For her birthday last year, we threw her a ninja princess party. She had just discovered the Disney princesses. She sort of smushed them together and asked us for a ninja princess theme. We had a cake specially made and everything."

I laughed a little. "I hate that I missed it. I missed so much."

"Hey, you couldn't help that," Stephen said.

"Maybe," I relented. I didn't believe it though.

"I miss her," Stephen said.

"I miss her, too," I agreed. "She was the happiest baby."

"That's why you invited me here?" Stephen asked. "To talk about Anna?"

I nodded. "I thought it would be a good way to honor her memory. That, and Brandi Burnett thought I needed to not shut out the people who shared my loss. I plan to reach out to your mom soon, too."

"That's good. I think she would like that."

I nodded. "So, what's new with you these days?"

"Well, I'm considering a job promotion," Stephen answered slowly as if he was thinking hard about what to say. "I passed a physical fitness test and checked all the boxes…"

"Congratulations! Did you take it?" I asked.

"I haven't decided," he said slowly.

"Why not?" I couldn't imagine why Stephen would turn down a promotion.

"Because it requires traveling out of state and sometimes over borders."

"Oh?" I wasn't sure what he expected me to say. I felt my heart sink in the most unexpected way. *Odd*, I thought. This was the first time I'd seen Stephen since Anna's disappearance. I didn't miss him when he was gone, but the finality of him taking a job that would keep him away on a more permanent basis felt abrupt. It felt like he was abandoning me.

"I haven't given them an answer yet." Stephen stood, picked up his plate, and carried it to the kitchen.

"Why not?" I asked. I dreaded the answer to this question. I knew the answer but there was something driving me to hear it. I picked up my plate, too, and followed him to the kitchen.

"I'm not sure." Stephen ran water over his plate, rinsing it off before he put it in the dishwasher. Watching him complete such a natural task seemed so intimate. For a moment, I pictured him living here with Carley. Suddenly, my mind pictured that it had been him and me living here together in this house with Anna as if time could be rewound. My heart fluttered. I remembered when I first met him and for one wistful moment, I would give anything to go back to that time. The time when we were in love. A time of total unawareness.

Stephen wordlessly took my plate, rinsed it, put it in the dishwasher, and shut it. Then he turned to me, giving me his full attention.

"Well, what's holding you back, Stephen?" I knew better than to ask.

"You," he said. I half expected him to remind me we were still waiting for Anna's DNA report to come back and the steps we would have to take when that happened. He didn't have to.

He was so close to me now. I didn't remember him moving. Maybe I was the one who had moved. He looked into my eyes and sighed. I could tell he was having a hard time obeying the boundary I had put in place for tonight.

"Well, you have my full blessing," I whispered. Neither of us moved.

"I keep feeling like I need to stick around to make sure you're going to be okay," Stephen told me. He reached out gently and put his hands on my upper arms to give them a gentle squeeze.

"Well, I'm fine, Stephen. Really, I am. I didn't know if I would make it when we first heard the news in the beginning and maybe I won't ever be exactly right again, but today, I'm okay." I turned my eyes downward, feeling emotional.

"Are you? Are you, really?" He was now ducking to look into my face.

Stephen put his finger under my chin and tilted my head upward until I had no choice but to look into his eyes.

"I—"

His lips were on mine. Warm and soft, he kissed me in the most natural way. I remembered this. I remembered kissing Stephen. It felt exactly like the last time we had kissed. The attraction I felt for him had not gone away. Attraction was never the problem Stephen and I had. I kissed him back. He pulled me close, and I snuggled into his embrace. It felt so nice to be loved again.

As he closed the distance between us, the keys in his pocket scraped my leg.

"Ow!" I said in surprise.

"I'm sorry," Stephen said as he mindlessly pulled his keys from his pocket, intending to continue the kiss.

I could see a small, folded piece of paper flutter to the ground.

"Oh, you dropped something—" I broke the embrace and bent to retrieve it.

"Paige don't—" Stephen said at the same time.

As I picked up the paper, it unfolded, and I saw my name. It was opened and I was reading it by the time I had straightened back up.

Dear Paige,
I guess neither of us is who we thought we were. I've made such a mess of my life. I can't drag you into that anymore. I'm the reason they found you. You could be dead now for all I know. All because of me. I'm sorry I doubted you. I don't deserve you. I'm going to get my shit together. Maybe the universe will bring us

back together some day. Until then, please know that I love you. I have since the first time we met, and I always will.
~James

I inhaled sharply and took a step back from Stephen. I re-read the letter. I looked up at Stephen. He said nothing, color flooding into his cheeks.

"What is this, Stephen? Where did you get it?" I asked as angry adrenaline flushed into my veins, making my body feel instantly hot.

"It was in your divorce papers the day you signed. It must have fallen to the ground. Only you didn't see it and walked off. I picked it up and followed you intending to give it to you. But you were in such a hurry to put distance between us, I didn't."

"I have spent countless hours wondering why my husband chose to divorce me." I felt my body start to shake. I could feel the anger take over now. "You knew all this time. You had this the day the papers were served, and you didn't see fit to hand it to me?"

"Paige, I know you're upset," Stephen attempted to put his hands on my arms once again.

I moved back as if his hands would burn me. "Don't ever touch me again."

"He doesn't deserve you," Stephen said passionately. "He left you when you needed him the most. He just disappeared. Come to find out, he's a druggy. If that's not bad enough, he serves you divorce papers on the worst day of your life. The day you learned about Anna. But you still agonized about why *he* left *you?*"

"That's not your business!" I sputtered. His words hurt. He wasn't wrong but it didn't make them easier to hear.

"Yes, it is, Paige! Don't you see? You and I are meant to be. I made a mistake, too. Years ago, I lied to you about my profession—"

"You were an undercover cop investigating me! You were paid to pretend to love me!" I interrupted, my voice raising.

"But I apologized, I explained. Everything changed and you know it. You knew I loved you—love you. But you could never just forgive me and move on." Pain was evident in Stephen's eyes as his chest rose and fell. "So, yeah, I held on to your note. I was planning to give it to you tonight. I just couldn't bring myself to do it."

"Won't you ever understand that a relationship founded on lies isn't a relationship that will last?" I raged. I shook the note at him. "This changes everything and you *knew* it would."

"I just kept thinking eventually the universe would throw us back together. You and me." He shook his head and lowered his voice, admitting defeat. "That's not ever going to happen, is it?"

"No, Stephen. James is out there somewhere working on himself. He was my perfect match. He made me a better person. Despite all his flaws, I love him. In my heart, I still feel married to him."

"Well, I hope he comes back to you some day. I hope you get your *happily ever after*," Stephen said in a voice that did not match his words. He looked sad. I knew this had been his last attempt to win me over.

"I can be quite happy by myself whether he comes back to me or not."

"I'm taking the job," Stephen decided. "You won't have to worry about my intentions anymore. Let's just call this what it is. A nice clean break."

"Deal," I said.

Then Stephen left. I followed him to the front porch and watched him get in his car. I went back in and shut the door behind me.

I sank down on my new couch and cried. I tried to determine why I was so emotional. Was I crying because I had feelings I didn't want to admit to myself about Stephen? Why else would I feel like the last person who actually cared about me had just abandoned me?

Before I could answer the question, there was a knock at the door. I quickly got up and wiped my face.

"Stephen?" I could see how white his face looked. He lifted his cell phone at me.

"Lieutenant Higgins just called. He has news. He won't tell me over the phone. He wants to see us in person."

"The DNA report," I said.

Stephen nodded his head.

Quietly, I grabbed my coat and followed him out the door.

19

CARLEY
DAY FIVE GONE

Carley had taken on a new hobby called internet stalking. This hobby, which was becoming more like an obsession, was not a good look for Carley, yet she couldn't seem to stop. She looked up Scott Milternett on Missouri Casenet, the state database of court records. At first, his background seemed cleaner than she expected. Nothing more serious than a few parking tickets, a divorce, and a civil disturbance.

"That's not so bad," Carley mumbled. Then she looked closer. Scott had a consistent number of charges that all seemed to stop abruptly two years ago. Before that, Scott had on average one to two charges per year for the past three decades. That is, until two years ago. No charges had been filed against Scott for two years.

"Pretty sure sending a few people down a hill in an explosion would look bad on this record." Carley's fingers drummed on the table. Then she remembered a few times Scott mentioned that he had made a deal with the cops. She wondered if Scott was supposed to stop doing bad things while he was working with them. *Too late.* She also wondered more about Demitri and if he was the kind of guy who would kill Scott if he knew about that deal.

Thank God she had ended things with Demitri. Carley could most definitely keep a secret and her loyalty would always be to Scott. No matter that he wasn't her real uncle. She was closer to him than her own mom and Scott had only been her mom's boyfriend for two years.

Carley sat back and remembered the time she had snuck out to a party and had been knocked out cold by a kid who most likely had his way with her. When she came to, she was in a dark room and called her mom to pick her up.

Scott had showed up in her mom's place. Instead of taking her home, they sat in his car and had a real conversation. It was the first time an adult had approached Carley like she was an adult. She was sixteen at the time, but more grown up than many other kids her age. Scott had made the next couple of years bearable for Carley. He'd made it easy to transition out of her mom's house to a place of her own. It didn't hurt that he had been giving her money to help set her up on her own.

Carley half-heartedly looked at a few internet articles about Scott that predated two years ago. There were plenty, but they always ended with Scott Milternett posting bail and coming home a free man.

If Scott did things, bad things like murder, while working with the cops, what had he accomplished when they weren't watching him? A shiver worked its way down Carley's spine. Scott must be very good at covering his tracks. Which meant there was a lot he wasn't saying to Carley.

Carley felt a little sorry for Demitri. But not sorry enough to tell him what she knew. Getting in the middle of this sick grudge match Scott was playing was the last thing she planned to do. What she was planning to do was stay far away from Demitri Abbott. She was not going to get pulled into the middle of anything.

Carley wondered vaguely if Scott Milternett's decision to become a narc had put them in a position of danger. All of them. Another chill went down Carley's spine. She thought of Anna who was safe here and at her private preschool where she learned things way above her pre-k grade level.

Carley began to think about an escape plan. How safe was *she* if she relied on Scott's protection, if Scott was thrown in prison, or if a criminal turned on him? She couldn't let anyone, not even Scott Milternett, take her down. If he went down, she needed to make sure he went down by himself.

20

PAIGE

DAY FIVE GONE

"Sit down, guys," Lieutenant Higgins told us after we arrived. It was late. Too late for a conversation like this.

We sat.

Lieutenant Higgins pointed to a report in front of them. "This is a hard conversation to have." He looked pointedly at Stephen and said, "I debated waiting to tell you at all until things finalized at the academy."

"What's going on?" Stephen asked. His voice sounded nervous.

"Though you haven't been privy to this investigation, you know we got the jaws of life down to the accident site and took those corpses out for DNA testing. We realized right away the corpse in the back seat was too damn big to be Anna.

"Finding her shoe on the ground that way, not to mention the clothes that were sprinkled all over the hilltop... well, it all felt a little too 'set up' for our taste. We didn't want to give you false hope. Then there was a backup at the lab on account of a tornado that ripped through southeast Arkansas the week before. The lab was busy processing and IDing a high count of bodies. So, it took longer to get our DNA evidence."

"What are you saying here?" Stephen asked.

I sat up straighter on the edge of my chair, hanging on the lieutenant's words.

"I'm saying those corpses don't belong to Carley and Anna. I'm telling you this because you have a right to know. But it changes nothing for you, Stephen. I won't allow you anywhere near this case. You need to go to Georgia and train for that job." Lieutenant Higgins rubbed the scruff on his face.

I tried to process these words. What did he mean *it changes nothing*? I looked at Stephen for an explanation, but he just stared dumbfounded at the lieutenant.

"I'm sorry, I don't think I understand. Do you mean my daughter could be alive and you are banning Stephen from finding her?" I could hear the dangerous way my voice pitched upward.

"Stephen doesn't work here anymore, Paige. We let him go because he was investigating against my direct orders. He's got a helluva opportunity to become a US Marshal and I'm not going to stand in the way of that. But he no longer works here, nor am I going to allow him to work on a case he's this close to."

I felt my anger rising. Stephen didn't mention he'd gotten himself fired. I stood abruptly.

"Fine time for you all to start playing by the rules!" I exploded.

Lieutenant Higgins looked startled.

"You allowed him to investigate my mom's murder, but you won't let him near this?"

"I was wrong to allow that, Paige. No need to have history repeat itself."

"The last superior who warned me off a case ended up guilty," I accused him irrationally.

"Woah, woah, woah. Paige, you need to calm down here," Stephen said. "Sit down."

I plopped down, feeling shocked.

"Whose bones are they?" Stephen asked.

"We don't know yet. That's the next thing they are looking into. We were able to determine there was no match for Anna and Carley. Now, we are looking through the missing persons database for a match," Lieutenant Higgins said. "I don't need to state the obvious, do I?"

"Please do," I said, trying to make my shocked brain function.

"This appears to be an intentional attempt to make it look like Carley and Anna are dead."

"But why?" Stephen asked. "Why would someone go to such lengths? Does that mean someone kidnapped them both?"

"You've been a detective for a long time, Stephen. Anyone you know who wants to get back at you?"

"No, not since we took down Lacose." Stephen shook his head in disbelief at the turn this conversation had taken.

"We plan to investigate this while you go train. When you're a US Marshal, I suggest you let us do our job. No more conflicts of interest. You've got to trust us here. Agreed?"

Stephen nodded slowly. "So, what's the plan? Where will you start?"

"With the last known place they were seen alive. We have your parents' testimony. We know what time it was when Carley and Anna left, and we know what time Carley's car was found. We just need to reconstruct a timeline of what happened from point A to point B. We'll look at your enemies. And yours too, Paige. We'll wait to see if they get a match on the DNA with the missing person database. Good old fashioned police investigation."

"You think they're alive?" Stephen whispered his question. But then he shook his head. "I can't hope for that and find out you're wrong. I can't grieve this twice. I lost my daughter in an instant. I just can't—" Stephen's voice broke.

Lieutenant Higgins came around the side of the desk and grasped Stephen's shoulder. "I know, son. I get it. Just let us do our job and we'll keep you posted on the rest."

"It's Carley," I stated with quiet certainty.

"What?" both men said as they turned to me.

"Carley kidnapped Anna and tried to fake their deaths."

"No way," Stephen objected. "Carley is stubborn and head-strong but she's not a delusional psychopath."

"Apparently, she is," I argued.

"Okay, you two. It's not a bad theory and it's one we've started looking into," Lieutenant Higgins admitted. "Stephen, why don't you give me a list of all known associates of Carley's. Let's see if we can find her or someone she knows."

"Unbelievable," Stephen shook his head.

I stood up. "Will that be all?"

Lieutenant Higgins shrugged. "Put together a list of enemies and we'll keep in touch."

I nodded but left the office. Lieutenant Higgins might be able to tell Stephen what to do but he wasn't going to tell me what to do. If my little girl was out there, I was going to find her and bring her home.

Stephen followed me out into the pitch-black night. Stephen put a hand out to stop me.

"You can't honestly be thinking about going to that training, Stephen. You can't leave at a time like this."

"They're handling this investigation. I've botched investigations I've been close to before. You heard him. He won't let me near this case. I lost my job over this. I don't even work for the Police Station of Little Rock anymore. I'm a civilian with zero authority. I'm not a US Marshal yet. I'll be in training for over four months."

I felt irrationally angry. "Fine time for *you* to start playing by the rules!"

"Paige, think about it. If I pass and become a US Marshal, my jurisdiction will supersede state lines. No one will tell me I can't investigate my daughter's disappearance on the side. What I do with my free time is my own business. But I have to leave so I can report to the training academy tomorrow morning."

"That's it? I'm supposed to sit here for the next four months or wait until someone calls me?" I threw up my hands. My mind was returning to a time years ago when Anna was kidnapped, and my lieutenant told me the exact same thing. Well, it would be different this time. Someone was going to find my daughter. I certainly wouldn't make any promises about not investigating.

"Paige, it was Lieutenant Higgins who solved your mom's murder. He's way more capable than me. If they haven't found Anna and Carley by the time I get back, I'll launch my own investigation."

"There's no time to wait—"

"You have to. You aren't an officer. These guys have been doing this for years. Now that they know this is a missing persons case, they'll find her."

"Like hell I'm going to sit here and wait. Every minute my daughter has been missing she's been in danger. Every day brings her a day closer to her death. If she's even alive at this point."

"Paige, please, you have to. You can't do anything to put your life in danger too," Stephen said protectively.

I snorted. "All of this goes back to your deranged ex-girl-friend. Carley's the one putting our lives in danger. Find Carley, you'll find our daughter."

"I don't think—" Stephen started but I interrupted him.

"Well, start thinking it. Carley kidnapped our daughter from your parents' house. At the very least, I'll make sure she hangs for *that* offense. You really think someone kidnapped them both after that point? Surely, no one else thinks Carley is a victim here. She stole my daughter and if you're too close to her to be objective in this investigation, then you're right. You do need to go do your training and remove yourself. Let the people who can bring her home do their job."

"I know what you're thinking. Don't do it, Paige. You're not a detective," Stephen warned me.

"That's the thing. You get to choose your academy training and I get to choose what I do next with my life too."

Stephen didn't even say goodbye. He just shook his head and got into his car and left.

I wasn't going home. Not yet. I was going to find my daughter.

21

PAIGE

DAY SIX GONE

The next morning, I knocked on the door to the Wilton's home. I'd opted to find a hotel room for the night. I wasn't surprised to learn Stephen had been staying with his parents. I knew they would have given me a place to stay as well. But I opted to be alone.

Linda Wilton opened it with a gasp of surprise. "Paige!" She exclaimed. "Please, come in."

"Thank you," I said as I entered her home.

She gave me a warm hug and had instant tears in her eyes. When she pulled back, I was reminded of how much she looked like Stephen. She was Anna's grandmother and they all looked so much alike.

"Can I get you some coffee?" she asked.

"Please," I nodded gratefully.

I followed her into the kitchen and sat at the bar stool as I'd done more than a few times while Stephen and I had been dating. I watched her busy herself with the coffee.

"You're not here to see Stephen, are you?" Linda asked perceptively.

"No, I'm not," I admitted.

"Good. He already left for his training. Listen, Paige, I need to ask you something that I have no right to—" Linda's voice broke as she started crying.

"Linda, it's fine. Ask me whatever."

"I let Carley take Anna. You trusted me and I let Anna go." Linda's tears streamed down her face. "Is it possible—can you ever forgive me?" She paused her actions and put her hand to her heart.

For a moment, my mind went back to that night. The night when we lost Anna. After a very long airplane ride with a layover, Stephen and I arrived at his parents' home to pick Anna up. I recalled in detail the look on Linda's face after we'd arrived.

Tears I tried so hard to blink away now spilled down my cheeks, mirroring Linda's, as I remembered that moment and the horror that radiated from my soul when Linda realized her mistake. Anna had been kidnapped. Again. Only this time, we would not find her mere days later.

Carley had come and had taken Anna from Stephen's parents' house. She'd told Linda and Bruce she was taking Anna to Stephen. She had lied, but Stephen's parents had no reason to doubt Carley. The last time they'd seen Carley and Stephen, they had been together.

What no one knew or understood was why Carley wanted Anna when Anna didn't belong with her. I still didn't know the answer to that question. Why had Carley wanted my daughter? She'd told Bruce and Linda she couldn't give them any details. She made Stephen's parents believe they were all still in danger and running to a new place. Her story fit the story Stephen had told his parents before he went to save me. Carley was conniving like that. Neither Bruce nor Linda questioned it. But that was where the true horror began.

Stephen had picked up the phone and called his police precinct to report the abduction.

Surely, this is all a misunderstanding, Stephen had reasoned. *We'll find Anna, and it'll be fine,* Stephen had said. He had actually thought Carley would have a logical explanation.

I nodded my head at Linda and got off my barstool. I gave her a hug. "I forgive you," I said. "You erred on the side of trust. You had no reason not to trust her. The fault is hers."

Bruce joined us in the kitchen just as we finished hugging. "Well, Paige, I didn't hear you come in."

"He doesn't hear that much these days," Linda whispered with a smile. She handed me a cup of coffee.

"Well, I heard that!" Bruce protested, pouring his own cup.

"Let's sit in the living room, shall we?" Linda asked once everyone was set up with steaming mugs.

Once we were settled comfortably in the living room, I asked the question that would explain why I was really here. "I assume Stephen told you about the development with Anna?"

Linda nodded, tears flowing freely down her face again.

Bruce put his arms around his wife and shrugged apologetically. "My wife, the crier."

"Rightfully so," I said. "You know I have a background working in a police precinct," I started. "It's what I did in Canada. May I ask you some questions about when Anna went missing?"

"Sure," Linda agreed. "Then what?"

"Then I plan to retrace the physical location and path to the accident sight, look at the evidence with a different perspective, and hopefully figure it out from there," I lined out my plan.

Bruce nodded.

"Ask us anything, Paige. We'll help any way we can," Linda assured me.

"Take me through the night Carley picked up Anna," I instructed. "Don't leave anything out."

"I can do one better. When the police initially started asking questions, I was afraid I might forget something. So, I wrote it all down." Linda got up and went to find the journal.

"Even better," I agreed.

Linda came back and opened the journal. Then she handed it to me. I read the passage:

Carley Smith came to the house at approximately 6:45 p.m. and greeted us cheerfully. I told her I didn't know she was coming but invited her in and gave her a big hug. She made a comment about Stephen being too busy chasing down bad guys to give us a call and tell us she was coming. I believed her. Stephen never called and he wouldn't have called if he'd been on assignment. Before I could comment, Anna flew into the room screaming Carley's name. Anna was so excited to see Carley! Anna asked her if they could go home now. Carley said yes, that was why she'd come. She said that daddy had found a safe place and wanted them to meet him. I believed her. I didn't know they had broken up. Anna didn't seem to know either. Anna started jumping up and down. Bruce came in and asked if they were leaving so soon. Carley said yes, and she would tell us about it, but the situation was a little touchy right now so she couldn't go into detail. I asked if everyone was safe. Carley said yes. We hugged Anna goodbye. Then Carley asked her if there was anything Anna wanted to take with her. I told her I'd pack up her bag. Stephen had sent Anna with an overnight bag. I packed it up and sent them out the door. Then Bruce and I walked out to the front porch to watch them go. They skipped down the street to the car – it was a navy-blue Toyota Corolla. Carley strapped Anna into her car seat in the back. Then Carley got into the driver's side and drove off. Anna waved as the car drove by. It was the last time I saw my granddaughter.

It was so hard to read. I asked if I could take a picture of it. Linda agreed. I had a two-hour drive ahead of me to Ouachita

Forest where they'd found the car and I wanted to make it while it was still morning. So, I planned to leave soon, but Linda detained me for a few minutes longer.

"Paige, the truth is, I'm glad you came in person. Thank you so much for your forgiveness—" Linda said.

"You're welcome," I assured her.

"It means a lot to me. You mean a lot to me."

"I know you didn't intend for anything to happen. You had no way to know. Truthfully, Stephen might not have even had time to answer a call or a text. We were on the run for our lives at one point."

"I did try to text him, Paige. You're right though, he didn't respond. But that wasn't uncommon."

"I figured. He was busy trying to save my life," I said these words through clenched teeth and tried not to blame Stephen yet again. His job had been to keep Anna safe. My job had been to keep me safe. He was always rushing in where he didn't need to be. Now we were in this mess.

"Thank you, Linda and Bruce. I know it's hard to relive that moment. We're going to find her."

"I hope you do. We'll be praying you do."

With that, I said *goodbye* and I got in my car. As I slipped behind the wheel, I picked up my cell phone to call Lieutenant Higgins. I buckled into the passenger seat as the phone rang.

"Did you find an overnight backpack in the Toyota?" I asked when he answered the phone.

"Let me check." The lieutenant seemed to be shuffling through paperwork. "No, no backpack, no bag of any sort. Why?"

"Linda Wilton said she sent Anna with an overnight bag."

"Right, but remember, the car blew up. Everything but those bones were incinerated," Lieutenant Higgins reminded me.

"Hmm… true," I acknowledged.

"What are you thinking about, Paige?" Lieutenant Higgins asked.

"I'm just trying to prove my theory. About Carley taking Anna. I know she still has her."

"We're already looking into it." Lieutenant Higgins said. "Paige, I really don't want you anywhere near this either. Things might get dangerous."

"Sorry lieutenant. You can't stop me from looking for my daughter." I hung up.

I felt like the lieutenant knew something he wasn't telling me. I knew he didn't really have to tell me, and he still took the stance that there were some things he *couldn't* tell me.

I sighed remembering when I worked for the police services in Canada. They had a system of entering all the information into a database that any employee could access at any time. Whether you were a police officer, detective, administrative assistant, or CIO, we could access all the case information. The solve rate was very high there. It would sure be helpful if I had a team like that behind me now. I thought of Mina, the crime analyst who had been my friend.

"Except one thing," I mumbled to myself. "I don't belong to the police force anymore." I felt instant concern, remembering my conversation with Brandi Burnett. Was I was doing the exact thing she warned me about? Was I slipping back into my old pattern of taking on personality traits that did not belong to me?

Still, I had to wonder. Why did my brain come up with logical pieces that others seemed to overlook? Maybe I was better at investigative work than I'd ever given myself credit for.

22

CARLEY

DAY SIX GONE

Carley's cell buzzed early, waking her up. She assumed it was Scott. She blindly reached for her phone. It was a mom named Michelle. Carley met Michelle the day Anna started her private preschool. Michelle's daughter, Hayden, and Anna had hit it off that day and they'd been best friends ever since. The two girls were going on a shopping trip with Michelle today for Hayden's birthday.

> Michelle: *Sorry to text so early but Hayden is so excited to see Anna. Can I come get her early this morning? I'll take them out to breakfast before the shops open...*

Carley hesitated for a moment. This was what she'd been grappling with since she'd arrived here. Dare she let Anna out of her sight? She had agreed to the birthday plans for the girls to play. But having Anna in such a public place as the mall without her was a different story.

On one hand, both Hayden and Anna would be devasted if Carley changed her mind. But what if someone spotted Anna in public and recognized her? Carley would lose Anna instantly. Then she decided she was being ridiculous and overprotective. She and Anna were from a different city, Carley reasoned. Who would possibly recognize Anna? Carley made a quick decision and texted back.

Carley: *Sure. What time? How about I send you all around in the Rolls today?*

The Rolls-Royce Cullinan belonged to Scott. It was part of Carlos' protective detail. It was fully loaded, complete with dark tinted windows.

Michelle: *Won't say no to that. Sounds fun. Is 7:30 too early?*

Then Carley texted Carlos.

Carley: *How about a day off body-guarding me to drive Anna around?*

His reply came quickly.

Carlos: *Of course. What time?*

Carley checked the clock on her cell. It was barely six in the morning.

Carley: *7:15. Can you keep tabs on them even when they leave the car? I'd prefer no one know you're watching them.*

Everything Carley had worked for, lied for, and helped kill for was wrapped up in Carlos and his ability to keep Anna safe right now. Carlos was capable, as he'd already proved to Carley in the short time he'd worked for her.

So, why did Carley have a feeling that something was about to go terribly wrong?

23

PAIGE

DAY SIX GONE

A fog had settled in a thin layer and hovered just above the ground. I followed the ranger through the long grass to the spot where Carley's car had come crashing down the hill less than a week ago. My shoes crunched where the morning dew had frozen some of the blades of grass. In less than a week, it would be December. It would just get colder from here on out. I didn't care about that or the cold wind that seeped through the legs of my jeans above my boots.

I felt a sort of dissociation from my feelings. It seemed crazy to me I had not come here with Stephen when I thought Anna was dead. I had chosen to look the other way, accept my worst possible fate, and move on.

Only I hadn't moved on. Despite all my best attempts, the pain of losing Anna hadn't gotten any easier. Sure, it helped when Dr. Burnett had come to see me. I was able to talk through those feelings, but I had never been able to fully come to peace and experience acceptance.

Now, as I followed the ranger, I began to see the remnants of the car crash in the grass. The car had been removed. But there was still a big, burned oval where the car had been on fire. When I looked up the hill, I could see clothes that were still stuck on trees. Stephen had told me about that. Anna's clothes had flown out the window as the car rolled. It was an image I couldn't get out of my mind at the time. It had haunted me. Now, it just confused me.

"When they took away the car, they took the clothes they could reach and boxed it all up. I need to figure out a way to get the rest of them out of the trees." Donovan, the park ranger, pointed to a few pieces of clothing while looking sheepish. Lieutenant Higgins had put me in touch with him when I asked exactly where the accident had occurred.

I nodded but I wasn't listening to Donovan. I was looking up where the road was high over our heads and trying to picture a car careening over the edge. I imagined it would fly over the trees for some distance before it hit one and flipped.

"How did the clothes fly out the windows?" I asked to no one in particular.

"Windows were opened," Donovan said.

"They were?" I exclaimed feeling perplexed.

"Yep, but I think just the back ones." He crossed his arms over his chest as he followed my gaze up.

"The crash happened about a week ago, at the end of November…" I pulled out my phone and looked at my weather app to find the exact temperature the night of the accident. "It was forty-two degrees that night!"

"Pretty cold to have the windows down," Donovan stated the obvious. "Did she smoke?"

"I actually don't know," I responded and added this to a list of questions I had for Stephen. Going back to my thoughts about the windows being down in wintry weather, I felt this proved my theory even more. It seemed like Carley had placed Anna's clothes in the car and rolled down the windows so the evidence would be sure to fly out before the car exploded.

"How high up is that?" I asked.

"That up there is about eight hundred feet," Donovan responded.

I tried to imagine the speed at which the car had to have been going to land right here at the base of the hill. Not very fast, I'd wager. But then I guessed even a slight miscalculation of the turn could send the car shooting over the edge. I shuddered, but not for my daughter. For the people who had been trapped inside the car as they rolled to a fiery death.

Who were they, I wondered? They were somehow connected to Carley but had Carley killed these people? That thought was more ominous than the last. How would Stephen, a detective, have missed her murderous tendencies? Unless she had help. This seemed like a big job to pull off all by herself. Of course, I didn't know Carley at all. I suppose she could have been a mastermind murderer who plotted to take my daughter, but I still couldn't figure out her motive on that.

If I was with the police force, I would request the pictures of the car accident. But I wasn't.

"Ma'am?" Donovan asked.

I looked up. He was looking at me with a questioning gaze.

"I'm sorry, what?" I asked.

"Do you have any more questions?" Donovan asked.

I shook my head and took a few pictures of the site from every angle. The answers weren't down here. I thought I might have to look up to find them.

I thanked the ranger and drove out of the forest and back up the hill. I drove slowly so I could scan for spots where a car might have sat before someone put it in neutral.

"Bingo!" I said spotting a scenic lookout. There was a small gravel drive designed for a few cars to pull off, sit, and enjoy the view. I parked my car. There were a couple of benches and even a viewfinder.

I fished out a few quarters from my car console and looked through the viewfinder. I could almost see the spot where the car had landed! My heart sped up in my chest and I changed my body positioning and looked down the road where I imagined the car flew over the side.

"Looks like the scene of the crime where the car started rolling," I mumbled, then I felt excited. Is this the starting point from where the car went over the edge? From the right angle, it was easy to assume if someone put a car in neutral, it would have rolled down the road which is a downhill angle, picked up speed, and flew over the edge, landing just about where Carley's car landed in the forest.

This only proved my theory. I knew Carley had my baby.

24

STEPHEN

DAY SIX GONE

Stephen felt like his heart had broken after he left Paige's house last night. He had been so sure they would end the evening together. Now he had no choice but to accept the facts. She had clearly communicated how she felt, more than once, and he had no choice but to accept it. He didn't feel the same way. That didn't matter.

All of that had led him on this road to Georgia to this last interview. If he aced the interview, he went right into training. This wasn't the way they typically recruited US Marshals. Stephen felt the rush of it all. More like he welcomed it. It was good to take his mind off the chaos happening around him. Chaos that he couldn't fix.

Stephen's cell phone rang, interrupting his thoughts. "Hello?"

"Stephen, it's Roger," Lieutenant Higgins began.

Stephen paused. In all his years, he'd only addressed his superior as Lieutenant Higgins. "Yeah, what's up?"

"I hear you're headed out of town?" Lieutenant Higgins asked.

"Yeah. I've got a final interview in Georgia. If I pass that, they'll put me straight into training," Stephen explained.

"Well, listen, I gotta ask you some follow-up questions about the investigation. Don't misunderstand. I'm not asking you to join back up. It's the opposite. I just need to ask you about Carley."

Stephen sighed. "Paige got to you, did she? You know she's not going to let you do your job, right? She figured out in Canada she's actually a good investigator."

"Yeah, sure wish I could get her to take a seat. She's out at Ouachita Forest right now. I fear this case is going to get dangerous," Roger said, getting serious.

"Dangerous how?" Stephen asked, hoping Roger would start talking.

"Nothing I can discuss with you," Roger stated directly. "I just need to ask you some questions about Carley. Paige isn't wrong. She's the last person seen with your daughter. They're both still missing. Any ideas where she might have gone?"

"The only connection I can think of is her uncle in Kansas City, Scott Milternett. But you remember that, don't you? Did you put a tail on Scott Milternett?"

"I had actually forgotten about that," Roger said, his voice trailing off. "I can always put a call into the authorities there, only..."

"Only, what?" Stephen practically snapped.

"You know we don't have jurisdiction there, Stephen. If I remember correctly, Scott Milternett made some immunity deal. He might be untouchable. I hate to say this but maybe this US Marshal job is coming at the best possible time. Once you get out of training, you'll have jurisdiction there. If Scott knows anything, you can get in front of him and ask."

"As if he'd tell me anything," Stephen snorted. "Truth be told, all of this is happening so fast, I almost didn't have time to process it all."

"You should know, Stephen, this training to become a US Marshal is a lot harder than you might think. I mean, you'll need to focus. You haven't been the most focused since Anna's disappearance—and rightfully so…"

"With all due respect, sir, I think I'm about to become pretty focused."

"Good. Glad to hear it," Roger stated.

"It's just that… I'm feeling a little unworthy of this position. I really botched the Mynart murder case. You fired me. Why would *they* want me?"

"You didn't botch it as bad as you think. You kept working every angle until it all fell into place. It took a while but you're like a chihuahua with a steak. You just won't let it go."

"Let what go?" Stephen asked feeling confused.

"Anything. If you find a loose string on a case, you won't sleep until you've chased it to the end. You just keep pushing and looking and asking questions until you're convinced you know the truth. You don't want anyone to get away with anything. Not even your ex-girlfriend."

"Let's not talk about that. Time to close that door for good."

"Probably best if you do shut that door."

"Also, I'm not sure I should be leaving Arkansas right now," Stephen worried.

"This is an opportunity you can't pass up. There's nothing you can do here," Roger assured him. "Go advance your career to the next level."

"Isn't it ironic the US Marshal position will lead me to Kansas City? Do you think they want me because of my connection to Scott Milternett?"

"No, and if you know what's good for you, you'll keep your mouth shut about your connection. Those connections of yours tend to cloud your judgement. They need someone with a clear head," Roger warned Stephen sternly.

"Noted." Stephen nodded. Roger Higgins was right about that.

Stephen never expected that one day he might be a US Marshal. He just needed to remove the doubt he felt over his own abilities to carry out the job once he finished training. Another thought surfaced. One that was more complicated than any others.

They say all things happen for a reason. Had Stephen's recent heartbreak, getting fired, and losing Anna all happened in order to free him for this moment and empower him to say *yes* to a job he did not feel qualified for?

25

CARLEY

DAY SIX GONE

Carley gently woke up Anna. Anna blinked owlishly at Carley. Her curly, frizzy blond hair stuck up around her head.

"I don't wanna wake up," Anna flailed her hands at Carley's face and willfully pulled the comforter over her head.

"Come on, Anna, I'm not really in the mood for this," Carley felt grouchy and tired.

"Go away!" Anna screamed.

"Stop yelling, Anna, and get dressed. It's Hayden's birthday and her mom is taking you guys to breakfast but I guess you don't have to go," Carley pretended to leave the room.

"What?" Anna flung the covers back quickly.

"Get up, Anna, or you'll miss Hayden's birthday." Carley came back into the room.

"Okay, I want to wear my purple dress." Anna jumped up and ran to her closet. She yanked down a purple dress with black stripes. Next, she pulled down a pair of yellow leggings that had big orange polka dots. Anna had thrown a fit in the store the day she saw the leggings and had to have them. Carley had relented.

"Purple, yellow, and orange? Are you sure you wanna go with that?" Carley asked doubtfully.

"Uh-huh! See," Anna said. She tugged the dress down and pulled the leggings on.

The color combo was not Carley's favorite to begin with but when Anna put the outfit altogether, it just looked busy.

"Okay, it's up to you on that." Carley had read it was important to allow a child to make her own decisions when she could and dressing herself was a step closer to independence. Even if that meant a hideous and busy purple, yellow, and orange combo.

"Can you fix my hair?" Anna asked after she was dressed.

"Come here." Carley sat down at the vanity and found an anti-frizz spray. She sprayed it on Anna's head and gently combed out Anna's curls with her fingers. "One ponytail or two?"

"No ponytails!" Anna announced loudly.

"Oh, Anna. It's more of a ponytail kinda day for you," Carley tried to suggest.

"No! No ponytail. I'm not a pony!" Anna giggled hysterically.

"You're right about that!" Carley smiled in spite of herself.

After the wrestle of getting Anna ready, Carley got dressed in some casual Saturday clothes herself. She wore a pair of yoga pants and a long-sleeved t-shirt with tennis shoes. She opted to pull her own hair back into a ponytail.

"Mommy, you're a pony?" Anna squealed with laughter when she saw Carley again.

"Clearly," Carley said dryly. They went downstairs together just as the doorbell rang.

"They're here!" Anna screamed and ran down the stairs to open the door.

"Stop!" Carley's voice was sharp and low.

Anna halted, shocked at the tone, and turned around in

surprise.

"Don't you *ever* open that door without my permission or first looking to see who it is." Carley checked the peephole then turned to Anna who still looked surprised and uncharacteristically still.

"Who is it?" Anna asked uncertainly.

"It's Michelle, Hayden's mom," Carley informed her. "You may open the door."

"Okay," Anna opened the door with a little trouble. "Hayden!"

The two girls skipped down the stairs outside and got into the waiting Rolls-Royce.

Carley looked at Michelle with sympathy. "She dressed herself today and she's a bit of a handful. Call me if you have any trouble."

"Of course." Michelle smiled big with excitement in her eyes, her confidence evident in the way her shoulders were pulled back and her chin was lifted. She winked at Carley. "Go have a cup of coffee and relax. I've got this."

Carley thanked her and went back inside. She moved the curtains to wave goodbye to Anna who was already safely in the back in the Rolls. *At least the Rolls has dark, tinted windows,* Carley thought for the second time that morning. Carley stayed long enough at the window to see Michelle climb in the car and Carlos promptly drive away.

Carley followed Michelle's advice and made herself coffee. There was a growing discontentment, a feeling of unease, in the pit of her stomach. It wasn't her battles with Anna this morning. It was a feeling that something big was about to happen and Carley would be at the center of it.

She sat at the bar in her kitchen, gazing out the window, lost in thought. She texted Scott to ask him to come to see her today. An immediate text came back for her to go to him.

Other than a few short outings, Carley really hadn't been

out of the house. She tried not to. For all her bravado, Carley didn't want to be spotted by anyone, either. Considering there were no funeral plans for her or Anna yet, it made sense to lie low. Not to mention, each time she left the house, Carley got the impression she was being watched. She always shook that off and chalked it up to having a bodyguard follow her around.

Finishing her coffee, she grabbed her car keys to the Mercedes-Benz GLS 7, another gift from Scott that showed up the day she did. She got in, started the car, and backed out of the driveway. Scott lived twenty minutes from Carley. It should have been a nice, easy drive but Carley found herself sweating profusely despite the air conditioning. She noticed a black car that seemed to be trailing her. When she switched lanes, the black car switched lanes. When she got back into the right lane, the black car did as well.

She slowed her car and tried to memorize the plates. It was a black BMW. It was sleek and sexy with tinted windows. She couldn't see the driver. Her adrenaline and perhaps fear, tingled down her spine. She was having a hard time breathing now. She took short, shallow breaths and focused on the road ahead.

Why was she so sure no one would spot her or know who she really was? While her car would have been found seven hours away, she had chosen to stay in the same state where Paige lived. Even the name *Carla* was too close to her name *Carley*. Why had she taken so many of Scott's ideas? She was beginning to understand how much smarter she was than Scott. Doubt wasn't her thing. She would work on ditching it immediately.

She could see the turnoff to Scott's private road that led to his private drive up ahead. From now on, Carley determined, she was going to trust her own instincts as if she was in this alone. Because she was. Scott had helped her get here and she needed to be grateful for that. But it was her and her survival skills that would keep her alive.

Thankfully, the BMW kept driving down the road when she turned off. She pushed the code to Scott's gate and the doors opened and shut behind her car. She drove down the long driveway that was lined with mature trees in full bloom. What a single guy like Scott needed with a house this big was beyond her but she assumed he had a reputation as head of the family to preserve.

Before she pulled up and Scott came out of greet her, Carley had decided the way to stay safe was to know more information. She was done hanging out in the dark about the life she was now involved in.

She got out of the car and allowed Scott to kiss her cheek. Then she entered his grand mansion. Inside, the main room of his house was deceptively big. The ceilings were twenty feet tall, and a grand marble staircase curved up the stairs into a loft. The room was an open layout though it was clear which part was the living area and which part was the kitchen and dining area. To the right was a kitchen where a large stainless steel double wide refrigerator lined the wall. A seven-foot serving island sat with decorative flowers and books. That was all Carley could see from her vantage point.

"How are you?" Scott asked conversationally. He motioned for her to sit down.

"I'm okay. Do you ever get the feeling that you're being followed? I'm starting to feel paranoid, Scott. I feel like I was followed here. I know I told you I didn't want to know too much about the business, but I think I need to know more."

"What? What do you need to know?" Scott asked her.

"You need to tell me who the bodies in the car were."

Scott lowered his voice. "Are you sure you want to know those details?" He rubbed his forehead.

Carley nodded but deep down, she wasn't sure at all.

"Those people in the car were a husband-and-wife con-artist team who were working in one of our affiliated casinos in

Kansas. They managed to steal over one hundred thousand dollars from the casino before they were caught and killed. They weren't supposed to die that night. One of my men botched the job. He came to me to clean it up."

"He, being Demitri?" Carley asked knowingly. She felt a little more at ease. At least the story seemed to fit with what Demitri had hinted at the other day.

"Your staged car accident presented a creative solution," Scott said as he nodded.

"Unless the cops test the skeletons for DNA," Carley said. She was suddenly furious with herself for not asking these questions before they sent the corpses down the mountain. Why hadn't she thought this through? But she knew the answer.

Think, Carley, think, she scolded herself. She made rash, emotional decisions all the time, but she was always able to get herself out of them. She'd come up with a solution now just like every other time before.

"There's something else you should know since we're being honest."

"Okay," Carley said.

"You don't need to worry about officials. If anyone ever pulls you over, or you get into any trouble, just drop my name."

Carley nodded, thinking she knew why, if the donations she had seen in the books was any indication. Still, they had to know what Scott was doing was illegal.

"We have agreements—the officials, and our family. We transport product across state lines, and they let us. They don't pull us over, search our trucks, or ask for licenses. We've all been amiable for years."

Carley looked at Scott like he had three heads. Then her phone started ringing. Carley looked at the caller ID and held up a finger. "I'm sorry, I need to get this."

Scott nodded.

"Hey, Michelle," Carley answered the phone quickly. "How's it going? Is she acting high-handed still? This morning was so rough!"

"Well, it's not about to get any better, Carla!" Michelle's voice snapped angrily.

"Uh-oh, what happened?"

"A security guard caught Anna stealing," Michelle said with clear disdain. "Anna blamed it on Hayden but when they reran the security feed for all of us to see, it was clearly Anna. They've got her in the security office and everything. I've never been so mortified! And on Hayden's birthday of all days!"

Carley's head started to pulse. "Really? She's only two. Does she really know better?" Carley knew Anna was fully aware as she edged closer to three years old every day.

Michelle made a noise that sounded like an indignant snort. "*My* daughter knows better. I don't know why *yours* doesn't!"

"Okay, I'm sorry about that, Michelle. Can you stay there until I get there? I'm on my way."

"Oh, trust me, they wouldn't let me go anywhere if I wanted to," Michelle stated and hung up the phone.

"I need to go. Anna stole something and a security guard pulled her into the mall office. Michelle is waiting for me to come get her." Carley grabbed the keys and stood to leave.

"Let me guess, the uppity private school mom shamed you for having a delinquent daughter?" Scott asked putting his nose in the air and walking on his tiptoes.

Carley giggled but then stopped. "Is Anna a delinquent?"

"No, she's normal. Kids test boundaries all the time. I'll hate to see her eat her words when *her* daughter pulls a stunt like this. Let me drive you," Scott was at her elbow. While the lack of privacy annoyed Carley, she remembered her earlier paranoia while she was driving and felt more and more like this was for her own protection.

"I'll be fine. I just need to pick up Anna. It's a private,

family matter. Surely you understand. I can drive myself."

"Not an option, I'm coming with you," Scott insisted, not accepting her answer. "Why did you drive here by yourself? I rarely drive unaccompanied anywhere. Where's Carlos today, anyway?"

Carley followed him out the door. "I sent him to play body-guard for Anna. Let's just take my car. It has Anna's carseat in the back."

"Fine," Scott relented. "But I'm driving." Scott got behind the wheel.

It wasn't long after Carley sat down, shut the door, and buckled her seatbelt before she found her anxiety increase. But it wasn't because of Anna's actions. She found herself looking at every car that passed. At one point, she slouched down in the seat.

"Are you really that worried?" Scott finally asked.

"Yes. I really think I was followed to your house," Carley admitted. "I just feel very anxious being out in public."

"Sounds like it's time to change your appearance," Scott stated.

"Change my appearance?" Carley asked with a frown.

"Yeah, if you're afraid of getting spotted, make yourself the opposite of what anyone looking for you would see, then blend into public."

"Will that work?" Carley wondered as she considered it. "What would you suggest?"

"Well, for one thing, you could go blond," Scott suggested.

"Blond!" Carley's eyes were big and full of disdain. She did not want to be blond!

"Yeah, and think about if there's any work you've ever wanted done to your face. Not because you need it, but because you've always wanted that work done."

"I'll think about it," Carley said. She could see the mall ahead and changed her focus.

26

PAIGE

DAY SIX GONE

After my trip to the accident site, I found myself at a dead end.
Where to next? I had no idea. I drove back to the police station.
I felt so tired. I remembered a time during mom's murder
investigation when I'd slept in a chair in the corner of the
police office. I was prepared to camp out again if it meant I
would be privy to information on Anna's case.

Just as I pulled into the parking lot of the police station, my
phone rang.

"Hello?" I answered.

"Hello, Paige?" a kind elderly voice inquired.

"Yes?" I responded, feeling curious.

"This is Marge from Animal Tales Veterinary. I just wanted
to give you an update on Molly, the golden retriever you
brought in yesterday."

"How is she?" I asked. "Did she make it through surgery
okay?"

"She did!" Marge exclaimed cheerfully. "She's such a sweet
dog. Her leg wasn't as bad as doc originally thought it
would be."

"Oh good!" I exclaimed. "I'll come see her when I get back."

"She'll be here. She's been a good office dog. We're looking for a home for her. They found the owner's wife and she's awaiting trial for murder."

"That's terrible," I said, remembering how this small town loved to gossip. My heart constricted as I said *goodbye* and turned off my car. I would love Molly to come stay with me. *Maybe someday…* I thought.

Maybe when we find Anna. I got out of my car, walked into the lobby, and rode the elevator up to the second floor. I found Lieutenant Higgins across the room. He made eye contact with me and held up a finger. He was talking to an officer. He pointed to his office, so I went in.

As I sat down, I saw a report sitting on top of the lieu-tenant's desk. I glanced out the door and could see he was still talking. I flipped the paper around. It was a DNA report. My heart quickened. I checked the date. The report named Carley Smith and Anna Wilton as negative.

"This is the report from the accident," I whispered. I read on. They got a hit on the missing persons database! My heart sped up. I took a quick picture, noting the names on the report. "William and Carolyn Abbott."

I had no more than flipped the report back to its original place and sat back down when Lieutenant Higgins walked in.

"Paige, how can I help you?" he casually turned over the report and eyed me suspiciously.

"I was just looking for an update on the investigation," I said making my eyes wide and innocent.

Lieutenant Higgins was quiet for a minute. "We're following every lead right now, Paige. We have some direction but nothing we can talk about."

"Then deputize me," I blurted. "Hire me and bring me in. I can help."

Lieutenant Higgins shook his head. "I wouldn't allow you to investigate something so close to you if you worked for me. As you know, it's why I let a damn good detective go. My advice to you? Go home, Paige. You'll be the first person we call if we find anything."

"Only, you have found something. You said it yourself. You have leads. But you're not telling me what they are. How can I trust that you ever will?" I challenged, crossing my arms over my chest.

Lieutenant Higgins shrugged. "You're right. We do have leads and we *are* following them. But there's nothing solid yet. I don't want to get your hopes up. The best thing to do, the *safest* thing for you to do, is to go home and wait for our phone call."

"Safest?" I whispered feeling horrified. "You think Anna is in danger?"

"She's been kidnapped, Paige," Lieutenant Higgins snapped.

I felt instant tears well up in my eyes.

"I'm sorry," he sank down in his chair. "I haven't gotten a lot of sleep lately. I mean, the safest thing for *you* to do is go home and wait. That's it. That's the only advice I can give you right now."

"I went to Ouachita Forest. I looked at the crash site. I think I found a point where the car might have gone over the edge."

"And?" he asked, clearly humoring me.

"There's a lookout on Scenic Seven at the top of the mountain. It's big enough for a few cars to pull off the road. From the right angle, it's easy to assume if someone put a car in neutral, it would have rolled down the road which is a downhill angle, picked up speed, and flew over the edge, landing just about where Carley's car landed in the forest."

"We've already investigated the entire area, Paige. Go home," he ordered.

I got up and walked out of the office feeling like my legs

were made of wood. His words replayed in my head. *The safest thing for you to do, is to go home and wait for our phone call.*

The chilling reality that made my stomach ache was this one question no one knew the answer to. How long would I be waiting?

27

CARLEY

DAY SIX GONE

Carley jumped out of the vehicle before Scott could turn it off. They were at a public mall and already she could tell it was busy with teenagers and parents.

"I'll be right back," Carley tried to jump out the door.

"Oh no you don't. I'm coming with you," Scott said firmly.

Carley kept walking. She didn't have time to argue. She found the security office quickly and her heart melted at the sight of her blond-haired angel sitting in front of a uniformed police officer.

"Anna!" Carley exclaimed. She told herself she was going to be firm, but Anna looked so scared right now.

Michelle stood in the corner with her hands folded over her chest looking very put out at the interruption to her daughter's birthday shopping.

The uniformed guard looked at Carley with disappointment. "Are you the mother?"

"Yes, I am."

"Your daughter decided to take something that doesn't belong to her."

The guard picked up a small stuffed animal and shook it at

Carley. Carley immediately recognized the small bear. It was a replica of a stuffed animal her dad had given her for her birthday last year. Carley's heart melted further but she knew better than to show compassion at a time like this. Three adults were looking at her to judge her response.

"Anna, I think I know why you took this. It's like the one your dad bought you—the one you left behind."

Anna nodded. Her eyes were full of remorse as she looked at the floor.

"But this bear isn't yours. You can't take things out of the store without paying for them. Next time, you need to ask. You know I would've bought you another one if only you would've asked."

"Can I have it?" Anna asked, taking Carley literal and looking hopeful.

"Not now! You tried to steal this. You don't get a reward. You'll have to be punished!" Carley turned to the guard. "Thank you, officer. Can I take her home? Do I need to sign something?"

Michelle made a rude noise in the back of her throat, making her appearance known. She pushed off the wall she had been leaning against and stood tall, waiting for all eyes to turn to her. Then she was quiet, expectantly waiting.

"Well?" Scott's voice came out surprisingly sharp. "Do you have something to say, Michelle?"

Michelle looked startled, as if she had not noticed Scott who had been lingering in the doorway of the room.

"Anna blamed this on Hayden. I think she owes Hayden an apology," Michelle snapped indignantly.

Carley knelt down by Anna. "Anna, when you stole the teddy bear, did you blame Hayden?"

"Yes," Anna admitted.

"You owe Hayden an apology," Carley ordered.

"I'm sorry, Hayden," Anna said instantly.

Michelle rolled her eyes. "She's not really sorry."

"Excuse me?" Carley stood up and glared at Michelle. "She said she was sorry, what more do you want?"

Michelle shrugged but seemed surprised that Carley would stand up to her this way.

"You can be offended and hold it against her forever if you want but if someone apologizes to me, I choose to forgive them." Carley turned to the officer. "Can we go?"

Michelle grabbed Hayden by the hand and stormed out of the office.

"Michelle," Carley called.

Michelle paused in the doorway. "You didn't drive yourself. Let me text Carlos to come take you back."

"No thanks, we'll get an Uber," she snapped and stormed off.

The officer scratched his head. "This is a little unprecedented. I've never had a child so young in here for shoplifting."

"Well, she wasn't successful, there's the bear. What do we need to do here to make this right?" Carley just needed this nightmare to end.

"Jack, surely you can excuse this one-time offense?" Scott's voice sounded behind Carley. "The child is two. Does she really know better?"

"Good point," the guard looked a little in awe over Scott Milternett's appearance in his office. He had the same look on his face as if he'd seen a celebrity and the celebrity knew him by name.

"This animal doesn't belong to you. You can't take things that don't belong to you, okay?"

Anna nodded.

Carley looked at the guard. "Please. Can we please just go home? I think we can take it from here."

The guard nodded. Carley took Anna's hand and walked her

out of the mall. Carley texted Carlos to tell him he was free to go.

When Anna was situated in her car seat in the back of the car, Carley got in beside her as Scott got behind the wheel. Carley looked Anna in the eyes.

"What have I always told you about that kind of stuff?" Carley asked with a stern voice.

"Don't get caught," Anna said promptly.

"Right. If you're gonna get caught, don't try it in the first place."

The drive home was quiet.

When Scott pulled back into his driveway and got out of the car, Carley got out of the back seat to get into the driver's seat. He looked sternly at Carley.

"Take your own advice. I was serious about changing your appearance. Go blond. Go see my surgeon. You're a beautiful woman, Carley. But if you want to stay *dead*, go get some work done. Talk to the doctor about his recommendations to enhance your image. I'll send you his number. Have him charge it to my special account."

Carley nodded. She wasn't opposed to this idea. Every minute she was out in public she felt exposed. She had always wanted to try Botox, not that she needed it, and she'd always wanted a nose job. The idea of going blond was going to take some getting used to though.

Carley re-started the car.

"Mommy, are you dead?" Anna giggled hysterically.

"Not yet," Carley said. But as she drove away, looking out the window without seeing the scenery passing by, she couldn't help but wonder if her death was closer than she, or Scott, could possibly know.

28

LIEUTENANT ROGER HIGGINS

DAY SIX GONE

Roger Higgins watched Paige Mynart leave his office looking dejected and sighed deeply. He put his hand over his face and combed over his beard. He wondered if she would let his officers do their job. Truth was, Roger hadn't slept well since Anna had gone missing. He felt more invested in this case than any other he'd had before.

He felt regret daily that he'd had to let Stephen go. Logically, it had been the right decision. He'd let Stephen get away with far too much for far too long. In truth, he should have fired Stephen for putting Paige in jail without following the evidence all the way through.

Still, the decision to let Stephen go hadn't been an easy one. Stephen had become like a son to him. The problem was other officers had noticed the favoritism and he'd heard their not-so-quiet grumbles. Roger had come to the conclusion that Stephen needed to be promoted or fired. So, he'd let him go and he planned to stick with the decision. His only consolation was this new opportunity for Stephen.

Roger pulled out his cell phone and dialed US Marshal Brix. He listened as the phone rang several times.

"Hey, Roger!" Brix answered. "Thanks again for that new recruit. If he works out, we'll owe you one."

"Speaking of which…" Roger awkwardly began.

"What's up?" Brix asked getting serious.

"Are you still in the area? I need a favor." Roger got up and paced the office.

"A favor or official business?" Brix asked.

"At this point, it's more of a favor. It's a sensitive topic. We need to tread lightly. If we go in too hard, it might scare off our suspect."

"Sounds intriguing," Brix murmured. "Whatcha got?"

"Well, we have a case here in Arkansas we think might have crossed state lines. A little girl has been kidnapped."

"You issued the Amber Alert protocols?" Brix checked.

"Of course. I put out a statewide alert as well. It's been over a week and no hits. I thought I'd approach this from a different angle. We suspect who might have taken her. But we can't find the suspect or any link to where she might be. The woman who we think kidnapped the girl is named Carley Smith and she has connections to Scott Milternett. Any chance you could look into the Milternett family to see if he's harboring Carley Smith?"

"Absolutely. Can you send me Carley Smith's ID so I can casually look around myself? I'll be in the area for the next week or two. You know Milternett is protected right? We could just pull him in and ask about it…"

"No, we don't want to tip anyone off. If she's there, we would like to go in and quietly rescue the girl. If he's harboring her and he knows you're looking for her, they'd just relocate her or hide her better. Could you follow him around a bit and see if you find anything?"

"Will do. I'll call you when I have something."

"Thanks, Brix. I appreciate it." Roger disconnected his phone. It was a long shot. It seemed a little too obvious. But

Roger had to follow the lead no matter where it went.

29

PAIGE

TWO MONTHS GONE

The first thing I'd done after returning home from Arkansas was interview for the job at the veterinary hospital. The second thing I did was bring Molly home. Molly had been following me around since I'd brought her home. She and I had already had plenty of "getting to know you" talks.

She was two years old as it turned out and she loved running in the yard. On not so chilly days, I would throw a stick for her to fetch and return to me. She loved her new home, and I loved her.

It was hard to believe two months had passed since my last trip to Arkansas. The holidays had come and gone. I'd spent Christmas break with Brandi and gone to dinner with Stephen's parents while I was in town. They were sweet and tried to cheer me up, but nothing distracted me from the obvious hole that no one could fill but Anna. Especially during the holidays.

I called or texted Lieutenant Higgins almost daily. The reply was almost always the same.

Lieutenant Higgins: *Nothing new today…*

I knew what that meant. It meant the trail was growing cold. While it should have been good news to find out it wasn't Anna in that car, it was excruciating knowing that she was out there somewhere alive but unreachable. The fact that there was no ransom note or demands led me to believe that either Carley had her well-hidden or worse. That or someone else had taken them. There was still a possibility that Anna was gone for good.

I only took solace in the fact that Carley, who I was convinced had taken Anna, knew her and cared about her. Stephen believed that if Carley had Anna, Anna was fine. He was convinced that Carley loved her. Enough that she had staged their deaths in an effort to disappear with her. He had some twisted fantasy in his head that it meant Carley loved Anna enough to try to be her mother. I thought it meant Carley was a psychopath.

That led my obsessive thinking to the next piece of the puzzle. The dead bodies in the car. While I knew their names were William and Carolyn Abbott, I couldn't trace any other information about them. It was as if they didn't exist. And no amount of questioning Lieutenant Higgins had gotten me any closer to solving that mystery.

So, I'd returned home and got the job as a veterinary resident. Molly was so happy to see me when I first walked into the clinic, everyone decided I should take her home to see how we got along. We got along great. She loved running top speed around the back yard and plopping tiredly on the back porch.

She had been my only companion as I restarted my veterinary program and worked to finish my online degree. Molly didn't like it when I went to the gym, shooting, or meetings because it meant she had to stay home alone. But she did get to go to work with me, so we spent a lot of time together.

I liked the quaint little veterinary hospital I was working for. I got along well with my co-workers. The outside of the office had a nice cobblestone front that made the place look homey. It was inviting. Once inside, the waiting room was roomy and had couches with throw pillows and a few overstuffed chairs. I felt like I could kick off my shoes, find a good book to read, and curl up all day with Molly at my feet.

The back rooms, where the work was done, were small. There were two exam rooms to see patients. The one doctor, who also owned the place, went back and forth between the two exam rooms.

It was my job to prep the patients and their humans. I would go in, talk to clients about their pets and relay information to the doctor before he went in. Then I shadowed the technician who prepared the vaccinations for the animals. I hadn't witnessed a surgery yet, but I was told it was coming soon.

Though my life was starting to take on purpose, I would always pine for the two people in my life who were obviously missing from it. I cried every day wondering if I would ever see my daughter and James again.

30

JAMES
TWO MONTHS GONE

James had been released from rehab. He was under strict instructions to touch base daily with his sponsor. James knew once he was out in the real world, he would experience frustrations. Wherever he settled, he needed to find a home group and attend regularly.

That was all fine but for now, he was taking things one day and even one step at a time. The first step was to find Paige. He had a pretty good idea of where to start. His divorce lawyer had found her at a police station in Arkansas. Literally. He walked right in to try to locate her, and she was there.

At first, James had no idea why she was at the police station. His first reaction to the news was excitement she was alive. The next reaction was heart-sinking. He quickly drew the conclusion why she was there. Stephen worked there. James had been right. Once he removed himself, Paige and Stephen got back together. It hadn't taken that long.

This was the sort of thinking that would spin James in the wrong direction. As his sponsor pointed out, it didn't matter what Paige did. James had released her. He had voluntarily gone to rehab to work on himself. That meant James shouldn't be in a relationship at all for at least a year.

Technically, his sponsor had pointed out, *no big life changes should be made at all until the year is up.* But it was too late. His divorce lawyer had already served papers to Paige. Paige had already moved on.

Was James launching himself into a place where he didn't belong immediately upon release?

Perhaps, his sponsor had agreed with him.

But then there was the issue of amends. James did owe both her and Anna apologies. He needed to do that in person. His sponsor had promised him he would be there with him every step.

When the plane landed in Arkansas, James got a rental car and drove to his hotel. One step at a time, James had decided. He had made it to Arkansas. That was enough for today. There would be enough trials for him on this journey. He was done for today.

Where James should have been feeling excitement to see Paige, he found instead the emotion of dread. There was a nice place in his mind that told him all would work out the way it should. But the fear deep in his heart asked what would happen if it did not?

31

CARLEY

TWO MONTHS GONE

Carley sat under the salon dryer chair with a hefty number of tin foils sticking out around her head. Prior to slathering the bleach product all over her hair, the stylist had cut six inches off Carley's length. The stylist had recommended heavy highlights to start off the process of turning Carley into a blond. This was Carley's second visit to the salon.

After Carley's hair was rinsed and shampooed, she found herself back at the stylist's station. The stylist blow-dried Carley's hair and showed her step by step how to style it straight. Carley had a natural curl to her hair, so she really hadn't needed a lot of time to get ready in the morning. Her hair could typically air-dry and go. But part of her new look would be blond, straight hair that fell just below her shoulders. This would require a lot more work.

Carley looked at her appearance in the mirror as the stylist worked. She had gotten Botox injections in her forehead, in her lips, and filler under her eyes. She had looked so different with those minor changes. As the stylist spun her around in the chair, Carley had to admit she didn't hate the blond highlights.

But it would take some time to get use to them. Mostly, she felt like she looked older and more expensive.

Her last phase was already in motion. Due to Scott's connections, the receptionist had found a quick opening. She had met with a plastic surgeon who showed her pictures of what she would look like with different noses. She picked her favorite and at the end of the week, her new look would be complete. She was looking forward to the change this would bring about. Carley had always hated her profile and thought her nose was not proportionate to her face. Now it would be.

If there was any consolation to this lifestyle, it was the way people who had money lived. She felt powerful and connected. Like it or not, Carley was now a "made" woman and she didn't even have to be married into the family to achieve that status.

All of this extra pampering was a nice surprise and Carley was finding she would like to maintain this new lifestyle at all costs. Even if it really did serve the purpose to keep her "dead."

32

PAIGE

TWO MONTHS GONE

I stood in my backyard throwing a stick to Molly and watching as she fetched it and brought it back to me. It felt nice to be in a moment of simplicity with a dog. Something as basic as a stick made Molly so happy. I wondered why I couldn't be the same way.

My cell phone rang from the pocket of my jacket. I shivered as the chill in the air suddenly made me cold. I pulled out my phone and looked at the number. It was Stephen.

"Stephen?" I answered, feeling breathless as the cold air began to whip around me.

"Hey," he greeted. "How are you?"

I knew what he was really asking about was my state of mind. I decided to be honest and let the tears fall. I sat down on the cold earth as Molly ran up to me with her stick.

"I just miss her, Stephen."

"I know," he said. "Roger said you were having a hard time. I talked to him today."

"Yeah, I talk to him every day... more like I check in with him every day but there's no news. I wish you hadn't left," I said suddenly, feeling so alone.

"I'm sorry, Paige. If I hadn't physically removed myself, I'd be doing what you're doing right now. I didn't know how much I needed this. It's been a good distraction."

"In what way?" I asked.

"This training is hard. But I can't help but feel I'll be stronger when I'm done. We're going to find her, Paige. I feel it in my gut," Stephen said.

"I just feel so helpless. It's like I've given up. I have nowhere else to look. Higgins won't tell me anything. Has he told you anything?" I asked.

"No, he wouldn't."

"I just feel like such a bad mom." I was crying again. Molly could see that I wasn't going to throw her stick again. She trotted over and sat down by me, sympathetically leaning into my side. I felt immediate warmth.

"You aren't a bad mom. And you're not a bad person either. None of this is your fault, Paige."

"Maybe someday I'll believe that." I wiped the back of my hand over my eyes.

"I hope you do. In the meantime, take care of yourself," he said kindly.

"You too, Stephen. Don't hurt yourself. I need you to come back to us."

Long after we hung up the phone, I sat on the ground staring at the sky. The best part of living in the country was the sunsets. As I watched the sun move lower over the horizon and the vivid colors splash across the sky, I could almost hope that we were going to find Anna and bring her home. But hope wasn't a luxury I could afford. Neither was time.

33

JAMES

TWO MONTHS GONE

James stared up at the ceiling of the small motel room he'd rented for the night. He knew coming to Missouri would be a mistake. He'd spent so much time tracking Paige to her home. Once he had some direction, she hadn't been too hard to find. James had started where his lawyer had found her—at the police station in Arkansas.

Once the lieutenant learned who he was, he'd happily given James her address in Missouri. James made him promise to keep it a secret.

I want to surprise her, James had said.

The lieutenant had agreed.

As the GPS on his phone had promised, it was a long drive. As he drove, his doubts assailed him, and he almost turned around more than once. Instead, he'd called his sponsor.

"I don't know what I'm doing," James admitted.

"Remember what you told me?" his sponsor had asked.

"Yeah, I need to make amends. I never should have abandoned her and Anna like that when they needed me the most." James stared at the scenery passing by as he drove without really seeing it. He needed to focus on the task at hand. He was not there for sightseeing.

"Making amends is for you. This is something you have to do with no expectations of her reaction. Whether she's mad, sad, apathetic—she gets to choose how to respond. Can you handle that?" he challenged.

"Yeah. But what if…" James trailed off, lost for a moment in thought. "What if she's moved on?"

"That's quite possible. You divorced her. She can move on and likely has."

"I know," James said. He just didn't know if his barely-out-of-recovery heart could handle it after all. He said *goodbye* soon after and hung up the phone.

Now as he stared at the ceiling of his motel room, he knew the answer. She *had* moved on. He had heard it with his own ears. Still wanting to surprise her, he'd parked up the road a bit from her house and walked closer. Just as he reached her drive-way, he saw her in the back yard. She'd been playing with a fluffy golden retriever.

She looked stunning. She was more casual than he'd ever seen her. Her hair was longer and a light shade of brown which was different than he'd remembered. She was wearing jeans that clung tightly to her legs and a sweatshirt under her jacket —the Patagonia jacket he'd given to her, and tall boots. Her phone rang and she answered it. He heard her say it was Stephen. James had stopped walking and listened.

It had confirmed everything he'd feared. Once James removed himself from her life, she'd resumed a relationship with the ex-boyfriend whom she thought was dead when she and James had met and married. James had no right to show up and muddy her waters again. Though the wind snatched some of her words away, he'd heard the ones that mattered.

I just miss… Stephen. His mind filled in the word the wind had wisped away. He assumed she said, *I just miss you, Stephen.*

I wish you hadn't left…

Don't hurt yourself. I need you to come back to us.

It confirmed his deepest fear. Now, he would leave her alone and let her live the new life path she was on. It's what some would call a living amends. He'd do the right thing for her from here on out.

He rolled over and off the bed feeling frustrated with himself. He dropped to the floor and did twenty quick pushups. In rehab, he'd allowed exercise to take place of his addiction cravings. The endorphins usually helped him kick into a better mood. Tonight, it didn't work. Tonight, he needed to admit he'd been lying to himself.

He picked up his phone and called his sponsor. His sponsor answered on the third ring even though it was late.

"Hi," James mumbled a greeting. He dropped his head in his free hand. "I'm calling because I need to admit something."

"Sure, what's up?" his sponsor asked.

"I shouldn't have come. I didn't come here for amends. I thought I did. But I heard her talking on the phone with another man. The one she was with before we met. I realized then I couldn't deny the truth anymore. I came here to get my wife back. Only she's not available anymore."

"That took a lot of courage to admit that. Good job. So, what now?"

"I'm leaving. I booked a flight to Canada. I'll leave tomorrow. I'm not ready for amends. That feels too final. Like a goodbye. I can't handle any of that right now."

"I understand. Try to get some sleep, James. Call me later if you need me." With that, they hung up the phone.

All James needed to do was get through this night. Then he'd gather what was left of his dignity and leave town. It seemed like a nice town, but it wasn't his home. He didn't exactly know where his home was, but he'd get on a plane back to his hometown. From there, he had plenty of time to figure it out.

He set his alarm for five in the morning to be sure he made his flight. It was an early one. The earlier the better. James didn't want to spend a minute longer in this town than needed now that he knew Paige had moved on. He needed to figure out how to do the same. He doubted sleep would be an option tonight.

34

PAIGE

TWO MONTHS GONE

"I'll be back in a few hours. You'll be fine," I assured Molly. "You do need some more dog food, so I'll stop by and do a little grocery shopping for you." I eyed the tub of dog food the vet had sent home with me, not sure what Molly had been eating.

I reached down to scratch her behind her ears. "Be good Molly, and I might surprise you with some new treats."

Molly gave a low bark in appreciation. She must know the word "treat."

"I'll be right back, I promise."

The cold air took my breath away as I went outside. I went back in to put on more layers. I laced up black boots that covered the pantlegs of my skinny jeans. The fur that lined the inside of the boots came out of the top right about at my calves giving me additional warmth. I sighed as I put on my Patagonia jacket, thinking about James the way I did every time I put on the jacket. Only now, I remember the matching coat he had bought Anna and tears clouded my vision.

It's a Canada coat, James had explained when he'd gifted it to me. *It's warm enough for the real cold.*

I hopped in my car and headed to the grocery store. I had

signed up for a self-defense class at the gym, and I still had a good hour before it started.

Though I'd been back for a few months, I was still new to the grocery store. I decided weeks ago I could no longer survive on pizza and coffee. I still had to search every aisle to find things I needed. I finally found the pet aisle and studied the different types of dog food brands and prices. I supposed that should be important to me.

"What is the best dog food for the price?" I mumbled. I kept reading the ingredients on the back. Finally, I took out my phone and texted the doc.

Me: *Sorry it's a Saturday but I'm wondering what's a good dog food for Molly?*

Doc: *I believe we sent Science Diet home with her when you took her. If you decide to change, you need to mix the two foods together until you run out the old food.*

Me: *Ok, thank you!*

I picked up a bag of Science Diet and looked at the back. Now I had to decide on chicken or fish…

"Excuse me, miss?" The words sounded so close to my ear. I could feel a presence standing just behind me.

His voice sounded familiar. I paused, still looking at the dog food but not really seeing what was right in front of me. For what felt like an entire minute, I allowed myself to imagine the deep, sexy voice of the man I loved.

My heart sped up and beat wildly in my chest. I was too afraid to look. Too afraid I would be disappointed. I wanted to stay right here lost in the memory. Then I smelled his cologne. It was light and musky, but not too overpowering. Was my mind desperately playing tricks on me?

"I think I know you, but I can't place where I know you from," he said.

I gasped then and looked up in surprise. It was James. I wasn't dreaming. He was real and in my grocery store in my small town where I lived. His hair was shorter than I'd ever seen it, but his black curls on top of his head were unmistakable. There was his adorable heart-shaped birthmark on his forehead. His deep blue eyes pinned me under his intense stare. I wanted to jump into his arms and kiss him but something in his body language held me back. There was a sadness about him. It didn't seem like we would begin where we left off and I wilted a little inside.

"James," I whispered. Tears filled my eyes, and despite his body language, I set the bag of dog food on the floor and closed the distance between us. I threw my arms around him. "Is it really you?"

"Yes, it's me," he said. He hugged me stiffly at first but then he relaxed into my tight embrace.

He's holding himself back, I thought sadly as I reluctantly broke our embrace. "What are you doing in town?"

"I came to see you." He rubbed the back of his neck.

"You've been waiting for me at the grocery store?" I asked with a teasing smile.

"No, I'm on my way out actually. I would have left already but I overslept and missed my flight. So, I came here to grab some food to get me by until the next plane takes off," James explained, looking sheepish.

"Which is…?" I felt breathless. I'd only just found him, and he was leaving again so soon.

"Tonight. There's a red eye to Canada," he said.

Of course there is. My mind replayed a time years ago when I fled this town and went out on a red eye to Canada myself. Some things didn't change, I supposed.

"So," I puzzled, speaking slowly, trying to understand. "You came here to see me, but you were going to leave without seeing me? What am I missing?"

"Maybe we could go somewhere and talk?" James asked quietly.

"Yeah, I live right down the road. You could come back to my place and—"

"Not your place," James interrupted. "I do want to talk to you alone. But I don't want to disrespect your relationship."

"My relationship?" I asked, my mind blank.

"Stephen." James shuffled a few items in his hands, and I noticed for the first time he really had been shopping. There was pain in his eyes. "I know you're together. I tried to surprise you last night. I drove to your place, and I overheard your phone conversation. I don't have any right to be bothered by that. I get it. I just have a few things I need to say, and I'll be on my way."

To my own surprise, I burst into laughter. Relief flooded through me. "That's what scared you away? Thank God, I thought it was something more serious. Stephen and I aren't together. He was calling to check on me. We're friends. That's it. That's all we'll ever be."

James exhaled a breath he'd been holding. He smiled a little in obvious relief. "I had no right to even be jealous…"

"Come over to the house. I'll make you breakfast," I offered with a flirty wink. "I've been very domestic lately."

Before we walked away, I grabbed the big bag of dogfood and a bag of treats. "Musn't forget this, or Molly will never speak to me!"

"You got a dog," James said with a smile. His tension seemed to have melted away. His eyes looked happy.

"Yes, I rescued a dog whose owner passed away. She's a beautiful golden retriever." I walked up to the conveyor belt and put the big bag of food on it.

"Does she get along well with Anna?" James asked.

His question took my breath away. I didn't know how to answer.

"That'll be seventy-two oh five," the cashier informed me.

I put my card into the chip reader.

James' question still hung in the air, and I knew he was waiting for my answer. It was about to be his turn to pay so I grabbed my bag of dog food and waited at the end of the register.

Then we walked out into the cold morning air.

"Here, let me help you with that." Without waiting for my answer, he grabbed the heavy dog food bag and followed me to my car. I popped the trunk and we set our groceries inside the car.

"Will you follow me home?" I asked.

"Yes, but can I do one thing first? Just for old time's sake?" he asked.

I nodded. There wasn't anything I would deny this man. My heart felt only love for him.

"Good," he closed the distance between us. He put his arms inside my coat and pulled me closer to him. I could feel his body heat warming my cold, shivering body.

I tipped my head up as he angled his head down. Our lips connected powerfully making up for a few years of lost time and heartache.

"That's what I thought," he whispered as he broke away looking concerned.

"What?" I said feeling worried.

"It was just like I remembered it." He smiled, repeating history.

"I'll see you at home, James." Those are words I never thought I'd utter again, and I hid them in my heart like little lost treasures.

35

LIEUTENANT ROGER HIGGINS
TWO MONTHS GONE

Roger Higgins had just gotten done with the morning meeting when his phone rang. It was US Marshal Brix.

"Hello," Roger answered quickly. He went into his office and shut the door.

"Hey, Roger," Brix answered. "Look, man, I didn't find anything. There's no Carley Smith who matches the description and ID you sent me. I ran surveillance for a couple weeks now…"

"Well, it was a long shot," Roger said letting out the breath he had been holding. "I should have known better than to think Scott Milternett would try something so stupid in plain sight of the cops. Especially when he'd worked out an immunity deal."

"I thought the same thing but hey, it was worth a shot, right?" Brix said.

"Sure. Have you heard anything about Stephen? How he's doing in training?" Roger asked.

"Yeah! He's a real rock star. Great recruit. Wish we would've found him years ago."

"Good to hear! Thanks for your help with this Brix. I really appreciate you looking around."

Roger Higgins hung up the phone and shook his head. They were running out of leads.

Where in the world was Anna Wilton?

36

CARLEY

TWO MONTHS GONE

Carley was up early. Since moving into her new house, sleep did not come easy for her. When she did fall asleep, she didn't stay asleep long. This morning, she found herself thinking about Demitri and wondering if she'd been too rash to throw him out of the house. Did she actually miss him? No, if she was honest, she knew she only missed the male company.

She sighed and threw the covers back from the bed. It was a bit drafty this morning, so she threw on a pair of sweats with her t-shirt and found a pair of fuzzy slippers. She made her way down the stairs and wandered around the house aimlessly.

She grabbed a banana and a water bottle and positioned herself in the study in front of the computer. She half-heartedly pulled up the accounting books and scanned through them, feeling restless. She didn't want to work. Maybe she should get a hobby. Maybe she should get a man.

She did an internet search. She found herself on the Missouri Casenet website. It was what she did when she dated back in college. *You can't be too careful these days,* her best friend at the time had told her. Carley had gotten lackadaisical when she left her college days behind with the excuse that she was an excellent judge of character. Maybe that was the case but when it came to men, she had terrible judgement. *Just for fun*, she told herself, *I'll look up Demitri Abbot*. It was inconclusive. She frowned. Maybe he wasn't from Missouri. She wasn't sure where he was from.

Next, she did an internet search on Demitri Abbott. Articles showed up, but they weren't about Demitri. They were about his parents. One article was dated today. Carley checked her watch. It was barely six. The article stated facts about the disappearance of William and Carolyn Abbott. They had gone missing on November 22. Their home held evidence of foul play and now the couple was missing. Their son, Demitri Abbott went to check on them after he noticed neither one of them were answering their phones or responding to messages.

Confused, Carley sat back and re-read the article. Why was this article just now coming out? Months had passed since November. But Carley knew how hard the local authorities tried to lock down all information and keep details from the media. Maybe it just now leaked out?

Then there was Demitri. He didn't act too concerned about his parent's disappearance. But what did Carley know anyway? It's not like they had taken time to get to know one another. She scrolled and clicked on another article. This one was more graphic in detail.

Carolyn and William Abbott were reported missing by their son, Demitri Abbott, on November 22. According to Mr. Abbott, he went to check on his parents after a series of unreturned texts and phone calls. The front door was not locked, and he entered to find a trail of blood, a piece of an earlobe, and a tongue on the floor. The couple was last seen working at the Kansas Town Casino on November 22. If you know the whereabouts of this couple, or any other helpful information, please call the tip line...

Carley re-read the part about the casino and felt tingly adrenaline flood her veins as Scott's words came back to her.

Those people in the car were a husband-and-wife con-artist team who were working in one of our affiliated casinos in Kansas. They managed to steal over one hundred thousand dollars from the casino before they were caught and killed.

Were Demitri's parents the couple they had sent down the ravine in her car? If so, did that make Carley an accessory to his parent's murder? *No,* Carley reasoned with herself, *the people in the back of the car were already dead.* Though their faces had been marred with blood that night, Carley could see the resemblance to the picture of the couple the article had featured. She could not, however, see any resemblance to Demitri.

Carley's hands shook as she began looking for more information. She wanted to read every article she could find now but the last article she had read had been the most informative. Two articles were all she could find. There would likely be more soon. It only took one journalist before all the others jumped on the story.

Carley felt her stomach turn, wondering what she'd gotten herself in the middle of.

"Scott," she whispered fearfully. "What have you done?"

37

PAIGE

TWO MONTHS GONE

"Molly, I'm home," I called when I walked through the door.

Molly ran at me with her tail wagging. She stopped suddenly and uncertainly when she saw James. James immediately put his groceries on a chair and knelt down to pet her.

"Hi, beautiful!" he greeted her after she smelled his hand.

Molly sat at attention as James scratched her head and pet her whole body.

"I'll let you two get more acquainted," I said as I went to start breakfast.

Ten minutes later, James and I sat at the table with eggs and bacon on our plates and large cups of coffee in front of us. We weren't eating though.

In truth, my stomach was full of butterflies and a desperate desire to keep him here as long as possible. But there was too much we needed to talk about. Molly now laid at James' feet under the table.

"Are you ready to answer my question now?" James asked.

"What question is that?" I asked, dreading what I knew needed to come next.

"My question about Anna. Paige, where is she?" he asked, concern evident in his eyes.

My eyes filled with tears. "She's gone, James," I whispered.

"What do you mean, *gone*? Do you mean Stephen got full custody when you went away? Is she in Arkansas with Stephen?"

I shook my head back and forth. "Anna was kidnapped, James. I've done everything I can do but the police ordered me home. I feel so lost—" my voice broke and tears puddled in my eyes.

"What?" James gasped, then covered his mouth with both hands when he saw my serious face. He instantly began to tear up as well. "How? What happened?"

"Stephen had this girlfriend who spent a year with him and Anna when I was in protective custody. She decided to take Anna —we don't know why. She picked Anna up from Stephen's parents' home. They didn't know she and Stephen had broken up and assumed she had Stephen's permission to take Anna. They let her go with Carley. We don't know where she was going, but her wrecked car was found a few hours from Little Rock. Originally, we all thought she'd missed a turn and went over the edge. It was in a mountain-like area where the roads are extremely curvy. If you drive off the road, that's the last anyone will see of you."

"She drove off the road?" he said in horror as he wiped at his eyes.

"We thought so until we got a DNA test. There were two bodies in the car, but they weren't Anna or Carley. I believe Carley took her and staged the accident to make it look like they were dead. The police won't let me investigate. And when I tried, I hit a dead end," I said. I started crying with him. James grabbed me and pulled me into his lap. He clung to me as we cried together.

"If I hadn't left, this wouldn't have happened," he said.

"James, I would never blame you—"

"You should. There are consequences for every action. I came to ask you to forgive me for leaving but this," his voice broke. "This is too big to ask for forgiveness."

"You know, guilt is one of the stages of grief. You'll get past it. I did. I'm so sorry you came back to this."

James put his arms around my waist and pulled me so close, there was no gap between us. His head rested on my chest, and I put my chin on his head. I wrapped my arms around his neck and held his head in place, my fingers combing through his hair. We stayed there so long, I felt like our bodies were meshing together and becoming one.

I identified with the sadness in James' soul more than any other emotion I'd ever felt from him. We clung to each other tightly, as if we were each other's life rafts in the midst of turbulent waters.

Hours later, I awoke on the couch feeling disoriented. I wasn't alone. I was curled up against James. His arm was holding me protectively. My body was curled up against his. I could hear soft snoring coming from him. Why were we sleeping in the middle of the day?

Then it came back to me. James had pulled me onto his lap and cried with me. When I couldn't stop crying, he had effortlessly picked me up and taken me to the couch where he'd laid me against him and just let me cry there. He smoothed my hair as he cried with me. I could feel his chest rise up and down in his own pain-filled breathing. That was the last thing I remembered. We must have fallen asleep together.

I crawled out from underneath his hand to let him sleep. From the bags I could see under his eyes, I guessed it had been a while since he'd slept well, and he needed the sleep more than I did.

Molly thumped her tail happily when she saw me enter the kitchen. The cold eggs and bacon were still on the table. She hadn't eaten them and sat almost like she was guarding the food.

"Good girl!" I scratched her ear. I grabbed one of the plates and went to her food bowl and dumped it in. Excitedly, she got up and ran for her dish. She had been well-trained. I'd give her that.

I was finishing clean up when I felt warm, strong arms hug me from behind. James smelled like heaven and for minutes, I just stayed in his warm embrace.

"Hi," he said into my ear, sending shivers down my spine.

"Hi, yourself," I said with a smile on my face.

"Can I take you out to lunch?" he asked.

I turned around, leaned into him, but pulled my head back to look up into his deep blue eyes.

"Right now?" I asked.

"Yes, now," he responded. "If we don't leave this house, I'm going to skip talking and take you right into the bedroom."

"I don't see a problem with that," I gave him my full blessing.

"I do. We haven't finished talking. I need to catch you up on where I've been and what my life looks like now. It's only fair that you understand what you're getting yourself into if you decide I can be in your life again."

"Of course you can be in my life again, James. I've dreamt about the day you would come back. I feel so lucky—"

James put up a gentle hand to my lips to stall my words. "I'm the one who's lucky that you'll even talk to me. But the things I have to say are important. We just need to get out of this house for now."

"Okay," I respectfully took a step back. "Let me get my things."

38

PAIGE

TWO MONTHS GONE

"Paige, there's no easy way to say this so I'm just going to say it. I'm a recovering alcoholic," James admitted. We were seated in a private booth back in the corner of the town's diner. We had already ordered, and the food had come out quick.

"James, I knew you were drinking—"

"And doing drugs. I really need to be honest with you," James interrupted. "About everything this time."

"Okay, you told me you did this before when you were divorcing your first wife. You told me things got dark, but it all got better. You did the same thing when you thought I'd murdered my mom. You don't think that's why you went off the deep end?" I asked, trying to wrap my mind around what he was telling me.

James shook his head as he took my hands in his hands.

I sighed. It was just what he'd always done when we were together before to warm my hands. Canada had been so cold.

He looked deep into my eyes. "I love you and you going to jail or WITSEC or wherever you were—none of it matters anymore."

I wanted to erase the pain of the past that showed up on his face. I wanted to fix his every life problem. If only I knew how.

"I didn't come here to get back together. I don't have a right to believe you would take me back. I need to tell you where I've been, and I need to ask you for your forgiveness. But you have to promise to hear me. You need to hear everything."

"I promise." It was going to be hard, but I planned on keeping my word.

"I spent the last two months in rehab in Maryland. There were no phones. They do that on purpose. I had the divorce papers sent before I left because I didn't know how long I'd be gone. I didn't have a right to ask you to wait for me. Not after what I'd done... Paige, Lacose found you because of me."

"I know," Paige said.

James nodded. "I went through a really hard medically induced detox right after that. I was lucky to get to the hospital in time. I never wanted—want—you to see me like that. I saw rehab as a solution but really, at the time, I think I was running away. I was so embarrassed. I learned a lot about myself in rehab. It starts with admitting I have a problem. I think I knew this about myself, but I intentionally lied to you about those DUIs in my background. Can you forgive me for that?" he asked, pausing to look for my reaction.

"Yes, I forgive you," I said, loving this man and his honesty more than ever before. "I wasn't honest about some things in my life as well."

"Well, we all hold back in new relationships. The problem is, we got married before we knew each other's secrets. I don't regret marrying you, Paige. But I don't think we really knew each other."

"I agree, but I don't regret marrying you, either." My mind replayed the beautiful cold, snowy garden where we'd gotten married in Canada.

"I also need to apologize for leaving after I saw Stephen

loading you in his cop car. You were so resolute. I got the sense that you really did it. I was thoughtless and I left you and I left Anna. I was only thinking about myself. I would've had so little time with her as it was. I just abandoned her." James wiped his eyes that had begun to leak tears again.

My own eyes started to overflow. All that time, I was feeling guilt over my own lies and was convinced I was the reason he'd left. But he'd left for his own reasons.

"Then I just got trashed because I couldn't deal with the pain I felt all the time without you. I just didn't want to deal with that while I was sober. I was such a wimp. I couldn't handle my emotions," James admitted.

"I forgive you," I told him as I leaned forward. "For all of it. Besides, I have plenty of my own sins to atone for."

"You do?" James asked.

"Oh yeah," I said. "You may want to catch that red-eye flight when you hear what I have going on. But not telling you when we met was me not being honest. In fact, I almost didn't text you the first night we met because I knew there was no way to explain what happens in my head."

"But you want to explain now?" James asked.

"Yes, I want you to know me, too."

"This is sounding more interesting by the minute."

"Okay." I took a deep breath. "So, my counselor thinks I have a condition called dissociative fugue. It's a condition where I sometimes black out and appear to be moving through life. But when those blackouts happen, I remember nothing of those times. People with this condition can take on a new identity. For instance, I'm not a cop or a CIO, that's really not me. I wear my hair long—"

"I love that," James interrupted.

"I don't wear a lot of makeup and the degree I'm working toward, and have been for a while, is a veterinarian. I ran to Canada because I thought I had killed my mom. I thought I had blacked out and killed her. All evidence pointed to me, and I believed it. I have a deep sense of guilt and shame and take on other people's issues as if they are my own. So deep is my shame, my subconscious mind conjures up ghosts of the past —"

"Ghosts?" James asked. "Like you can see actual ghosts?"

"I can see actual people who are dead, yes. I'm not sure if they are there or simply in my mind," I admitted, feeling so vulnerable. But I wanted to take the band-aid approach and rip it off quickly and get it over with.

"Woah, what's that like?" he asked with some reserve. He looked now like he was observing me, studying me. "Do you see people you know or just figures and shapes?"

"First, I saw my mom. You should thank her because she's the one who convinced me to text you the night we met."

"Wait, so they talk to you, too?" his eyes were serious, and I could tell he was trying to understand.

"Yes, they do. I officially said *goodbye* to my mom, and I haven't seen her since. But then Darby showed up. Remember her? Anna's nanny who Lacose killed in Canada?"

James nodded slowly. His eyes were big.

"Since I've been back in the house, I was tortured by the ghost of Ray." I wiped sweat from my forehead. This was so hard to talk about to someone other than Brandi.

"Ray? The man who tried to kill you?" James seemed to be searching his memory.

"Yes, he was also my biological father. But I killed him," I reminded him.

"So, I bet he's not a nice ghost."

"Yeah, it was pure torture. It got pretty dark for a while."

"What did you do about it?" he asked.

"Well, I have a friend who's a counselor, she was my counselor, as a matter of fact. She came and stayed with me, and we worked through it."

"Have you seen any ghosts lately?" he asked.

"No, no ghosts at the moment," I confirmed.

"And on the fugue… do you do that often?" he squeezed my hands anxiously. "Black out?"

"Ow," I said.

James apologized and smiled sheepishly as he lightened his grip.

"It's not daily. It's magnified with stress and alcohol. I just try to keep the stress level light and rarely drink."

"Okay, so no alcohol for either of us!" James announced, seemingly happy to have common ground.

"What do you do to stay sober?" I asked. "Is there some sort of plan?"

"AA meetings and daily check-ins with my sponsor," James lined out his plan.

I felt comforted to hear this. Even though I hadn't seen James when he was under the influence, I had talked to him enough on the phone in the height of his addiction to know it would be difficult to coexist with him should he start again.

"Well, we're a mess." I said.

"Life is a mess," James said.

"Should we be messy together?" I asked.

"We can try it. Tell you what, why don't we take one day at a time?" he suggested.

"I like that," I agreed.

James kissed my fingertips. His kiss warmed me, heating me from the inside, and exciting me. Sudden memories came to me of those lips kissing other parts of my body, starting with my lips, and trailing down the length of my body.

I laced my fingers into his, noticing the way our hands fit perfectly together. Like they were made to find one another, come together, and never be apart again.

After lunch, James took me home. We walked to my door hand in hand. I fiddled with my keys, attempting to open the door with my one free hand. James wrapped his free hand into my hair and gently pulled my head back, so I had no choice but to look him in the eyes. He didn't have to ask for permission. I was his. I would always be his.

His lips landed on mine, softly at first. Then the kiss deepened, becoming more passionate. I responded with urgency. I felt like I would wake up and he would be gone so I never wanted to sleep again. I supposed that was always a possibility. All we had was today. This moment right now.

Somehow, I managed to open the door to the house.

Once inside, I started shedding clothes. I threw my shirt off first. Then I ripped James' shirt off. I could feel the warmth of his body against mine as we kissed. My heart beat faster in my chest. This is what I'd been missing. Him. Us.

My boots and jeans were the next two items to hit the floor. Then his jeans. We were leaving a messy trail of clothes but neither of us cared. That's when James scooped me up, like he had earlier when he'd carried me to the couch. Only now, his intention was to find the nearest bed. The nearest bed he could find happened to be in the master bedroom. But this time when I entered the bedroom, I didn't feel afraid.

In this room with him, I saw only the defined muscles in his stomach, his bulky arms, and his enlarged pecs. His body was more defined than I remembered. I felt excited that the love of my life had come back to me. There was a freedom in knowing each other's secrets and loving each other despite them. It deepened our sense of intimacy. The connection felt unconditional.

I laid down on the bed and crooked my finger at him. He shed the last of his clothing and approached me gently. He slid my body to the edge of the bed and slipped my panties off. He began to kiss the places where my panties had been. His tongue found its way inside me, excruciatingly slow at first. I arched and moaned with pleasure. It had been far too long since he and I had made love. The way his hands felt on my body had become a distant memory. Only now, I remembered everything. I remembered the way my body heated under his touch from the inside out.

When I was wet and desperate for him inside me, James paused. He climbed onto the bed beside me, his body resting right up against mine, and he looked me in the eyes. I could feel the heat from his body warming me.

"I love you, Paige. I never stopped. I thought about you day and night. I fantasized about this moment. Will you take me back?"

I nodded, breathless and dizzy with happiness. "You were always here," I tapped my heart.

James put his hands around my back and unclasped my bra, releasing my breasts which he promptly began kissing.

"James, I love you, too. I've always loved you."

"I know," he smiled as he rolled his body on top of mine.

I wrapped my legs around him and arched my back up to meet him. I gasped as he took me in one firm but gentle movement. He made love to me until I screamed in sweet release. He was soon to follow. Then he collapsed on the bed next to me. He pulled my body against his and cuddled me so close, I could feel his heartbeat thumping against my back.

We only slept for a few hours at a time before we were making love again. We loved each other as if this was our last night on Earth and we were choosing to spend it together.

"James?" I whispered somewhere around midnight. "You're gonna miss the redeye."

"To hell with the redeye. I'm never leaving you again!"

39

CARLEY
TWO MONTHS GONE

Carlos drove Carley and Anna to school every morning. She was thankful Carlos drove because the school drop off and pick up line would have been enough to instigate severe road rage in Carley. Instead, she used the time to talk to Anna about the school day and learn if there was anything new. Though Anna was not a morning person, there was a point when she got very chatty.

Anna waved cheerfully as Carlos opened the car door for her and she took his hand to get down out of the big SUV.

"Carla, is there anywhere you need to go before we return home?" Carlos asked her as he did most mornings.

"No, thank you, Carlos. Home is fine."

Carley pulled out her phone. Now that she knew where Demitri Abbott was from, she could do a quick background check on him. She quickly found he had a rap sheet of multiple trips to jail, a DWI, and assault. The assault charge gave her pause. That one made Demitri seem dangerous.

"On second thought, Carlos, can you take me to Scott's house?" Carley asked.

If Carlos was surprised, his voice didn't indicate it. "Sure thing."

Carley called Scott just as they pulled down his drive. He sounded groggy.

"Scott, did I wake you?" Carley asked.

"No, I'm up. Is that you I see in the driveway?" his tone sounded a little put out.

"Yes. I need to talk to you," Carley announced.

"Clearly," Scott responded. "I'll be down in a minute."

Once inside, Carley made herself comfortable on the couch. She was wearing a pair of jeans, a t-shirt, and her hair was piled on her head in a messy bun. She didn't usually dress up for school drop off. She slipped off her ballet flats and tucked her feet under her.

"Your nose looks amazing!" Scott commented.

"Yeah? It's all healed up," Carley smiled. She loved her new look.

Scott looked at her expectantly knowing Carley had come for a reason.

Carley was having a hard time knowing where to begin. In her usual blunt way, she spilled it. "I internet stalked Demitri Abbot," Carley blurted out.

Scott's eyebrow lifted. "And?"

"His parents are missing, Scott, and they bear a strong resemblance to the couple we sent down the mountain!" Carley took a deep breath. "I need to know, were those people William and Carolyn Abbott?"

"Yes, they were," Scott said calmly.

"Ohmigod!" Carley said, her eyes wide with panic. "You killed his parents?"

"No," Scott said slowly as if speaking to a child. "They were dead when I picked them up. I told you. My assignment was to transport and get rid of the bodies. That's all I know."

"Who killed them?" Carley pushed. She was starting to

have a fuller understanding of Scott's *exporting* business. When she was young and in school, there were rumors that The Milternett Family Organization trucking company exported many things other than products and services. Now she had experienced one of his *services*.

"I don't know who killed them," Scott answered.

"Who gave the order?" Carley shot back.

"That's confidential," he told her with a warning glare in his eyes.

"Does Demitri know?" Carley asked.

"That's Demitri's story to tell." Scott's face had taken on a gravely serious look and Carley wondered if she was on shaky ground.

"Why did you tell me they were con artists who worked for the casino?" Carley narrowed her eyes.

"Carley, most of this is none of your business and the more you know, the more guilty by association you become and the more it puts the entire family in danger. So, I don't like telling you details. If you must know, there's plenty of history between the Milternetts and the Abbotts and it's been ugly and drawn out. At the end of the day, only one family could survive, and we were lucky it was us."

"When you put it that way, it sounds like you saved Demitri from going down with his family." If Carley romanticized the story, Scott could still turn out to be the hero.

"You could say that. He was given a choice. He chose to join our family."

Carley felt relief. That didn't sound nearly as ominous as she'd imagined. She nodded her head and got up to leave.

"Don't rush out on my account," Scott said, suddenly lighter and jovial. "Stay for breakfast?"

Carley waived a hand. "No, I need to get back home." She bent and kissed Scott's cheek.

As she left, Carley looked over her shoulder feeling as if

someone was watching her. She could not see the dark eyes that watched her retreating form as she left the house, but she could sure feel them.

40

SCOTT MILTERNETT
TWO MONTHS GONE

"Did she buy it?" Demitri asked as he stepped out into the open. Carley had interrupted an early morning business meeting between Scott and Demitri. He had been around the corner and had heard the whole conversation.

"Yes, for now," Scott said frowning. "She's a clever girl. I might have underestimated her. She's much smarter than you or me."

Demitri laughed. "Speak for yourself. I could kill her if you'd like?"

"God, no!" Scott said with a horrified laugh. Partially because he thought Demitri might have been serious and partially because he hoped he had been wrong.

"Just say the word and I'll take care of her," Demitri assured Scott.

"That's my niece, Demitri. She doesn't deserve to die." Scott crossed his hands over his chest.

"And my parents?" Demitri's pupils dilated so his brown eyes suddenly looked black. "Did they deserve to die?"

"I believe you're the one who needs to make peace with that one," Scott answered.

"I don't like it," Demitri said. "She knows too much."

"She's under my protection."

The two men stared until Demitri blinked. Lifetime grudges were hard to move past. Scott knew time would tell if Demitri would be able to move past his resentments. Clearly, Demitri was living with the regret over his own actions.

Scott had to stop himself from shaking his head. Sometimes, he could swear that Demitri Abbott was two completely different people on any given day.

41

CARLEY

THREE MONTHS GONE

Carley helped Anna into her *birthday ballgown*, as Anna called it when they went shopping. It was a shimmery aqua blue and green and resembled her favorite princess. Despite Carley's best efforts, Anna had remained loyal to the princesses. Carley had to remind herself that she was not trying to control or change Anna. As a parent, it was her job to guide Anna into the adult she eventually would be.

That began with allowing Anna to get the crazy princess ballgown for her birthday. In fact, there wasn't much Carley said *no* to Anna about. It was important that she allow Anna to make her own decisions.

It wasn't exactly Anna's birthday. Not for another month anyway. But Scott had proposed the idea to Carley and Carley hadn't turned it down.

"Anna doesn't know it's not her birthday. It'll give you a chance to show off your new look and I can introduce you to the rest of the family."

Carley was feeling adventurous. She'd agreed. She needed something to break up the monotony of being home all the time. Then she broke the good news to Anna that her birthday was coming up.

Thanks to Scott's planning, this was becoming quite the event. Luckily, Anna wanted a big party. Big parties, Carley knew, meant lots of gifts. Scott assured Carley there would be lots of cousins there around Anna's age.

Not a lot made Carley nervous, but this party sure was getting to her. Since Scott was throwing the party, he had taken care of the invitations. He'd invited the family. She sighed. She was going to have to get used to it she supposed. She'd heard this family loved to party.

"Hey!" Anna protested suddenly. Anna had managed to get an arm caught under one of the three layers of the fabric and was trying to push her hand out where the head was supposed to go.

Carley giggled suddenly at the hilarity of the situation. Anna's hand had emerged through the neck hole completely covered in fabric. It looked quite alien.

"It's not funny!" Anna yelped.

"I'm sorry, you just look like a monster of satin and shimmer," Carley tried to keep the laughter from her voice as Anna started jumping around.

"Help!" Anna cried.

"Okay, I've got you. Calm down," Carley said but took a second to pull out her phone and take a picture of the satin princess monster. Then she reached up under the dress and repositioned the fabric. When she was convinced Anna's arms and neck were lined up correctly, she pulled the dress back down.

Anna's face was red from all the effort. She wore a pout, and she crossed her arms over her chest when Carley smiled at her.

"Not funny!" Anna said again and stomped her foot.

"Okay," Carley agreed amiably. She spun Anna to look in the mirror. "You look…"

Anna's curls were sticking up with static from the tussle under the dress. Anna started combing through her hair.

"Come here," Carley said. She spritzed Anna's hair with anti-frizz spray and ran her fingers through Anna's hair.

"Let's go!" Anna said excitedly after she slid her feet in a pair of ballet flats.

Any nervousness Carley initially felt slipped away the minute she walked through the door at Scott's house.

Carley remembered the twenty-foot-tall ceilings and grand marble staircase that curved up the stairs into a loft where some party guests were already in deep conversation and looking down on the people milling below. The open room was decorated with party decorations. The room colors matched Anna's dress which were also her favorite colors – aqua blue and green. Everything seemed to shimmer like Anna's dress as well. Yes, this was a party made for Anna.

To the right was a kitchen where a large stainless steel double wide refrigerator lined the wall. A seven-foot serving island sat filled with food such as a large sub sandwich, pizza, chips and dip, macaroni salad, pasta salad, regular salad, and a nacho bar.

There was a huge balloon arch against the wall with an instant selfie photo booth. There were silly hats and sunglasses to try on and take fun pictures. In the middle of the room was a chocolate fondue fountain. On the table beside the fountain were marshmallows, fruit, and candy ready to be dipped into the chocolate. Beside that was a two-tiered birthday cake that seemed to match Anna's dress. Atop the cake was a plastic princess with the same color dress as Anna's. Just beyond that and against the wall was a table mounded with birthday presents.

"Is this for me?" Anna whispered with big eyes.

Carley felt the same awe. She nodded. Just then, a pretty little girl with two brown piggy tails ran up to Anna.

"Hi, I'm Ariel," she grabbed Anna's hand.

"She has a princess name!" Anna gasped, looking at Carley.

"Do you want to come play?" Ariel asked Anna.

Anna looked at Carley in question.

Carley nodded. "Go!" She watched Anna run off with the girl.

Scott was suddenly by her side. "Well, what do you think?"

"It's a lot! You didn't have to do all this," Carley said. "I mean, thank you. You just… didn't have to."

"This is nothing!" Scott laughed jovially. "We kept it toned down as you requested."

Carley could only imagine what they must do when they went all out.

"Come, let me introduce you to some of the ladies." Scott took Carley by her elbow.

Carley's apprehension returned. She generally wasn't that great at conversing with women. Her strong personality seemed to turn women off at times. But Carley refused to conform, so there was nothing she would do about it.

"Carley, meet, Gianna, Lizbeth, Lauren, and Dinah," Scott rattled off their names quickly.

Carley's heart sank as she tried to memorize who was who but failed to retain their names. Each woman was made up with sleek hair, big makeup, dressy clothes, and most of them were in heels. Thankfully, Carley had thought to wear a dress herself. She got the distinct impression that cosmetic surgery had a lot to do with their beauty. Carley fit right in.

Scott left Carley to chat with the women. There was an awkward pause before a redhead turned back to the group as if there had been no interruption.

"Anyhow… Ariel turned to Lewis and whispered quietly in his ear, but I could hear every word. I kid you not, she said…"

Carley tuned out the conversation as her eyes searched for Anna. She had lost sight of her for the moment. She was starting to feel overprotective and paranoid. Her heart beat faster when she couldn't immediately spot her. She felt a concerned hand on her arm.

"Hey, are you okay?" a woman with brown hair and big eyelashes was asking her. All eyes were on Carley.

"Huh?" Carley focused on the women.

"Are you okay?" she asked again.

"I'm sorry," Carley mustered up as much politeness as she could. "I've just lost sight of Anna and she'd never been here before... I just feel like I should go look for her."

The women gushed in sudden sympathy. All of them clucked that they understood and started scanning the small crowd on Carley's behalf.

"Here, why don't I show you around the place and let's see if we can spot her?" the redhead said. Without waiting for Carley to agree, she grabbed Carley's hand and started the search tour. "I'm Lizbeth, BTW."

Carley smirked at the way Lizbeth used the trendy abbreviation for *by the way*. Lizbeth seemed younger than the other women and might have even been Carley's age. With this texting era, it made sense but felt misplaced in this world. Still, Carley appreciated the attempt.

Before they got too far into the tour, Carley could hear shrieks of giggles. The redhead smiled knowingly at her, and they followed the sound into a large playroom. There was a trampoline in the middle of the room and five children, including Anna, were bouncing and laughing.

"There they are," Carley sighed, feeling relieved.

Anna caught sight of her. "Hi, mama!" Anna yelled. "Watch this!"

Carley waved. It seemed important to Anna that Carley watch her. At least until Scott called that it was time to cut the cake. All the kids immediately hopped down and ran for the living room.

"Is it chocolate cake with white icing, mama?" Anna asked as they followed they kiddie train.

"Of course," Carley said. "That's your favorite."

Carley and Lizbeth joined the group of women and watched as Scott positioned himself behind the cake with a cutting knife.

"Are we ready to sing happy birthday?" he asked.

"Yeah!" all the kids yelled loudly.

The room burst into song and Carley watched Anna who was surrounded by a new group of friends. She smiled but looked uncharacteristically bashful as the crowd focused on her.

"See this step stool? Come on up here," Scott requested.

Anna did as she was told. The height from the step stool made her tall enough to reach the three candles on top of the cake.

"Make a wish and blow out the candles!" Scott said.

Anna closed her eyes for a second, leaned close, and blew out the candles.

Everyone cheered for the little newcomer who was clearly enjoying her party.

The women watched as Scott began cutting the cake and putting the pieces on plates. Carley popped over to offer assistance. Scott waved her off with assurances that he had it and she just needed to go enjoy herself.

She helped Anna find a place near her to sit and eat her cake before she rejoined the women, who had started telling funny and embarrassing stories about their kids. Carley found herself laughing and letting her guard down. She was surprised to find she was enjoying herself.

"How about you?" the group turned to Carley, putting her on the spot.

"Oh, I don't know…" Carley tried to think quickly on the spot. Then she had a burst of inspiration. "Okay, I've got something." Carley pulled out her phone and showed the picture of Anna all tangled up in her birthday ballgown.

Amidst the peels of laugher, Carley heard a shrill scream. Everyone went still. All eyes looked for the source, including Carley. It didn't occur to her that Anna might be the screamer. Until she saw the small child with her fists balled up at her sides. Anna's face was bright red, and her eyes narrowed hatefully.

Before Carley had time to react, Anna grabbed the phone out of her hand and threw it destructively on the floor with all the force a three-year-old body could muster. Carley heard the screen crack as it hit the ground.

All eyes turned to Carley to see her reaction. Carley froze. She was mortified. Slowly, she began to process how mad Anna had been earlier when Carley laughed about her dress.

Carley bent to pick up her phone and paused in front of Anna's face. She had half a second to think about her reaction. She just needed to stop the drama before any more unfolded.

"I'm sorry, Anna Banana," Carley whispered. "I didn't mean to laugh at you. I just thought it was cute."

"I hate you!" Anna whispered back. Her eyes were dark as she glared meanly at Carley. Anna stood with her arms crossed. Then her expression changed to one of triumph. Clearly, Anna felt she had won whatever game they had been playing.

"Anna, you want to open presents?" Scott interrupted, rushing in to whisk Anna away before Carley could say more.

The party resumed and Carley could feel the women's gazes avert from hers as they actively tried to pretend nothing had happened. Carley's face burned and she turned from the party.

She found a bathroom and locked herself inside. Her body shook from head to toe. She had no way to know for sure, but she got the distinct impression that she had reacted the wrong way.

She had been so sure letting Anna be Anna was the best

way to go. But what if Anna decided to be a mini manipulator? What would Carley do then? She looked at her phone screen. It was cracked. Anna had thrown it down hard enough to break her phone.

Carley hated the thought of trying to change Anna through unnecessary force, especially when Anna was mostly a good kid. Anna had just been rewarded for bad behavior in front of the entire family. Maybe this mom thing was a little harder than Carley had imagined.

When she was calm and collected, Carley left the bathroom. As she walked back into the room, she could feel dark eyes on her. She looked up to see Demitri Abbott looking down from his place on the loft.

What she failed to see was that Demitri's eyes weren't on Carley, they were on Anna.

42

PAIGE

THREE MONTHS GONE

While it was true that I was enjoying James' company and we'd settled into a nice routine, Anna was never far from my mind. I still texted Lieutenant Higgins every day and asked if there was any news. But I had gone so long without hearing anything, it was a shock when a lead presented itself.

It was one of those lazy Saturday mornings. I was lounging on the couch, curled up next to James, drinking coffee. Molly lazily laid at my feet. James flipped on the TV just in time to catch a breaking story.

> … Demitri Abbott reported to the authorities that his parents, Carolyn and William Abbott of Gayena, Kansas, went missing on November 22nd. According to Mr. Abbott, he went to check on his parents after a series of unreturned texts and phone calls. The front door of the Abbott's home was unlocked and slightly ajar. He entered to find blood in the living room. And his parents were nowhere to be found…

"Turn that up!" I stood up suddenly, my attention riveted to the screen.

James looked surprised but did as I requested.

...until recently when a DNA report confirmed their bodies had been discovered in a car accident that occurred in Ouachita Forest. Authorities confirmed a dark blue Toyota Corolla drove off the road two days after the couple was reported missing. What Carolyn and William Abbott were doing in that car remains a mystery. More to come...

James looked at me expectantly. I held up one finger and texted Lieutenant Higgins.

Paige: *I'm coming to Arkansas. We need to talk.*

Lieutenant Higgins: *About?*

Paige: *About the big story that just broke. And why I had to hear it on the news instead of from you.*

I turned to James. "I'm going to Arkansas. That just gave me the missing piece."

"The missing piece?" James asked looking confused.

"Yes," I said. "The car they mentioned is Carley's car. Before I hit a dead end, I saw the DNA report on Lieutenant Higgins' desk. The actual bodies in the car were William and Carolyn Abbott. Until today, I had no additional information about them. I searched for months but could never find who they were or where they were from. Lieutenant Higgins isn't exactly sharing info. Now that I know where the Abbotts are from, I can go do my own investigation in Gayena, Kansas."

"Count me in," James said as he threw on his shoes and looked for his coat.

My gaze fell on Molly who was still lounging peacefully on the floor. I picked up my cell phone and called Marge, the manager at Animal Tales Veterinary Hospital. She answered in a cheerful voice.

"Hi, Marge. It's Paige. Sorry to bother you on a Saturday—"

"Oh, Paige, you're never a bother. Is everything okay?" she asked.

"It's okay." I took a deep breath. I wasn't used to telling strangers my business, but it was necessary to keep the veterinary residency. "It's going to sound like a crazy story, but a few months ago, my daughter disappeared. There's an ongoing investigation and I need to go to Arkansas right now."

"Oh my lands!" Marge exclaimed. "That's terrible! How long has she been missing?"

"A couple months," I felt the familiar burn in my chest of unshed emotion. "I don't talk about it much if I don't have to."

"Well, you do what you need to do, honey. How can we help?" Marge asked, her voice laced with sympathy.

I paused. I was still getting used to the southern hospitality and gossip that went hand in hand around here. Still, I had no choice but to trust her.

"Maybe. I need to take off for a bit and I was wondering if I could drop Molly at the clinic until I get back?" I knew the clinic opened for half the day today.

"Certainly!" Marge agreed quickly. "I'm on the way up there to open up. I can meet you there. Anything we can do to help out. You just take your time and go find your daughter."

"Thank you, Marge," I hung up the phone and found James waiting but ready to walk out the door.

"Hold on, James. I need you to understand that what we're about to do might not be perfectly legal," I warned. I wiped my forehead, feeling the sweat beading up.

"Oh?" James paused. "How illegal are we talking?"

A plan was beginning to form in my mind, but I needed a bit more thought.

"I'll tell you my idea on the way. In the meantime, we need to pack an overnight bag with some specific items."

"Okay," James agreed.

We made quick work of packing, we dropped Molly off at the clinic, and hit the road.

Hours later, we pulled into the police station.

James stopped me before we got out of the car. "Paige, I guess the only part I don't understand is why tell Lieutenant Higgins anything about your plan? Aren't you afraid he'll stop you?"

I shook my head. "He can't stop me. I'm a civilian. I like to give him a nod by telling him just enough information about what I'm doing and where I am in case I get into trouble. I don't have a badge and I know this could get dangerous. Despite the fact that he won't keep me informed, I still want to keep him informed in case—"

"Something happens to you?" James asked.

"Exactly. That way he can continue the investigation from there." I explained as I walked into the station. James trailed after me. It was a Saturday, but Lieutenant Higgins agreed to meet me at the station. James and I walked right into his office and shut the door.

"Paige," Lieutenant Higgins nodded at me. He offered James his hand.

James shook it and sat expectantly.

"What can you tell me about the people who were found in the car? Carolyn and William Abbott? What have you found?"

Lieutenant Higgins hesitated.

"It's all public record now and reporters will only find more information from here. You might as well tell me everything." I didn't have much time.

"We notified the police station in their county when we got the DNA report. Yes, their names are William and Carolyn Abbott, and they are far from home. They lived in Gayena,

Kansas. There's a casino that sits on the border of Missouri, Arkansas, Oklahoma, and Kansas. They had connections to that casino. They didn't own it. It's owned by an Indian tribe, but we know they had some position of power there. But that's all we know so far. The authorities in their county are aware of them and said they would take it from there."

I nodded. "So, you told them about Anna and the connection?"

"Yes, and they promised to look into it. It's out of my jurisdiction, Paige."

"Well, it's not out of mine," I got up and crossed my arms over my chest. "What did they say when they got back to you?"

"They haven't yet. During the initial conversation, they said they had an idea of who was involved in the death. When I asked them about Carley and emailed over her information, they said they didn't believe she had any ties to the case."

James squeezed my hand which he was still holding.

"Could they be lying? Covering up what they know?" I asked.

"Paige, I know your history and I know why you don't trust law enforcement agents. But there's really no reason for us not to collaborate."

I shrugged.

Lieutenant Higgins looked at me knowingly. "I need your word that you won't go undoing the work we've done by launching your own civilian investigation. You need to trust us to do our job."

"With all due respect," I found my voice. "I don't know anything about the work you've been doing. My daughter is out there somewhere. She has been for months. I'm tired of hearing about your jurisdiction rules. Not to mention, what will you do if she's out of state?"

"As I said, I notified the police department in the Abbott's town. They will notify us of any development as they investigate that on their end. Our focus here will be interviewing and re-examining the evidence until we come to a conclusion. Is there a reason you think Anna might be out of state?"

I nodded. "Do you have a paper map of Arkansas?"

Lieutenant Higgins nodded and pulled out a current Rand McNally Road Atlas from a bookshelf to the left of his desk. "What am I looking for?"

"Can you show me the route from Little Rock to Ouachita Forest?" I requested.

Lieutenant Higgins nodded and opened the map. Once it was spread over his desk, I stood up to study it. James stood next to me. I put my finger on Little Rock, which was easy to find since it's the capital, and I traced the route to Ouachita Forest.

I paused. "There's where the car was found in the Ouachita Forest." Then, I continued to trace my finger up to Kansas. "It's a straight shot from Ouachita Forest to Gayena, Kansas. I don't understand the connection to the people found in the car. But someone put a lot of effort into making it look like those bodies were Carley and Anna's. It looks like they used the opportunity to dispose of the Abbott's bodies. It might have worked if we didn't live in the age of DNA extraction. Could they have kept on driving up to Kansas?"

"Anything is possible at this point, Paige," Lieutenant Higgins stroked his beard scruff again. "Do I have your word that you'll let us do our job?"

"No. I'm sorry. I can't sit around and do nothing anymore. There's nothing you can do to stop me. I'm a concerned citizen." I crossed my arms defiantly.

"Paige," James put his arm around my shoulders. "Maybe he's right."

I turned with a look of annoyance. "With or without you, I am going to the crash site. Who knows where we'll go from there? You can come with or go back home."

James put his palms up. "I'm with you. No matter what." No doubt he was remembering the time I was ordered home when Anna was missing as an infant.

Lieutenant Higgins met my eyes. "I know enough about you through Stephen, Paige. I know it will do me no good to tell you *no*. So, here's what I'll tell you instead. If you find anything that we, or the Gayena Police Department can move on, please keep me informed. Also, if you find yourself in danger, don't hesitate to call."

"Only if you agree to keep me posted with any news you find on your end," I shot back.

"Deal."

Relief washed over me. It was good to know I would have some support or backup. James and I shook hands with Lieutenant Higgins and left the station.

"Where to next?" James asked as he got into the car.

I didn't even hesitate. "We're going to Gayena, Kansas."

43

CARLEY

THREE MONTHS GONE

Carley had accepted an invitation to have coffee that morning with the women of the Milternett Family Organization. Carley was now calling them the *wives*. She wasn't allowed to call them "princesses" per Scott. He had informed her that the term "princesses" was an antiquated term overused in Hollywood for mafia-wife stereotyping. So, she was now calling them *the wives*. She remembered them from Anna's birthday party but not by name. She would have to work on that during this visit.

The redhead, Carley remembered, was Lizbeth but she only knew because she was the one who'd walked around with Carley when Anna was out of her sight. Which had happened again, come to think of it. Carley scanned the room.

Lizbeth put her hand on Carley's hand to reassure her. As if reading Carley's mind, she leaned forward.

"She's with Ariel. She'll be fine. Ariel will show her around. She really liked Anna when she met her at the party," Lizbeth assured Carley.

"Thank you," Carley said, allowing herself to relax. She turned back to the conversation. She felt so lost on the gossip. She sat still and listened in an effort to understand.

"Has Ralph not made it home yet?" Gianna, a pretty brunette, asked Lauren, who was a blond with golden low lights in her hair.

Lauren cast her eyes downward but not before Carley saw the sparkle of tears. She shook her head.

"How long has he been gone?" Dinah asked. She had jet black hair and long, thick eyelashes. She looked thoughtful.

Lauren sighed. "Two days. Don't get me wrong. He's been gone that long before and a little distance is nice," she paused and looked around. The wives nodded in agreement. "But he usually tells me where he's going. Or at the very least when he'll be back."

"Was it the feds?" Gianna asked.

"Nah, he would've been out by now. They're such a joke. Every time they take him, he's back out in less than a day."

"Anything strange happen before he went missing?" Dinah asked.

"Well, something did happen, but you gals have to swear not to tell anyone!" Lauren's eyes were full of fear. She looked at Carley. "I don't know you yet but you're Scott's niece. Can you keep a secret? Even from him?"

"Of course!" Carley said, too interested to think that through. She was, however, very good at keeping secrets.

Lauren lowered her voice practically to a whisper. "He and Scott got into a fight."

"Oh!" collectively the wives murmured and gasped in horror.

"I know," Lauren fanned her eyes. "I'm so worried!"

"How do you know?" Lizbeth asked.

"I could hear them. It was after midnight, and Ralph's loud voice woke me up. Scott had come over and they were in the downstairs office. Ralph was yelling so loudly I could hear him all the way upstairs!"

"Did you hear anything else?" Lizbeth followed up her

question. "Do you know why?"

Lauren shook her head. "When I came out of the bedroom and called downstairs, I heard Ralph say, *You gotta go*. Then Scott came out. He looked up to me on his way out and apologized. The next morning, Ralph left for work just like every other day. It was the last time I saw him."

Gianna, who was sitting closest to Lauren, pulled her kindly into her arms and hugged her. "Oh, honey, I'm sure it's nothing. He's Scott's brother after all. Brother's fight. I'm sure he's on his way home as we speak."

"I hope you're right!" Lauren said as tears fell down her face.

Carley's heart was pounding. Scott was dangerous. She could tell from their reaction. She tried to remember Lauren's husband, Ralph. She looked around for pictures since they were all in Lauren's house. She spotted a picture of a large man. Lauren was a little plain herself, but her husband didn't really match her well. Not only was he large, but he was also bald and looked like he might be twenty years older than her.

Now that Carley understood the gravity of Lauren's missing husband situation, she realized this whole get together might have been by design to be a support system for Lauren. She felt impressed by how the wives seemed to band together in Lauren's time of need.

Learning more about Scott these days was opening her eyes to who he really was. Scott was a much scarier individual than she had originally perceived him to be. Was Scott involved in Ralph's disappearance the same way he had been involved in the disappearance of Demitri's parents?

Carley felt panic rise within her. Her whole life was enmeshed with Scott Milternett now. It had put her in a far more dangerous spot than any other man she'd been involved with in her life. She couldn't help but wonder, as she watched Lauren cry, how the hell she was going to get out of this.

44

CARLEY

THREE MONTHS GONE

Later that same afternoon, Scott had called an emergency family meeting. Sitting in the living room at Scott Milternett's home, Carley found herself surrounded by the Milternett Family Organization employees. She looked around the room, watching the quiet buzz as everyone talked in whispers. Some paced, some sat perched on the edge of their seats, others stared off into space. All seemed on edge. Not one person in the room seemed calm.

The only exception was Scott Milternett who was weaving his way around, seeming to work the crowd. After making his rounds, he stood up in front of his large fireplace that had a cobblestone face spanning two stories high. He stood and motioned for everyone to sit. The dull roar quieted.

Carley scanned the room one more time. Not only were the employees there, most of whom she had met, so were the wives. Lizbeth sat beside Carley because she had appointed herself Carley's unofficial new best friend. She had been very welcoming.

The rest of the wives sat in a clique on the couch comforting

Lauren, who sat at the center. Gianna and Dinah sat on either side of Lauren, each of them with one hand on Lauren's shoulder and the other grasped in one of Lauren's hands.

"I know everyone is worried about my brother, Ralph, but I would like to deal with facts and squash the rumors. First things first, I am not responsible for the disappearance of my brother. There would be no reason for me to harm him. He's a valued member of our team. Yes, we argue. But we're family."

Carley's pulse quickened and she felt instantly anxious. She glanced quickly at the wives to see if anyone was looking at her. She hadn't said a word to Scott, but he seemed to know exactly what they had talked about.

Lizbeth must have sensed Carley's discomfort and leaned over to whisper. "Don't worry. No one thinks you said anything. This family talks. There are no secrets."

Carley let out the breath she didn't know she'd been holding. Before Scott could say another word, the front door opened and slammed shut quickly. Carley turned and made eye contact with Demitri Abbott. Demitri barely glanced her way before he addressed the room.

"Sorry I am late," he said loudly in that smooth Italian accent. "I misread the time."

Scott did not look happy but went on with the meeting. Demitri sat at the one remaining barstool at the kitchen that looked out on the open living room.

"As I was saying, we will be dealing with facts instead of rumors or hearsay. So, let's work a timeline for who saw Ralph last."

Slowly, one person after another began telling the last dates they had seen Ralph. The last known person was his wife, Lauren, who saw him in the morning when he left for work two days ago. No one had seen him since.

"Abbott?" Scott called out. "Did you see him after that point?"

"No," Demitri cleared his voice. "I did not."

"What about the feds?" someone suggested. Everyone started talking at once.

Scott held up a hand. "I have been in communication with all my contacts. None of the officials have Ralph in custody. Not the feds, the police, or the US Marshals. Which means Ralph is a 'missing person.' Now, we can launch an actual investigation with the authorities. Show of hands who wants to do that?"

Five hands went up.

"Okay, majority says *no*," Scott ruled. "We keep it in the family. Which means *see something, say something.*"

Everyone around the room seemed to be nodding. Scott adjourned the meeting and people got up and started conversing. Carley stayed right where she was. She chanced a glance at Demitri.

She hadn't seen him since she learned that she'd helped conceal the identity of his dead parents. She still didn't know if he even knew his parents were dead. She didn't usually have a guilty conscience but right now, her conscience was stabbing her hard. She felt guilty and sorry for him at the same time. Then Demitri turned to her and locked eyes with her. She wondered if he had sensed the compassion she felt. His expression was ominous.

Carley remembered the last conversation they'd had, and it made sense why his gaze seemed so angry. She'd thrown him out of her house after telling him she wouldn't be paying his trumped-up invoices. She had cost him quite a bit of money. Never mind the fact that it wasn't his to begin with, nor did he deserve it. No doubt Demitri didn't see it that way. She guessed he only saw her as an obstacle to getting what he wanted.

Still, it was hard to be too angry with him knowing that his parents were recently deceased, and that it might be Scott's doing. Her mind returned unbiddenly to the first night she and

Demitri had met. There was something dark and erotic about him and heaven help her, she actually missed that.

45

PAIGE

THREE MONTHS GONE

During the drive to Kansas, I fielded questions from James on what had happened in those final moments when Lacose had shown up at the safe house. James and I had spent a year apart when James was in Canada and I was in a safehouse in Georgia. I told him about my bodyguard, Joe, who was a US Marshal. That he'd been shot and killed trying to protect me when I broke out of custody and ran. I told him about how Ludwig Lacose and Johnny Jenkins were sitting at the safehouse waiting for us.

"I don't understand why you even went back," James puzzled. "You were free. What on earth made you do that?"

"I spent the majority of my time in WITSEC writing in two journals. One of them was for Anna and the other was for you."

"You wrote to me?" he asked.

"Yes, I kept thinking if I got out alive, I'd work every day to earn your forgiveness and become worthy of your love. I wrote to you almost every day for a year."

"You thought *you* needed to be forgiven?" James was incredulous.

"Oh, James. There were so many things I was dishonest

about. The dissociative fugue, my mother's death and the full impact of that, and the ghosts I sometimes see. I still hate saying those things out loud."

"Well, at least you didn't rat out the location of the woman you love to the very people who were trying to kill her," James smarted.

"You win?" I laughed. Only he could make a joke out of a sad situation.

I went on to tell him I'd killed Johnny and that Stephen had thrown Lacose out the wall of windows after several gunshots had cracked it pretty good first. Then Stephen had almost fallen the same way Lacose had—through the window. I told him how I had saved Stephen's life.

"Kinda makes you even, don't you think?" James had asked.

"What do you mean?" I asked.

"I mean, neither of you owe each other a thing now. You left him to die at one point but then you saved his life."

"True," I responded.

It took us five and a half hours to arrive in Gayena, Kansas. We had passed the big casino on the way. I pointed it out to James. It must be the one Lieutenant Higgins had mentioned that had four states bordering it. It was most likely the one the couple had connections to. I made a mental note to come back to that place if we needed more answers.

For all our earlier light-hearted banter, our mood changed dramatically when we arrived at the hotel in Gayena. We were tired and starting to feel the seriousness of our task. This investigation would either bring us closer to Anna or shut down our leads.

I did a Google search once we were checked in and comfortable in the room. I didn't expect to find much more news, but the Abbott family were apparently a big deal in the area. One newscast had spawned several articles about their disappearance.

"Listen to this," I said as I proceeded to read what I'd found. "Carolyn and William Abbott were reported missing by their son, Demitri Abbott, on November 22nd. According to Mr. Abbott, he went to check on his parents after a series of unre-turned texts and phone calls. The front door was not locked, and he entered to find a trail of blood, a piece of an earlobe, and a tongue on the floor—"

"Really?" James interrupted. "Gruesome, eh?"

"Very," I shuddered. "So, we now know the rest of the story. Clearly, they were injured badly enough to maim them, then transported five hours down the highway before they were sent down the mountain to a fiery death."

"Did they say anything else about theories on why or who?" James asked.

I shook my head. "No. I'm surprised they released this much information to the media. They usually try to keep some details hidden so they are sure when a suspect reveals those details. Oh, wait! Maybe it was way worse than this and they were holding back other details?"

"Whoever did this seems like a real sicko," James stated. "I feel sorry for their son. I can't imagine finding that in my parents' house."

"I know. Remember, these people died in Carley's car so maybe the sicko is Carley." My stomach tightened and I suddenly felt like I was going to be sick. I didn't voice my next thought. *Carley, the sicko, has Anna.* James didn't voice it either, but I saw his jaw clench. "Actually, the timeframe doesn't put Carley in the house with the parents at all. She went straight from Linda and Bruce's house to Ouachita Forest. Maybe someone met her with the Abbotts? Afterwards, I assume she drove to Kansas. That's only a hunch."

"I don't suppose that article tells us where the Abbotts lived, eh?" James joked.

"Of course not," I smiled at his attempt to be funny but

zoomed in on a picture of the house just in case. "Huh! There are numbers on the mailbox as clear as day!"

"You jokin'?" James asked.

"No, 1352. But it doesn't say a street."

"We know it's somewhere in Gayena, Kansas. I wonder how big the town is?"

"I think it's pretty small," I mused. I typed in *Carolyn and William Abbott, 1352, Gayena, KS* to Google. "No way!" I exclaimed.

"You found it?" James asked.

"I did. You really *can* find anything on the internet."

"Scary," James said.

"I'm starving but I also want to take a shower," I announced.

James' eyes lit up. "If you take a shower, I'll have to get in with you and we won't leave the hotel."

"Do they have room service?" I giggled a little, happy for the light distraction.

"Surely," James said as he looked around. "But when do you want to go check out the Abbott house?"

"Soon. After dark," I said immediately. "We'll have to break in and it's easier to go unnoticed after dark."

"Sounds dangerous," James said as he closed the distance between us and pulled me into him. He kissed me, gently at first, then with more longing.

"I brought my gun with me, and I know how to fight," I said, pulling back for air. "But you don't have to go."

"Are you kidding me?" his eyes sparkled now. He held me tighter. "I wouldn't miss this. I love seeing you in action, babe."

I liked the sound of this nickname. I also liked the feeling that James and I were in this together. It was nice not having to do everything alone. I felt his hands creep up my shirt and in mere seconds, my shirt was laying on the floor. I returned the favor.

Our expert hands worked quickly to remove our clothes. Our bodies were touching as we stood close to each other, James' chest was against my back. He had wrapped his arms around me and was nuzzling his face into the crook of my neck. It sent chills of delight down my body.

He kissed my neck, starting at my shoulder, and worked his way up to my earlobe. It was slow and seductive. My hands reached back for him and found his muscular legs. I rested my hands on his outer thighs, feeling the warmth of his body against my hands.

"Are you okay?" he asked me. His question brought an unexpected surge of emotion and my heart melted that he cared so much about me.

"Aside from missing my little girl who might be out there with some psychopath?" I asked.

"Yes, aside from that," he said. He spun me around to look into my eyes. He seemed to be searching them for something.

I sighed, feeling emotional. I hugged him, loving the way our naked bodies felt pressed against each other. "I'm glad you're with me. I'm so used to doing hard things alone. It's nice to have someone I love with me for support."

"Speaking of hard things…" James wiggled his eyebrows comically.

I laughed before standing on tiptoes to kiss him. I broke for the shower and turned it on. James followed me, pinning me against the wall and kissing me while the water got hot. I slid away from him and into the now steamy shower relishing the way the hot sting hit my sore, tired body.

James got into the shower with me and shut the door. Immediately, he lathered up his hands and ran them over my wet, naked body. I returned the favor. When our hands had roamed over every inch of our bodies, cleaning as we went, I seductively leaned forward, putting my hands on the wall, wiggling my bottom playfully, looking back at him.

It was all the invitation he needed. He took me from behind. Slowly at first, our bodies slippery with hot water. Then he thrust deeper and harder hitting all the right angles until I screamed out in delight. Minutes later, he gasped in satisfaction having found his own release.

We toweled off and lounged on the bed. Clothes were not needed as we cuddled and fell into a brief nap. As it turned out, the hotel did have room service and we stayed in until almost dusk.

We didn't want to be seen around town or to draw any attention to us. In fact, the one car trip around the block of the Abbott home needed to look like an innocent drive by. So, we drove by slowly.

As luck would have it, we got a lot of information in that drive around the block. There were two entrances into the house and a few windows on each side. The windows were the small, old-fashioned kind that opened from the top and dropped down. They would not be a good way in or out of the house. The front entrance faced the street where several houses all sat in a row lining the street.

The houses were all the same, wooden shingles, white shutters, and accents, with a nice big porch with steps leading up to the house. Though they were the same cookie-cutter houses, they varied in color. They all had the same straight sidewalk that led to a mailbox. The yard was sectioned off by a waist-length picket fence that had a clasp on the gate door so the fence could easily swing open if invited in.

We turned the corner at the next street and drove around so I could see the back of the houses. Each house had a privacy fence in the back yard with a similar gate and clasp. Some of the fence gates had padlocks. The only house that didn't have a privacy fence was the Abbott home. They had a driveway that came from the back of the home and led to an outbuilding that I assumed was a garage of sorts.

Directly across from the Abbott driveway was a park. It was easy to see that this setup gave easy access and a bit of privacy to those coming and going at the Abbott home. That is, if anyone was still going there at all, given the present state of the missing Abbotts.

Then we went back to the hotel and waited. We watched as the room got progressively darker. I glanced out the curtains, satisfied to find it was a dark, moonless night. Only then, when nightfall came, did I don the black clothes I had brought. I had warned James we might need them, so he also put on the black clothes he brought. I put my gun in the holster on my hip, and we got in the car.

46

PAIGE

THREE MONTHS GONE

We drove to the Abbott's house in the dark. We knew better than to drive right up to the property, so we found an inconspicuous place at the park nearby. Before we got out of the parked car, I tossed James a small flashlight. I had one as well. I always carried a small flashlight in my glove compartment and had shoved one in my overnight bag before I left the house.

It was a straight shot from the park to the house. I felt so thankful for that dark, moonless night. I crossed my fingers that the darkness combined with the black clothes we wore would be enough to keep us concealed. As we parked the car and got out, I did an inventory. *Cell phone with fully loaded battery, check. Flashlight, check. Gun at my hip in the holster, check.* I tossed a pair of rubber gloves to James then I put on my own pair. We were prepared. Still, I felt jittery. There was no reason to think anything might go wrong. We were just breaking into a house on a dark night. A home that should be unoccupied.

We hurried through the grass, keeping our feet light, jogging on tiptoes in case a nosey neighbor spotted movement. But even the homes with a light on inside had curtains on the windows and we would have seen them move. I figured we were in the clear.

When we got to the back door, I pulled out a little tool I used to pick locks. I had graduated from credit cards to an actual tool that worked ninety percent of the time when I'd worked in the police services in Canada. The door opened without a hitch. We were inside.

I paused and James paused with me. He was clearly following my lead. I listened for any sounds of movement. I let my eyes adjust to the darkness. I could see curtains on these windows similar to the neighbors. Still, I wouldn't chance using the flashlight unless we absolutely needed to.

I walked forward and heard the floorboard creak. I froze. James bumped into me. When no lights went on after a minute, I walked forward again. I mostly wanted to get the layout of the house and check to be sure no one was in here sleeping.

What I noticed was how empty the house was. The furniture was minimal. So far, we had made our way through the backroom, a laundry room, the kitchen, and two bedrooms. One bedroom was empty and the other had a bed and belongings. Had the Abbotts been in the process of moving?

Then we turned the corner. The stench was unmistakable. An odor hit our noses at the same time because I could hear James gasp behind me. As I cautiously moved forward, I understood what the smell was before I fully entered the room.

Even in the darkness, I could see the massive amount of blood stained into the floorboards. Yellow tape still stuck to the wall but where the front door was, the tape was now lying on the floor as if someone had walked through the front door, causing the tape to unfix itself from the wall and flutter to the floor.

This was no "blood smear" as the article I had read suggested. It was a full out massacre.

When two people lose this much blood, how could they still be alive?

I wondered. *If they weren't alive after all this, why send them down a ravine in a car?* Then the answer came to me. *To conceal their bodies.* Whoever did this wanted to give the appearance that these people had been killed and taken randomly. Then they used the bodies to make it appear they were Carley and Anna. *Well, that was a stupid idea,* I realized. Clearly, this person hadn't thought about DNA testing. What was the connection? I failed to make any.

When I could not stand another minute, I turned and found James had already backed himself out of the room. He was inching toward the one bedroom that held furniture. I followed him into the room. It was curious that this room still held belongings as if someone had recently been here. I noticed a computer table in the corner of the room. In the front of the table sat a chair with a hoodie draped over it.

Cautiously and quietly, I opened a few doors to the computer table. The first drawer I opened held supplies. I shut it quickly. The next drawer held pictures. It was a drawer full of them. Now, I turned on my flashlight and scanned them. There were pictures of the man and woman I had seen in the article. These were pictures of Carolyn and William Abbott. Some of them were framed. Some of them had a dark-haired boy in them and several showed the same boy at various stages of life.

I noticed how different the boy looked from his parents. He had olive-colored skin, black hair, and dark brown eyes. Carolyn and William were fair. They both had light skin and what looked like green eyes. I remembered a biology lesson about eye dominance and knew two parents with green eyes did not ever make brown eyes. I shrugged. The son must have been adopted.

I shuffled the pictures to see more. Then I saw one that was ripped in half. I easily found its match. William and Carolyn were on one side of the rip and the son was on the other side of the rip. I saw a big, red 'X' marked through William and

Carolyn's faces. I shoved the picture halves into my back
pocket.

"Paige!" James hissed suddenly.

I looked up, surprised that he wasn't right at my elbow
where I had last seen him.

"Car lights!"

I could see the temporary illumination now. A car had
pulled into the driveway and in minutes someone would be
coming into our exit door. I looked around. We were too far
from the living room and the thought of running through a
blood-stained room to escape didn't sound smart.

I waved my hand for James to follow me. I quickly went out
into the hallway and pulled open a door, thinking it was a
closet. Then I heard the backdoor open but not close. It
sounded like the person had paused with the door still open. I
stepped into the closet and was surprised to find there wasn't
floor beneath my feet. There was a step.

My foot hit the stair hard, making a noise. I was instantly
off balance. James reached out to steady me. I shot him a
grateful look, aware that without him, I would have tumbled
down the steep stairs. I moved downward as quietly as possible. James soundlessly shut the door behind him and followed
me.

We could hear footsteps overhead. The gait was irregular. It
sounded like a step and then a shuffle. Step, shuffle, step, shuffle. Maybe whoever was up there was injured and dragging a
foot? It was truly black down here and the musty smell of basement, and maybe mold, hit my nostrils. I chanced a quick
glance around with my flashlight.

We both saw a door across the room and made haste toward
it. It wasn't fully closed. It was opened half an inch, but we
swung it open just as the basement door opened. We could
hear a grunt followed by a groan. We dove behind the door.
James made a noise of surprise. I could only hope the grunts of

the person at the top of the stairs were loud enough to cover the noise James had made.

We were in a tiny closet that housed the water heater. It was designed to hold only the water heater. There wasn't room for two people, but we had no choice but to make ourselves squish uncomfortably into the space. James had found a place behind the door, by the hinges. I was closer to the doorknob. I pulled it shut.

Only, the door didn't shut. At first, I thought a piece of James' clothing was wedged in the door. But then I remembered the door was opened a little to begin with. It didn't quite sit right in its frame. I leaned against the wall trying to make myself flat to fit in with the shadows, but I could see out the half inch crack in the door. I tried to manually shut the door the rest of the way, but it didn't budge. I could only hope if someone came down the stairs, they couldn't see me.

Before I could finagle the door anymore, sudden light flooded into the basement. It was as if someone had turned the hallway light on above. First, I heard, then saw, a person come rolling down the stairs. The person was a large, rotund, bald man. I put my hand over my mouth. A fall like that could kill a person. It didn't. The man groaned at the foot of the stairs and looked upward.

"What do you want from me?" he yelled loudly.

I heard the reply before I saw the abuser. It was loud, erratic laughter. The sound sent chills down my spine.

"I suppose I could ask you the same question, you fat fuck!" yelled the man walking down the stairs.

The large man at the bottom of the stairs shook visibly.

I could hear each step as the abuser slowly and deliberately descended the stairs, as though he was playing on the man's fear.

"Demitri!" the man on the floor exclaimed, his voice a mixture of groveling and pleading. "We're on the same side."

"Are we?" Demitri asked. "Are we really?" He leapt down the last few stairs and landed on the man lying on the floor. Demitri beat the man's face with his fists.

Even from this angle, I could see the slim build and the black hair of the attacker. From the man's words, I put together quickly that Demitri Abbott was this big man's tormenter. I tried to make sense of it. Had Demitri found his parent's murderer? Had he taken the law into his own hands?

When he was done punching the man, Demitri stood and dragged him to the middle of the basement.

"Get up!" Demitri shouted.

"I can't!" the man cried out, panting.

Demitri kicked him hard in the gut. "Get up!" he screamed. Now Demitri was facing my direction, and I could see his wild hair and crazed eyes. His top lip was pulled up in a snarl. He almost seemed animalistic. He squatted down and put his face in the other man's face. "There's plenty more where that came from so get up on your feet. NOW!"

The big man rolled to his side and got to his knees.

Demitri kicked him again.

"Ugh!" the man made a guttural noise.

"There's a chair right here," Demitri said. "I need you to sit in it."

The man now did as he was told, his face showing extreme pain. Once he sat down, Demitri roughly grabbed his hands and tied them with zip ties. Once the man was tied down, Demitri back handed the man, his hand connecting powerfully with the man's face.

"Now," Demitri said, "you will tell me everything you know."

"I know what you know!" The man was now crying. "You're the head of operations. We're on the same team!"

"False! I'm a fucking figurehead. You're the real head of operations. Don't think I don't know you're all playing me!"

Demitri yelled. He backhanded the man again. This time blood went flying and I heard something clatter on the basement floor. Was that a tooth?

"What do you want?" the man asked pitifully.

"Where does Scott Milternett keep his cash?" Demitri demanded.

"In the safe at his house. You know that."

"Keep lying!" Demitri kicked the man between the legs and the man gasped, shocked at the pain and unable to speak for a minute.

"He keeps it in the Greenfield Village House," the man choked out.

"Now we're getting somewhere," Demitri said in a normal voice. "Carla's house? He keeps cash stashed at his niece's home?"

The man nodded slowly and defeatedly. "There's a fake panel in the study. It has a small vault. All the cash you would ever need."

"Good man. Is Carla in on this? Is she a spy? Was she sent to get information out of me?" Demitri's voice was going up and he looked posed to strike again.

The man shook his head. "I didn't even know Carla until she showed up."

"What's the code to get into the safe?" Demitri asked.

"Zero, seven, nine, four," the man breathed.

"There you go, was that so hard?" Demitri asked mockingly.

The man shook his head.

"If you told me the wrong code, I'll kill your daughter," Demitri threatened.

"She's four!" the man protested.

"And? I killed my own parents for less than your betrayal. Care to change your answer?"

"Zero, seven, nine, five," the man corrected. "Why did you

kill your parents?" The big man was still shaking, and his teeth chattered, making it difficult for him to speak clearly.

Demitri smiled proudly. "If you must know, they weren't really my parents. They stole me from my real parents and had them killed. I was too little and weak to fight back."

"S-s-orry to hear that," the captured man stuttered.

"No need to feel sorry for me. I only told you because I'm going to kill you." Demitri took out a gun and pointed it at the man's temple. "Just like I killed them."

"Demitri, no! I told you. I told you the truth!" the man shrieked.

"If you're lying about the code this time, your daughter will join you in the afterlife." With that Demitri pulled the trigger and I squeezed my eyes shut and put both hands over my mouth. I knew what I would see if I opened my eyes. I didn't want to see blood and brain matter, so I kept them shut.

I heard the tone of buttons on a phone beside me. It sounded loud. I saw out of the corner of my eye that James had called 911. I frantically waved one hand at him as Demitri paused and looked in the direction of the heater room.

47

PAIGE

THREE MONTHS GONE

Miraculously, Demitri's footsteps receded from the basement. I could hear them go up the stairs. For now, we had not been spotted but how were we going to get out of this house alive?

Only after I heard Demitri's footsteps retreat upward on the basement stairs did I turn to look at James. His eyes were wide with fear.

I imagined my eyes looked the same way. I put my finger to my lips. We could hear loud footsteps overhead. It sounded like someone was pacing. Then I heard a deep voice from above. It sounded like Demitri was talking on the phone, but I couldn't hear the words.

I wiped my forehead, which was sweating profusely. I felt frozen to the spot in fear. I tried to make my brain work. It felt like it was on overload trying to process all the information I had heard. I was frozen in terror. Would I remember all of this after we got out of here? I had been repeating the names and place I'd heard over and over in my brain. *Scott Milternett, Greenfield Village House, Carla...* They made no sense to me now, but it might make sense to someone else. Demitri Abbott killed his own parents!

I leaned against the wall. We needed to wait until the footsteps upstairs stilled before attempting an escape. That's when I assumed he would be gone or sleeping. Before I could whisper the plan to James, we heard the sirens. They were so loud, we could hear them all the way down in the basement. How many cop cars were here? Thank God for James' 911 call. I nearly sagged with relief.

Then I heard Demitri's voice. "Thank God you're here, officers! Come in." There was fear in Demitri's tone. This sounded all wrong. I felt confused. Weren't they here because of James' 911 call?

We could hear them on the stairs. Several pairs of footsteps stomped down the steps. Had they already arrested Demitri? *When should we come out of the closet,* I wondered? I glanced at James. His eyes were full of question and confusion as well.

"Oh, no!" A tall, broad man exclaimed as he came into view of the dead body.

"I know," Demitri said sounding scared. He was facing the door to the heater room where we were still trapped. His face wore a scared expression as well. There was actual fear on his face! "As you know, I got the okay to start cleaning up the place—"

"Yeah, sorry to hear about your parents, Demitri. You've really been through the ringer," an officer stated with sympathy in his voice.

"Thanks, Sarge," Demitri said with downcast eyes. "Anyway, this guy was here when I got here."

"Jesus!" The man said shaking his head. There was a woman with them, and she crossed her hands over her chest.

What in the world was Demitri doing? Was he really going to pull this off? I looked at James and locked eyes with him. Before I could give a sign to move, Demitri turned his back to the closet and lowered his voice.

I could barely make out what he was saying. I caught a few

words like *hiding* and *still here*. Comprehension dawned when I saw the two officers pull their weapons suddenly and look in the direction of the water heater closet.

Before I could give James a warning glance, the door flew open.

"Get your hands up where we can see them!" the female officer yelled. She grabbed my arm and pulled me. I willingly walked out of the closet with my hands lifted. She patted me down and found my gun. "She's armed."

"This one's clean," the other officer announced after pulling James out in the same way.

"Turn around and place your hands in the air," the lady yelled at me. It was unnecessarily loud given our proximity.

I obeyed her instructions. My mind was racing. This looked bad. Very bad. This must mean that Demitri had figured out we were here. We did not have permission to be here.

"I'm going to remove your holster. Keep your hands up. I will shoot you if you move."

Harsh! I thought, *if only you knew the real murderer was cowering behind you.* I felt the holster slip off my hip. She removed my cell phone at the same time. This was all an innocent misunderstanding. Surely, we wouldn't go down for this. But even as the thoughts surfaced, I answered them. James and I had just been found in a closet wearing all black clothing and gloves and I had a gun they likely assumed was the murder weapon. This could not look any worse.

The officer brought my arms down. She handcuffed my wrists. "I'm going to remove your gloves and place them in a plastic bag."

An evidence bag, my mind said.

I could see the other officer taking off James' gloves in the same way.

"You are being arrested under suspicion of murder. You have the right to remain silent. Anything you say can and will be used against you in a court of law. You have the right to an attorney. If you do not have an attorney, one will be appointed for you…"

The words continued as they led us up the stairs but at the mention of an attorney, I felt a little hope. I had a very good criminal attorney. Surely Sandra Stockman could get us out of this. They couldn't have actual proof because we didn't do this.

They led us up the stairs and through the back of the house. The night air was considerably colder than when we entered the house earlier that evening. This time as I was placed in a cop car, James wasn't standing on the outside with bewildered eyes. He was sitting right beside me.

"I'm sorry," I whispered.

"We're in this together," he whispered back.

"No talking!" the female cop yelled. She turned on the car and began backing out of the driveway.

I watched the road with unseeing eyes. Tears of frustration spilled down my cheeks. Why did my story always seem to end with prison?

The precinct was tiny. When we got there, a female officer took me into a single stall bathroom and had me take off my clothes. She handed me a jumpsuit. She immediately bagged my clothes.

When I exited the bathroom, a small lady who looked to be in her forties started swabbing my hands. James was next. I knew from my experience as a CIO in Canada that officers do this when they suspect you fired the gun. Even with gloves on, the procedure dictated a hand check. Next, they fingerprinted us. Last, they took our mugshots.

After we were officially booked, they threw us in empty cells. James was in one and I was in the other. Luckily, the cells were right next to each other. The doors clanged shut in the most final and unforgivable way.

"Excuse me, officer, can I use the phone please?" I asked.

The officer groaned. "Right now? Do you know how late it is?"

"Yes, right now, please," I requested. From the time I had spent in prison, I knew my rights. They had to allow it. I also knew that I didn't just get one phone call, I could have three. This would work to my advantage since I didn't have Sandra Stockman's phone number memorized and they had taken my phone.

First, I called Brandi Burnett. The phone rang three times before she picked up. Because I was calling out of state, I had no choice but to call collect. I knew the recorded message Brandi would hear and crossed my fingers she would accept the call. She did.

"Brandi?" I said. "It's me, Paige."

"Paige? Are you okay?" her voice sounded groggy. I supposed I should be happy she hadn't put her phone on silent for the night.

"Hi. No, I'm not okay," I could hear how small my voice sounded to my own ears. "I can't go into detail right now, but I need Sandra's number. I'm afraid I'm in some trouble."

"Oh no! Do you have a way to write this down?" she asked.

"Hang on," I said as I looked at the guard. "I need to write down the phone number of my lawyer. Can you help me?"

The guard looked annoyed but then turned to the pretty forty-something brunette sitting behind the desk. I hadn't really looked at her when she was dusting our hands. She threw the guard a sticky pad and a pen.

I shot the woman a grateful look. Then I repeated the number so the guard could write it down. I thanked Brandi with promises to call when I could.

Next, I dialed Sandra. Sandra picked up on the first ring.

"Hello?" Sandra greeted.

"Sandra, it's Paige Mynart," I said.

"Paige? You're calling me collect from a jail in Kansas. I

would ask if you're okay but clearly you are not. Don't give me any details, I'll set up a time to call tomorrow. You're too far away for me to get you out so you'll have to stay there for the night. What are the charges?"

I wasn't surprised that she responded this way. She was a criminal lawyer, and she was probably used to clients who repeatedly broke the law. Still, I gulped feeling anger and embarrassment all roll into that one word. It was the same word that held me in jail the last time. I choked as I said it.

"Murder."

48

CARLEY
THREE MONTHS GONE

Carley had awoken late and not even the sound of the alarm clock had gotten her up. Instead, it was Anna crawling into bed with her and curling up with Carley that had alerted her they should be up by now. The sun was streaming in the window a little too brightly for a Monday morning.

"Anna! What time is it?" Carley asked, feeling panic instantly rise up.

Anna stared at Carley. "I don't know time!" Anna giggled.

"Of course you don't know time. You need to get dressed. We're going to be late to school." Carley threw back the covers and threw on yoga pants, then grabbed a long-sleeved t-shirt.

"I am dressed, mommy!" Anna said. "See!" She stood up on the bed to display her newest fashion trend. She was wearing a pair of jeans with bright pink terrycloth shorts over them paired with a red shirt.

Carley groaned. She sure hoped Anna's weird taste in clothes changed for the better someday. Then she shuddered remembering some of the clothes she wore as a teenager. She knew it could always be worse.

"Come on, Anna! Grab your backpack. We need to hurry," Carley commanded.

"Okay!" Anna ran into her room and reappeared with a vintage My Little Pony backpack. She ran ahead of Carley down the stairs.

Carley noticed Anna's backpack was opened about the time the zipper came undone and everything spilled out on the stairs. Carley slipped on falling crayons that had popped out of the box when they hit the floor. She came down hard on her back.

"Damn it, Anna!" Carley exploded in pain and frustration. She lay still for a minute, assessing the pain with closed eyes. After the pain subsided, Carley sat up. While she would be sore tomorrow, Carley had gotten lucky that nothing appeared to be broken. Maybe just bruised. She checked her limbs gingerly as she sat on the step.

"Anna?" she called. Her voice was softer now. "Come help mommy pick this stuff up. We don't want to be late to school."

Carley looked around. Anna was not in sight.

"Damnit, Anna," Carley muttered quietly as she used the staircase railing to get to her feet. "Come out, come out, wherever you are!"

Anna went through a phase where she hid a lot when she was younger. She used to say she was the *best hider* and that she was a *ninja*. She never really grew out of it, but Carley had noticed it wasn't something Anna had brought with her to the new house. She hadn't hidden from Carley once—until now.

Carley walked slowly from room to room looking behind long curtains, inside the pantry, in closets, and under tables. None of the usual places produced Anna. Finally, Carley turned to the study. She looked around slowly, as she had the other rooms, scanning the room for signs of little feet. She didn't spot anything.

She almost turned around when she got the feeling she was

being watched. Behind Carley's work desk at the back of the room, there was a panel that looked like it wasn't quite lined up with the rest of the paneling on the wall. Carley crept forward, frowning. This had never looked like anything but a wall before.

Carley touched the wall and put her fingers in the gap. It was an opening! There was a space where one side of the wall should have met the other side, leaving no holes. But there was a hole. Carley used her hands to pry it open. It opened easily. The panels were actually sliding doors.

There Anna sat in the corner with her knees drawn up against her forehead. Her arms were wrapped tightly around her knees, and it sounded like she was crying. Carley got on her knees and tapped Anna on the shoulder.

"I found you!" Carley said in a singsong voice, hoping Anna would forget that she had yelled at her. She really didn't want to apologize. Especially to an almost three-year-old child.

"Go away!" Anna shouted. "You're not my mommy! I miss my mommy!"

"Anna, I'm sorry!" Carley said softly. "I'm sorry if I scared you. I fell and I got hurt."

Anna looked up. She had tears spilling from her eyes. She wiped them and looked at Carley with concern.

"Are you okay?" Anna reached out and patted Carley's arm.

"Yes, but my bottom sure hurts!"

Anna giggled.

"You ready to get out of here?" Carley asked.

Anna nodded.

Carley pulled Anna into her arms. Anna was small for her age, so it was usually easy to pick her up this way and get to her feet. Today, Carley struggled because her tailbone was in more pain than she originally thought. But with some effort, she straightened. Anna was clinging tightly to Carley with her arms around her neck.

Before she could turn around, she found herself face to face with a large safe that was camouflaged into the wall. That must be what the fake wall paneling was hiding. Then she noticed a tiny red blinking pin light just above the safe. Upon further inspection, she noticed the light was angled downward. Right on—

"My desk!" Carley gasped. The realization made her feel chilled. Had someone been watching her work this whole time? Carley could only think of one person who might rig up something like this.

"Scott!" Carley said through gritted teeth. She closed the paneling so it butted up against the other side and looked like the wall again. She looked through the paneling to see if she could tell where the red light was now that she knew there was a camera. She could not. She still felt violated and angry at Scott. She calmed when she realized the camera was likely to record only if anyone accessed the safe. Still, there were so many things Scott was *not telling* her. Too many things these days.

"Anna, how did you know this wall opened up?" Carley asked.

"One day I tried to find you. I bumped the wall. It opened and I hid," Anna said into Carley's neck.

"You've hid here before?" Carley asked.

Anna nodded.

"How many times?"

Anna, still snuggling her head into Carley's neck, turned to Carley and showed her three fingers.

"Three times?" Carley asked.

"Yes, one time I hid from Carlos," she whispered.

"Carlos!" Carley exclaimed. "Did he find you?"

"No. He looked at the wall a long time then went away."

Carley took out her phone and called Anna's school to tell

them Anna wouldn't be in today. Carlos would not be driving them anywhere until Carley got to the bottom of this.

The chills had returned. What if Scott didn't employ Carlos to protect Carley but to spy on her? The fear quickly turned to anger. She wanted to go confront Scott now, but she knew she needed to wait until she had a good plan.

49

CARLEY

THREE MONTHS GONE

Carley was on edge as Scott walked into her study. She sat at her desk watching him with a new perspective. Scott looked dark, moody even, and his eyes had a hardness to them she'd never noticed before. Was she safe with him? If both Scott and Carlos turned on her, she didn't know if she could defend herself. When had her own home become so unsafe? Oh yeah, when Scott had installed hidden cameras in it.

Should she proceed with caution or just be blunt? Carley had not decided.

"Where's Carlos today?" Scott asked, having received a text from Carley to let himself in. She knew he had a key.

"I gave him the day off," Carley said.

"Why?" Scott asked, his irritation showing.

"Because I don't trust him," Carley responded.

"This again?" Scott's voice rose a notch. "We went over this. You need someone to keep you safe, especially after Ralph's disappearance—"

"Still no word?" Carley asked.

Scott shook his head, looking defeated and older. Carley

thought Ralph's disappearance might be why his appearance had a harder edge today.

"What's the real reason you let Carlos off today?" Scott asked.

"Anna told me she hid from Carlos the other day because she was afraid of him. Do you know where she hid?" Carley asked.

Scott's eyes narrowed but he shook his head. He clearly wasn't in the mood for guessing games.

Without taking her eyes from Scott's face, Carley reached behind her and opened the paneling. Scott's eyes looked surprised but only mildly.

"Anna found that?" he asked with a smile.

Carley nodded, waiting for an explanation.

"I thought it was only a matter of time before you found it. I had no idea that your smart daughter would be the one to figure out this fake wall. Did Carlos find her?" The smile on Scott's face left and he looked suddenly horrified.

"No, he didn't. I'm not sure what he was even doing in this room to begin with. It's off limits."

"Indeed," Scott agreed stiffly.

"I'm just gonna ask. Is Carlos here to spy on me? And is that camera on me to watch what I'm doing?" Carley decided to be blunt. It was always best to be direct.

"Jesus, Carla! I can't have *you* mistrusting me, too. Everyone in this ungrateful family is trying to pin Ralph's disappearance on me. Now you're accusing me of spying on you? No, okay, I am not spying on you. Carlos is as good as fired. You'll never see him again. I'll send you a replacement as soon as I can."

Carley nodded. *Never see him again?* She didn't ask but she knew what that meant. She swallowed hard.

"Shut that paneling door behind you," Scott commanded wearily.

Carley obeyed with curiosity.

"Do you think a camera can see through an inch-thick wood paneling?"

Carley studied the paneling and shook her head. She didn't think so.

"Well, there you go. Think it through next time. The camera triggers an alarm on my phone if it senses motion which can only happen if this panel gets opened." Scott showed Carley the alarm on his phone. "I knew you found this. I just didn't have the energy to call you."

"Did it trigger the camera when Anna hid in here the other day?" Carley wondered, feeling curious.

"No," Scott frowned as he pulled out his phone to check the camera. "Maybe she's too small to have triggered the alarm though the movement of the wall should have turned it on. I must have missed it."

"Can I help you interview the guard you send? He will be in my house after all." Carley crossed her arms over her chest, feeling firm on her request.

"Yes, but I already have someone in mind. I'll let you meet him, and you can tell me if you are comfortable with him." Scott stood up. "Anything else?"

Carley stood up with him, feeling bad for doubting him.

"Thank you." Carley felt a little ashamed of her suspicions. Scott looked like he was in bad shape. "Get some sleep, Uncle Scott."

"I can't sleep with family out there unaccounted for."

Carley watched him leave. She didn't understand the responsibility and burden Scott must feel. He was in charge. That meant he needed things to be under control. Looking at it from his perspective, she could understand his struggle.

Still, Carley couldn't help but feel something was amiss and Scott Milternett was at the core of it all. Which meant she was too.

50

PAIGE

THREE MONTHS GONE

Sandra sat in front of me and James. How she managed to get the time to drive five and a half hours with her busy schedule, I'll never understand. James and I discussed money after I called her. I still had some money from my mom's life insurance, though I had used quite a bit of that to get me out of the last murder charge brought against me.

James had inherited quite a bit of money in addition to his grandfather's company so we knew we could cover Sandra's fee. It would be a small price to pay for freedom.

Sandra waited until the door shut and the blinking recording light turned off. Then she leaned forward, wasting no time.

"You're in a lot of trouble you two! It is not to your benefit to take this to trial. A jury would have you fry for this. Before we talk about what I know and your options, I need to know— did you do it?" Sandra pulled her jet-black hair off her neck as if the humid questioning room made it stick to her. Her blue eyes assessed us coolly.

"No, no we didn't," I answered. James was looking stunned

and scared. Rightfully so. I would have felt the same way except I'd been through this before. The last time I thought I was guilty. This time, I knew I was not.

"Good. I would rather defend someone who is truly inno-cent." Sandra opened her manilla folder. I considered her words and thought, *As opposed to someone who was guilty?* It was terribly naïve of me to think she didn't ever defend a guilty person. Sandra shuffled through some papers.

James and I sat quietly waiting.

"Here it is…" Sandra mumbled. She produced a scratch piece of paper with notes. She picked it up. "They found you hiding in the closet in the same room where a man was found beaten and murdered. It was not your house, nor did you have permission to be there. Paige was carrying a gun. You were dressed in all black and wearing rubber gloves. When the cops showed up, Demitri Abbott, who inherited the home, met them at the door. He told them he'd come to the home to start getting the house ready to sell. He said he heard a noise, went downstairs, and found the dead body in the basement. He felt certain the criminals were still in the house. Then they found you in the closet. What am I missing?"

"What is the name of the dead man?" I asked.

"They have identified him as Ralph Milternett. Do you know Ralph?"

"No, but—"

"But, what?" Sandra asked sharply.

"That's not the first time we heard the name Milternett tonight."

"Oh?"

"We saw who murdered Ralph." I really didn't want to tell her that. In the past, my knowledge of a criminal who committed murder had gotten me placed in protective custody. I shuddered. I never wanted to go back to protective custody.

"Really? Who?" she asked.

"It was Demitri Abbott. He also admitted to murdering his parents, Carolyn and William Abbott. He told Ralph before he killed him. He also asked Ralph questions about Scott Milternett, a safe at Greenfield Village House, and someone named Carla. After Ralph gave him the information Demitri forced Ralph to tell him the location of a safe and the safe code. Then Demitri killed him."

"I see. Maybe you need to start at the beginning. But first, how did you know the man was Demitri Abbott?" Sandra asked.

"I knew from the article they had a son named Demitri Abbott. In one of the bedrooms, I saw pictures of William and Carolyn with a boy at various stages of his life. I could tell from the photos, some of which showed the boy more grown up, that it must be their son. When Demitri came downstairs while we were hiding, I recognized him from the photos. Plus, Ralph called him *Demitri*." Then I remembered something else. "I took the pictures. They were in the back pocket of the pants I was wearing. The picture had been torn in two with a red X through the side with the parents on it. Demitri was on the other side."

Sandra shook her head. "I'm sure that will be submitted into evidence."

"Evidence of what?" I asked. I looked at James. Would this establish some sort of motive for us to be in the house? Did it make it seem like we were trying to find a way to frame Demitri?

"I think you need to tell me why you were in that house. Don't leave out any detail." Sandra's nails made a tapping sound on the cold metal table, her impatience evident.

"It all started when we got the DNA test back from the people who were killed in the car crash thought to be Carley and Anna—"

"Let me guess? The DNA did not match Carley and Anna?"

I shook my head *no*.

"Then whose DNA was it?" Sandra asked. Her fingers stilled, her curiosity was piqued.

"Carolyn and William Abbott."

51

CARLEY

THREE MONTHS GONE

Carley was dressed in head to toe black with the rest of the family. It was a closed funeral with heavy security. The news of Ralph's murder had come to the family three days ago. Lauren, Ralph's wife, was inconsolable. Carley could hear her crying from the back of the church.

Carley's opinion of the wives was changing. She had been so judgmental about the motivations behind a young wife marrying an older, large man who just happened to have a lot of money. But it was now clear to Carley that Lauren really had loved Ralph.

All the police would tell them was Ralph had been found murdered and that it was part of an ongoing investigation. The family was beside themselves with anger and fear. Who would do such a thing? It was not lost on anyone that Ralph was Scott's brother. If anyone wanted to hurt Scott, this was a good way to do it.

After the announcement of Ralph's death, Carley had managed to find a few minutes alone with Scott.

Do you really not have any leads on who might have done this?

Carley had asked him, feeling spooked. She was feeling just as vulnerable as the rest of the family.

What's that supposed to mean? Scott had whirled around and looked her dead in the eye, his anger evident.

Only that you told us at the family meeting you had contacts inside the feds, police, and the US Marshals. Do they really not know anything? Carley had challenged him.

If I knew, you'd know. Everyone would know. You mistake your place. Don't assume for a minute you and I share more information than anyone else in this family. Then he'd stormed off.

Except that Carley and Scott *did* share more information than anyone else. They had a secret no one else knew. Anna was not Carley's daughter. Scott's words had left Carley feeling chilled. Should she doubt Scott's loyalty to her? She was finding this family had no secrets. Was it only a matter of time before her secret came out?

She turned her attention back to the service when she heard a whisper to her right.

Did you hear? Ralph was shot in the head. That's why it's closed casket.

Carley took in a sharp breath and discreetly got up from her aisle seat. Was it only a matter of time before she was next?

As she left the stuffy sanctuary to get some air, she could feel dark, intense eyes boring into her back and following her every movement. She looked up in surprise to find Demitri Abbott watching her every move.

52

PAIGE

THREE MONTHS GONE

We had spent ninety-six hours in jail by the time James and I were requested in court. Sandra was able to set a preliminary hearing for us while she was in town. I should have known that Sandra would make good use of her time while she was here. Once we were in the courtroom, it was obvious she intended to bring us home.

It was a good thing, too. She explained to us they could hold us for up to twenty-four hours without evidence but due to us being found in such close proximity to the murder victim, they had extended our stay to ninety-six hours. They either needed to move us to the next step, which was closer to a trial, or let us go.

Once in the courtroom, it became clear that Demitri Abbott would not be in attendance, which calmed my fears a little. I didn't particularly want to be faced with that violent killer. Nor did I want him to see our faces in daylight. While we waited in jail, I had several nightmares of his dark, animalistic face.

It soon became apparent that the state attorney intended to do everything in his power to keep us incarcerated. He was tall and had a commanding stature. His hair was brown and slicked back with gel. He might have been handsome if he didn't wear that brooding, mean face.

When the judge called the state attorney, Rick Boston stepped forward to present his opening statement and evidence. He was so polished, he almost had me believing we'd committed the murder. I guessed that didn't mean much considering my chronic guilty conscience tended to take on crimes and offenses that didn't really belong to me. I wiped my forehead, beginning to sweat as Rick Boston closed his opening statement.

"Paige Deffer and James Friesen were found in the closet at the home of the deceased couple, William and Carolyn Abbott, with a gun in the same room as the murder victim. Demitri Abbott *might* have been the next victim had the police not shown up when they did. Clearly, they broke into the house and were up to no good. Maybe they were returning to the scene of a crime. Maybe they had been planning to frame Demitri for murder—"

"Objection," Sandra yelled. "Speculation."

"Sustained," the judge said. Even I knew a reprimand from the judge was a win for him as long as the attorney created reasonable doubt.

Rick then went around explaining each picture, submitting them into evidence, one by one. When he was done, he presented my gun in a plastic bag.

"This gun is registered to one Paige Mynart, resident of Missouri." Then he submitted that into evidence. Around the room, there were graphic pictures that had been blown up and lined up on easels. Ten pictures showing the dead body from every angle decorated the courtroom. They showed the basement layout in proximity to the closet where we were to where the murder victim lay when he was found. Rick submitted these into evidence as well.

By the time he was done, I slumped low in defeat. I chanced a glance at James and saw that he, too, looked worried.

"Nothing further, your honor," Rick sat down with a smirk on his already smug face.

Sandra stood to give her opening remark. "It is the position of the defense to prove that the evidence does not point to my clients, nor does it definitively show guilt on their part. While they may have been in a home where they did not belong, they found themselves in the wrong place at the wrong time for purposes we plan to explain today. I plan to submit a police report to clarify my client's lack of involvement."

I heard Rick Boston chuckle in his seat. I understood his arrogance. He got up and gestured to the pictures around the room. "A man is dead. Brutally murdered. Paige Mynart and James Friesen were found hiding in the closet in the same room where Ralph Milternett was killed. Paige Mynart was carrying a gun on her hip. If they did not kill this man, who did?" he challenged.

Then Sandra got up. She pulled out a police report and began to read. "Neither Paige Mynart, nor James Friesen had gunpowder residue on their hands after they were arrested and checked. Neither did the gloves on their hands nor the clothes they were wearing, which indicates they were in the closet at the time the murder occurred. The gun, while registered to Paige Mynart, is not the weapon that was used to kill the murder victim. The gun clip was full, indicating no bullets were fired. The bullet fired did not match the bullets loaded in Ms. Mynart's Glock 43x. A ballistics expert noted the striation of the bullets, which indicated a different gun altogether was used as the murder weapon.

"I pulled the records from the nine-one-one call to see what number it came from, and it is a phone number from Canada. Further investigation concluded the nine-one-one call did not come from Demitri Abbott at all but my client here, James

Friesen. If James were guilty of murder, why would he call nine-one-one?"

Next it was time for us to tell our story. James and I each took the stand, but we only told the story we rehearsed. Sandra warned us strongly not to make accusations about Demitri. He wasn't on trial here, we were. We only needed to explain the bizarre circumstances leading up to the terribly bad decisions that put us in the house. Which is exactly what we did. James and I both told the same story about Anna and how she had been missing and presumed dead. When the DNA came back as not our daughter, Anna, we decided to investigate on our own in case Anna was being held at the home of the deceased couple who were found dead in the car.

"That's quite a story," Rick Boston sarcastically said when it was his turn to cross examine me. "So, it didn't occur to you that breaking into the home of a deceased couple could implicate you in their murder? How do we know *you* didn't send them down the hill in that car crash?"

"Objection!" Sandra yelled.

"Sustained," the judge called.

I'd never said the crash was premeditated. The couple could have stolen Carley's car and wrecked it for all anyone knew. The fact that Rick Boston seemed to know what had happened only further convinced me that we'd heard it all correctly. Demitri had a hand in his parent's death.

I answered the rest of Rick's questions and sat still next to Sandra as James took the stand and told the exact same story. Then the judge asked if Rick had any more witnesses. Rick said *no*. The judge turned to Sandra and asked her the same question. Sandra shook her head *no*.

The judge sat quiet for a moment, deliberating.

"This is a difficult decision to make," the judge began. "In America, you are innocent until proven guilty. While there is no evidence that Paige Deffer and James Friesen committed the murders, the fact remains they were found in the closet in the very same room at the time a murder occurred. I can't overlook that. I am sentencing a trial by jury six weeks from today with bail set at five hundred thousand dollars a piece. Court is dismissed."

I felt Sandra stiffen beside me. I saw her wide, surprised eyes swing to me. Before she could say anything, guards were grabbing my arm and lifting me roughly from my seat. They had handcuffed my hands behind my back. I saw them do the same thing to James.

"Do you have money for bail?" Sandra asked quickly.

I laughed bitterly. "One million dollars. No. I don't have that."

Sandra sighed in defeat. "I'm sorry, Paige. I rarely lose. I don't even know what to say right now. Trial by jury is not good. This town seems to have an affinity for the Abbotts. I'm a little out of my element here."

Tears sprang to my eyes. If my lawyer, this bad ass woman who rarely lost a case felt defeat, what hope did we have in front of a jury? It was all happening again. Only this time, we might go down for murder we didn't commit. If Rick Boston had anything to say about it, we might go down not only for Ralph Milternett but for the murders of William and Carolyn Abbott. *Bad people deserve the bad things that happen to them.* This proved it. I was still a bad person.

53

PAIGE

THREE MONTHS GONE

They took us back to our cell at the county jail. We were right back where we had started, in the cells where they had been keeping us for the past four days. I'd heard horror stories about waiting for trials in federal prisons. I'd never been to prison, only jail. It looked like Sandra Stockman had pulled some strings so we would be able to wait our time here, in two jail cells, separated only by metal bars. At least we would be together.

Before the guard put me in the cell, I asked for a phone call. He escorted me to the phone. It was the same old-school phone on the wall that I'd called Brandi Burnett on when we first arrived.

"Paige?" Lieutenant Higgins greeted. "Sandra Stockman called me a few days ago," Lieutenant Higgins started talking immediately. "I knew you were in a load of trouble."

"Yeah, we are," I admitted, wondering if he was going to lecture me for the mess I was in right now.

"Well, I called the police chief there on the force after that. He didn't have any new information about Anna. But he did brief me on Demitri Abbott. I understand you've had a run-in with him."

"Yes, but nothing I can talk about right now," I said. Sandra had briefed me before she left about not saying a word to anyone without her present. "What do you know?"

"He's part of a much bigger investigation being headed up by the feds. They aren't allowed to touch him, but they also watch him like a hawk. I'm only telling you so you know you're safe to return home. He did see your faces and I'm sure he thought you would go down for the murder. But if Demitri Abbott crosses into Arkansas, they will immediately alert me."

"That sounds great, but we aren't coming home any time soon." I sniffled as tears filled my eyes.

"Oh?" he sounded shocked. "I didn't hear that."

"We have to go before a jury in a month. The bail is set at a million between the two of us."

"I'm sorry to hear that," Lieutenant Higgins said. "In the meantime, Paige, as bad as this timing is, we need to talk about Anna."

"What about Anna?" I asked, clutching the phone like it was a life raft.

"We've followed every lead we could possibly track down, but the trail is cold." There was a tone of finality in his voice.

"So, what? You're just gonna give up?" I heard my voice pitch in a dangerous octave.

"Until new evidence or a lead comes to light—yes. We've been diligently searching for the past few months. There are other cases we need to put our time and resources toward."

A sob caught in my throat.

"What about the DNA report? It's the whole reason we came here. What if it's connected to Anna? There has to be a connection, right? There has to be a reason they were in Carley's car..." The thought that Demitri might somehow be connected to Anna's disappearance was horrifying. For a minute, I couldn't catch my breath.

"I've turned it all over to the police department in Gayena. If there's any more information, they will let us know."

"But my baby…" I gasped.

"I'm sorry, Paige," he said.

I hung up the phone and I was sobbing by the time I got back to the jail cell.

"Talk to me," James said softly. He put his fingers through the bars.

"They've done everything they possibly could to find her. They're giving up. And we couldn't find her," I sobbed. "It's like two years ago all over again except it's been so much longer! If only they would've moved faster, we might have been able to find her. This is what you need to know about me, James. Bad things happen to me. I am bad."

"Remember when you asked me about God, Paige?" James asked suddenly. He was sitting on his cot with his head leaned back against the wall.

I nodded. We had been looking for Anna then too. We had gone into a church to say a prayer. I'd asked James if he knew God.

"I have a connection with a higher power I call God. I believe that's what's keeping me sober. Even with all this new stress… I don't feel like I need a drink. Maybe you need to start seeking to find your higher power. You need to give this to God and put the outcome in God's hands."

"But what if it's not the outcome I want?" I whispered.

"It's out of your control, Paige," James responded.

It's out of my control, my mind pondered the words. They had bounced around in my brain, forming a new concept I really hadn't considered before. Those words were still with me. *This is all out of my control.*

I'd never felt so powerless in my entire life.

54

CARLEY

FOUR AND A HALF MONTHS GONE

"Mommy, you look so pretty!" Anna said excitedly, then she immediately pouted. "Why can't I come to the party?"

"Anna, we talked about this. You're too young for this party. You be good for Fria," Carley told her.

"Or what?" Anna sassed. "Fria is boring!"

"Anna! You take that back!" Carley put her hands on her hips trying to look stern.

"No! Boring, boring, boring! I want to dress up for a party." Anna stomped her foot and crossed her arms over her chest.

"Well, no one said you couldn't dress up." Carley rummaged through Anna's closet. "Ah ha! Here it is! This is perfect for tonight."

"What? What?" Anna started jumping up and down.

"It's your birthday ballgown." Carley took it off the hanger and dropped it over Anna's head.

Anna wiggled with her arms overhead, trying to find the arm holes. Finally, her head popped out of the top. The frizz that came off her blond curls stood up with static electricity. "I need high heels like you."

"Okay, let's go," Carley led Anna to her closet and opened

the doors to her vast selection of shoes. Carley had never owned so many shoes in her life. Shoes that sparkled, shoes that added four inches of height, boots, flats, wedges. It was like she had an entire shoe store right here in her closet.

"I want those," Anna pointed to Carley's feet.

"Oh, well that's a hard *no*, child. These things are worth more than your life."

"Hey!" Anna protested.

Carley rolled her eyes. "It's a joke, Anna. Lighten up."

Anna picked a different pair and put her feet in them. She shuffled her feet as she walked. Carley closed the closet door but not before peeking at her appearance. She truly did look stunning in her tight black shimmering cocktail dress. Her shoulder-length, highlighted hair was curled and swept over to one side. Her makeup was just a touch darker than normal. She wore bright red lipstick. The earrings that dangled from her ears were a combination of white gold and diamonds.

The short skirt of her dress cut off a good four inches above her knees and on her feet were three-inch Jimmy Choo black satin high heels. She looked like royalty. Hell, she practically *was* royalty. In the five months she had been in this family, she had risen in the ranks. She who controls the money, controls the family, she had learned to believe.

Luckily for Uncle Scott, Carley was also fiercely protective. The bond they had was thicker than blood. There was a secret between them that no one must ever know. Neither of them wanted the truth to come out. The truth about Anna and the dead bodies who'd taken her place in the car the night Carley and Anna had come into the family.

"Okay, Anna, I need to go," Carley kissed Anna's cheek and took her hand firmly in hers knowing Anna was about to throw the world's biggest fit. Carley quickly found Fria and said *goodbye*. She met Brian, the new bodyguard, and her driver at the car. Though she had hated having a driver in the beginning, she had come to love it. The windows were tinted and bullet proof. It was the one place she could lay her head back and relax.

When she arrived at the party, the music was already pumping with a live DJ spinning inside. She could hear it as she walked in. Carley smiled at this. She was probably the youngest family member to attend but this family partied like they were Carley's age. Nothing but the best for Uncle Scott's birthday party.

Two very large bodyguards stood at the door to the non-descript brick building.

"Name?" they asked.

"Carl—Carla Milternett," she stumbled out but smiled flirtatiously at the guard to cover it.

"You can go in," he winked back at her.

Once inside, there was a staircase that led down to a basement. It was dark with soft lights and candles lit for ambiance. The dance floor was a classy black-and-white-checked marble, raised slightly from the rest of the floor. A few people milled about on it talking. Some people already sat at the high table-tops, sipping wine out of sophisticated flute glasses. Everyone was dressed in their best.

Carley immediately found the bar along the left side of the room and ordered a dry red wine. She wasn't much of a drinker at these events, but she could most certainly hold what she did drink. Still, she planned to pace herself for a long night ahead.

"You look gorgeous, mi amour," Demitri Abbott was suddenly standing a little too close for Carley's liking. His warm breath by her ear sent shivers down her spine. Damn her body for betraying her. She had created a nice power hold over Demitri, and she didn't plan to give that up. She accepted the drink the bartender handed her.

"Thank you, Demitri," Carley said as she stepped away to

put distance between them. She smartly moved through the crowd until she found Scott.

"Happy Birthday, Uncle!" Carley hugged him and kissed his cheek.

"I was wondering if you'd made it yet," Scott was already in high spirits. "Do you know everyone here?"

Carley turned and scanned the room. It was nice to find that she did know most of the people in the room. She hesitated and pointed out a few she'd never seen before.

"Those are two of Kansas City's finest boys in blue dressed in business casual, here only for tonight. They're on security detail to keep the party under control should anything go awry." Scott winked.

Carley smirked. Of course, Scott had uniforms in his pocket. "What could possibly go awry?"

Scott turned serious for a minute and frowned. "You know the investigation of Ralph's murder is still underway. Any of us could still be a target since we don't know a motive. It does leave his position open for some promotion from within—but let's not talk business at the party tonight."

"Speaking of which—" Carley mumbled, watching as Demitri Abbott weaved his way in their direction. "Don't tell me, Demitri is a candidate for promotion?"

The look on Scott's face answered her question.

"Why does that not surprise me?"

"Go easy on him, Carla," Scott used her fake name. "He could very well work his way into that position, but don't close your eyes around him. He's waiting to pounce."

"Don't I know it." Carley made a face of distaste.

"Still, it wouldn't hurt you to be friendly to him. Maybe make a little effort?"

"How about *you* sleep with him if you're so crazy about him," Carley snapped and walked off right as Demitri walked up.

"Your niece hates me," she heard Demitri gripe to Scott as he threw his arms around him and kissed his cheek. "Happy birthday!"

"She'll come around," Scott replied loudly enough for Carley to hear him.

Oh brother, she thought, *now he was sending her messages to buddy up to Demitri?* Even after the stealing scandal that happened when she first took over? She couldn't begin to understand why Demitri could be important to Scott, but she'd just have to take Scott's word.

Carley found the group of wives and hugged them all. She hugged Lauren a little longer than the others feeling surprised she'd made it out. Her dress was beautiful, but her hair and makeup were plain. Come to think of it, she didn't wear much makeup at all. Carley quickly discovered why. Lauren's eyes never seemed to stay dry long enough.

Carley had more tolerance tonight and found herself laughing and listening to the gossip. She had to admit that her focus was a bit forced in effort to keep it from straying to Demitri Abbott. In truth, she couldn't care less about the things the wives talked about, but she had learned it was her obligation to fit in with them. She liked them well enough. She felt compassion for Lauren and a little admiration that she was functioning, even if she did excuse herself to run to the bathroom a few too many times. But to not fit in with the wives meant their sharp, gossipy tongues would turn on her and that was something Carley could not afford.

"What about Demitri Abbott?" Gianna's words got her attention.

"No one really knows his story," Lizbeth pouted. "He sort of just showed up out of nowhere. No wife, no mistress, no boyfriend. He just gets his job done and keeps to himself. Look at him, though. Hottest guy in the room, hands down."

The wives nodded.

"What do you think? Don't you agree, Carla?" Gianna nudged Carley hard in the ribs, knocking her breath out of her.

"First of all—ow! And sure, he's okay," Carley shrugged as she sipped her wine.

"Okay?" All heads said in unison and turned to her.

Great, that's all I need, she thought, *more attention.*

"Yeah, okay, he's hot. But I've had hotter." Carley actually found herself comparing Demitri to Stephen in her mind and was shocked to find she really did think Stephen was just a little more her type.

"I don't believe it. Dish!" Dinah, the black-haired beauty challenged her.

"Think six-three, muscular, blond curly hair with deep blue eyes and dimples."

"Huh, yeah, that is not Demitri at all. That's your type? Not me. Tall, dark, and handsome all day long. Speaking of which…" Gianna pointed discreetly with her head.

They watched as a beautiful woman approached Demitri. He talked to her, but Carley noticed his eyes seemed to be searching the crowd. He nodded and answered her questions, but it was clear he was searching for someone.

"Who is that lady?" Carley asked, feeling more curious about someone who looked like that but held no interest for Demitri.

"I think she's a girlfriend—" Gianna started to say.

Before they could confirm it, one of the truck drivers stalked up to the woman and grabbed her hand. Demitri shot him a thankful look. We all laughed a little, still watching Demitri walk through the crowd.

As if sensing their attention, Demitri looked up at them and made eye contact with Carley. Carley felt her pulse quicken. She saw him switch directions and move toward them.

"I'm gonna go check on Lauren," Carley excused herself and quickly made her way to the bathroom. She shut the door behind her and took a deep sigh of relief. She couldn't duck him forever and Demitri seemed determined to talk to her. She just hated the idea of everyone thinking they were an item. Because they weren't. Nor would they be. Carley could hear gentle crying coming from a bathroom stall.

"Lauren?" Carley called, tapping gently on the stall. "Are you okay?"

"Yes," came the whisper.

"You don't sound okay," Carley responded. "Do you need anything?"

"A ride home. It was too soon to come out," she said sadly. She opened the door and Carley could see that her face was red and splotchy.

"I could text Brian, my driver, right now and have him come give you a ride home?" Carley suggested.

"Would you really?" Lauren asked with appreciation in her eyes.

"Sure," Carley pulled out her phone. Brian responded instantly. Of course he would take Lauren home. "Come on, I'll introduce you to Brian and he'll take you home. Will you be safe there alone, though?"

"Yes, trust me. No one wants me dead. I don't know anything. But I have a nice alarm system and can have someone at my house in minutes if need be."

Carley walked out arm in arm with Lauren for support and found Brian. Once Lauren was off with Brian, she turned and found herself face to face with Demitri Abbott. What was his problem with distance tonight?

"May I have this dance?" he gallantly bowed to Carley. Carley was close enough to the wives to see them standing with their mouths gaping as Carley stood, inwardly fuming and mortified. Carley had sat her wine glass down somewhere, so her hand was free. Carley put her hand in Demitri's and allowed him to lead her in a slow song.

"What the hell, Demitri? Are you stalking me?" Carley arranged a pleasant look on her face, but she was anything but happy about the gap of distance he kept trying to close. "This is all those women will talk about for the next week. Do you know how hard I work to *not* be the center of their gossip?"

"Dancing is nothing to gossip about. If I kissed you, on the other hand," Demitri leaned his face downward, pausing to make sure the wives saw him, then kissed Carley's cheek instead.

"Cut it out. I'm still mad at you," Carley hissed through clenched teeth as she smiled pleasantly for anyone who was watching.

"I owe you an apology. I did take advantage of your family. I underestimated you. Please, won't you forgive me?" his Italian accent was sexy, and his suit hugged all the right places on his muscular but trim body. He pulled her closer to him so her breasts were snug against his hard, defined chest.

"Please, stop groveling. You're just trying to get into my pants again," Carley attempted to switch the subject.

"Yes," he agreed. "I am. I can't stop thinking about you. For months I can't sleep at night because our one night together makes me hard just thinking about it. Please, say you'll forgive me so I can start working my way back into your bedroom."

"Jesus, Demitri, could you be any blunter? That was *not* romantic," Carley tried to act annoyed but a man who said exactly what he wanted without mincing words was someone she could get used to.

"I think you mean graphic. Could I be any more graphic? Yes, I've thought of a thousand ways I want to ravage your body. Would you like to—"

"Calm down, Demitri. Normal men compliment women. They bring them flowers. They take them out to dinner." Carley took a step back to put a little distance between them.

"You're right," Demitri said, looking around. He put his

warm hand on the small of her back and touched her bare skin where the dress was cut low down her back. He guided her to a table. He pulled out a chair for her. He made a grand, sweeping gesture for her to sit down.

He left but returned a minute later with a flower centerpiece and a plate with appetizers. He held up one finger and left again. This time he returned with a glass of wine.

"You were drinking red, yes?" he asked.

"Yes," Carley agreed. She had popped a peppadew into her mouth, not realizing how hungry she was. "Ohmigod, this is so good! Thank you. Go get yourself a plate."

"I'm not hungry. I'm content to watch you," he said with intensity.

Carley rolled her eyes but kept eating.

When she was finished, Demitri grabbed her hand and leaned forward.

Carley resisted the urge to reclaim her hand.

"You look stunning tonight," he began. "I thought you were pretty as a brunette but as a blond—wow! Tell me, do you have more fun?"

"That's for me to know and you to find out. In the meantime, I'm getting more appetizers. I'll be right back." Carley found the food and piled her plate high. She was famished and she didn't care who noticed. Despite her thin frame, Carley loved to eat. She was on her way back to the table when she saw something—or someone, rather—who stopped her in her tracks.

She heard Demitri say her name as she approached the table, but Carley wasn't listening anymore. She happened to glance up the stairs at the two men who had walked through the door when she spotted them. With their jeans, nice shoes, and suit jackets, she guessed them to be off-duty law enforcement. But one of them she knew—intimately.

It was Stephen Wilton.

55

STEPHEN

FOUR AND A HALF MONTHS GONE

As Stephen walked into the large building, the contrast from the sunlight outside made him squint into the sudden darkness. Fresh out of training, he had officially started his career as a US Marshal. As fate would have it, his first official assignment was to attend Scott Milternett's birthday party. Stephen had been surprised by this. As a police officer, he'd never been invited to a criminal's birthday party before.

He even paused a minute to shake his head and consider the odds of this. It seemed bigger than fate considering Scott's connection to Carley. As Stephen considered this turn of events, he thought about Paige's predicament. Roger Higgins had called Stephen to give him an update. Paige and James had gotten into trouble for investigating on their own and were awaiting a jury trial for murder. A lot had happened in the short period of time he was gone.

James was back. That news stung Stephen's heart. He wondered how much time and distance he would have to put between him and Paige before her rejection didn't hurt his heart so badly.

They're in jail for murder? Stephen had asked. *I think you need to back up and tell me the whole story.*

Roger Higgins had explained he and Sandra Stockman had visited to prepare for the jury trial and the full truth came out. *The media blew the story wide open, and Paige learned it was William and Carolyn Abbott who were in that car. She found their home. She assumed Anna was connected to them and broke in. She found blood and gore all through the front room. While she and James were snooping around, Demitri Abbott came home. They hid in the closet in the basement and watched him kill Ralph Milternett, Scott's brother. When the police showed up, Demitri Abbott flipped the script and said he'd come home to the murder and suspected the murderers were hiding in the closet. Paige and James were arrested on suspicion of murder. Not even Sandra Stockman could convince the judge to let them go. There was no hard evidence they did it, which works to their favor moving forward, but the judge set a jury trial. It'll be up to a jury to convict or let them go free.*

Stephen whistled lowly. *They saw Demitri Abbott kill Ralph Milternett?*

Yep, they said he admitted to killing his parents too, Roger said.

Why would he do all that? Stephen asked.

Paige thought it had something to do with his parent's adopting him. But he killed Ralph because he needed access to a safe that belongs to Scott. Once Ralph gave him the combination, Demitri killed him. The story got a little fuzzy after that. Paige kept repeating words over and over.

What words? Stephen asked.

Scott Milternett, The Greenfield Village House, and Carla... She said them over and over again like a broken record.

Did the police find anything out about Carley when they looked into Scott? Stephen had asked.

They didn't find anyone named Carley Smith who fit her description, Roger had answered.

Then came the phone call from Paige. The one that tore his heart in two.

Stephen, there's nothing more I can do, Paige had said. She was crying. *Lieutenant Higgins is shutting down the search. I have to let go. James says I have to give it to a higher power—to God and trust He will bring Anna home. Maybe He'll use you to bring our baby home.*

He was in reference to *God*. Paige hadn't ever been religious before. Truth be told, Stephen had never really thought much about God before either. But now, as he received his first official assignment, he had to consider that maybe, just maybe, his steps were being ordered by someone higher than himself. That was for sure. Paige's God.

It was then that Stephen's new deputy director, Rob, had briefed him on the situation within the Milternett Family Organization. Scott Milternett was under protection. Years ago, Scott had made a deal and had gotten immunity. He'd promised to give them Demitri Abbott. A promise Scott had not yet made good on. But they were convinced Scott got them closer every day. So, the real target of observation was Demitri Abbott. In order to keep Scott protected in his world, his people must believe that Scott owned the law enforcement officials and not the other way around. For years, it had been true. Then there was a *changing of the guard* so to speak. When Scott realized he could no longer manipulate or buy off the new line of officers, he came in and made a deal.

The timing had been strategic, Rob continued. *This new, competing family had moved into the area and were threatening the existence of the Milternett Family Organization. Scott wanted to serve up the Abbotts on a silver platter. With the new partnership, we warned Milternett that he couldn't do so with illegal means.*

"Then it will take a little longer," *Scott had told us.* Rob smirked a little. *We were okay with that.* Then Rob leaned forward, and the tone of the meeting changed. *There's something you should know about Demitri Abbott,* the deputy director looked Stephen dead in the eyes. The other Marshals sitting at the table sat up taller, looking spooked.

Let me guess, Stephen had smirked. *He's dangerous.*

Do not lower your guard around him, Wilton. We believe Demitri Abbott has multiple personality disorder. We've seen at least three different personalities emerge over the course of the time we've watched him. One is a charming Italian who's a successful businessman and has a way with the ladies. Another personality is a scared little boy. The last one is truly terrifying. He takes on animalistic characteristics. He lacks logic and wants only to destroy everything in his path. The local law enforcement has learned to appeal to his scared little boy personality. This is where he's the most controllable.

Stephen had sat back, processing his words and feeling truly terrified but not for himself. His mind went back the story Roger Higgins had told him. Stephen had been impressed that Paige had found the Abbott's abandoned house in Kansas. Until he heard she'd broken in.

He also thought Demitri was clever in that moment when he shifted the focus to Paige and James who were in the closet. Now Stephen wondered if it hadn't been *clever* as much as a personality shift. Maybe when the cops showed up, the scared little boy personality had no knowledge about what the animalistic personality of Demitri had done.

The words Roger said Paige kept repeating were about Demitri Abbott. She said Demitri had grilled the man about *Scott Milternett, The Greenfield Village House,* and *Carla.*

What do those things mean? Stephen had asked Roger.

I don't know. Paige just said Demitri asked Ralph Milternett, who was tied to a chair, at gunpoint where a safe was. The man said the words Greenfield Village House. Then Demitri asked if Carla was a spy. If she was working for Scott Milternett. The man said he didn't know. And Scott Milternett appeared to be the ultimate target.

Stephen had taken notes. At the time, he had a few weeks left of training.

I have to give it to a higher power—to God and trust He will bring Anna home. Maybe He'll use you to bring our baby home.

Even now, Stephen clenched his jaw, hearing her desperate words replay over and over again in his head. He debated telling the deputy director what he had learned from Paige. But he held back. Paige wasn't the most reliable witness now that she was wanted for murder. He also remembered Lieutenant Higgins' words of warning when they first discussed this job.

If you know what's good for you, you'll keep your mouth shut about your connection to Scott Milternett. Those connections of yours tend to cloud your judgement. They need someone with a clear head.

He'd be as clear headed as a dad of a missing daughter could possibly be.

56

CARLEY

FOUR AND A HALF MONTHS GONE

Carley grabbed Demitri's hand and led him to the ladies' bathroom. She looked back to make sure no one had spotted her. She pulled him in with her.

"Anyone in here?" she asked as she led him into the quiet room.

There was no response. She locked the bathroom door behind her.

Before she could blink, Demitri had pushed her against the wall and was kissing her. Demitri put quick hands down the back of her dress. Carley put her palms on his chest and pushed Demitri away. Confused, Demitri formed a question, but Carley shushed him and held up one finger.

"Hang on," she said with panic in her voice.

She took out her phone and texted Scott.

Carley: *What the f*** is Stephen Wilton doing at your party???*

There was no way Scott would be looking at his phone in the middle of his party. She needed a plan to get out of there.

She needed to think. She'd just sent Lauren home with her driver.

"I need your help," Carley choked out her words. She hated asking for his help. She knew it would mean she'd owe Demitri a favor on his terms.

"Oh?" Demitri's eyes narrowed.

"I need you to take me home. Right now. Is there another way out of here or is the front door the only way?" Carley quickly took off her heels, juggling them in her hands. She dropped her phone in her purse.

"Are you inviting me to come home with you?" he asked with an arrogant smile.

"Yes, Demitri, I'm inviting you over. If you get me out of here undetected, you can stay. All night," Carley whispered huskily as she closed the distance between them. Her lips softly brushed his. "Please, the way back into my panties? Just don't ask me any questions and do me this one favor."

"I know a way," he said, his eyes full of lust and excitement.

Carley exhaled in relief.

"Okay," Demitri put a finger up and opened the bathroom door looking both ways before he casually exited. He waved for her to follow before the door swung shut.

Carley did the same thing, looking both ways. The bathrooms were at the back of the building and Demitri opened a door that led to a dark hidden stairway. The two of them ran as quickly as they could without tripping up the stairwell. Demitri opened the door and they burst out into the sun which was setting and casting a hazy glow across the sky.

"Over here," Demitri pointed to the sleek, sexy BMW sitting in the back parking lot.

For a moment, Carley hesitated. She remembered the day she was followed by a car that looked just like this one. Demitri took her hesitation to mean she was waiting for him to get the door. Carley looked back toward the building anxiously weighing the alternative to leaving with Demitri. She could not go back in there now. Stephen Wilton was like a bloodhound. He would sniff her out the minute she re-entered the party.

She sat down and buckled her seatbelt. Once inside Demitri's car, speeding away from the party and heading toward her house, Carley began to breath normally again. Demitri Abbott might just have saved her life.

57

STEPHEN

FOUR AND A HALF MONTHS GONE

Stephen paused at the top of the steps that led down into a large open building.

"What is this place?" Stephen asked his new partner, Booker, as they walked in. Booker was shorter than Stephen. He was sturdy and muscular. He had an attitude that said he did not play games.

"It used to be a dance club. It was run by some of the younger Milternetts but then it got out of hand. Lots of fights, drinking and drugging... After a while, the family shut down the club and made this an event center."

Stephen nodded. The place was decorated classy and had a chill, dark vibe with lots of candles and low lighting. His eyes had adjusted as he found his footing and followed Booker down the stairs.

"Play it cool, man, and follow my lead," Booker said curtly.

Though he followed Booker through the room with ease and confidence, Stephen's eyes were scanning the room. He was looking for Demitri Abbot. He didn't see him anywhere. Then he found himself in front of Scott Milternett.

"Scott Milternett, this is our newest Marshal on the force,

Stephen Wilton," Booker introduced them believing it was for the first time.

Scott's eyes showed recognition but before he could mention that, Stephen put his hand out.

"Pleased to meet you, sir, and happy birthday." Stephen had grasped Scott's hand firm but amiably. "And might I say, condolences on your niece, Carley's, untimely death. Carley and I go back aways."

Scott instantly looked sad, and his eyes shifted down to his feet. "Thank you. Yes, it's a tragedy to die so young."

Stephen nodded but stared intensely into Scott's eyes. Stephen didn't know Scott that well. In fact, Carley was the one who talked to him after he'd showed up randomly with an arrow through his stomach in Stephen's backyard over a year ago. Carley had practically been living with Stephen at the time.

Still, Scott Milternett knew exactly who Stephen was. Scott had given Carley a heads up that Ludwig Lacose had put a contract on Stephen's life. Lucky for Stephen, Scott had chosen to warn him through Carley instead of taking on the contract himself. He owed Carley's relationship with Scott for that one.

"Stay, have a drink. You are welcome in my family," Scott said warmly.

As they walked away, Booker gave him a weird look.

"You know Milternett?" he asked sharply.

Stephen shrugged. "I knew Carley, his niece." He didn't invite further discussion.

Long after Booker said *goodnight,* Stephen stayed and roamed around the party. He'd finally given up looking for Demitri and changed his strategy. He started listening to conversations. He skillfully stood in places where no one really noticed him. He blended in and tried to make sense of what he was hearing. He thought with all the drinking going on someone would say something valuable.

He made his way to a group of women standing together

who looked like they might be gossiping. His ears perked up when he thought he heard Carley's name spoken. Then he listened to the whole sentence.

"… did you see the way Demitri walked up and claimed Carla like she was some prize?"

"Yeah, some prize," a pretty brunette snorted. "She's a little standoffish if you know what I mean."

"You're just jealous," a woman with jet black hair and big eyelashes retorted.

"Hell, yeah, I'm jealous. What does she have that I don't have?"

"More like what do you have that she doesn't—a husband!" the black-haired beauty sassed back.

That got a dirty look.

Carla and *Demitri*? Stephen's ears perked up.

That's when the pretty, albeit curvy, redhead noticed Stephen. She was a little old for Stephen, but she wasn't wearing a wedding ring and Stephen thought she might be a good source of information.

"Well, hello, who do we have here?" she'd asked Stephen while looking him up and down. "I know everyone at this party, but I've never seen you before in my life."

Stephen smiled his most charming smile and stuck out his hand. "I'm Stephen Wilton."

"Well, hello, Stephen…" she said to him as she tucked his arm in hers. "Don't wait up, girls."

Stephen allowed himself to be taken to the bar.

"What are you drinking, Stephen Wilton?" she purred.

"I'll have a seven and seven," Stephen ordered, knowing he'd nurse the hell out of that drink.

They found a semi-quiet bench to sit on where Stephen could observe the rest of the room from a distance. It was a very big room. It had a marble dance floor in the middle of the big open space. There was a large disco ball overhead that was currently flashing strobe lights to the beat of the music the DJ spun. Several people danced. The rest of the room had standing tables with barstool chairs and lower, more intimate tables sat further from the dance floor where Stephen assumed people could hear better.

Greenery and white faux orchids lined the walls and tables. It was simple but elegant. There was a chocolate fondue fountain over by tables of catered food. Stephen had checked it out earlier. There was more food than anyone in this room could eat in a week.

"So, clearly you're new here," the redhead leaned close to his ear. "I'm Lizbeth. Let me explain who's who in the room."

"Great," Stephen said back. "I'd really like that."

58

CARLEY

FOUR AND A HALF MONTHS GONE

Carley sat watching out the picture window in her big, dark room, her bottom settled firmly into an oversized soft, plush chair. She was wearing a thin, silk robe which did little for warmth, but she didn't care. Her knees were drawn up to her chest and she hugged them tightly while trying to think of a solution.

"Fiore, come back to bed," Demitri's voice sounded from somewhere in the mound of plush comforter on her king-sized bed.

"Fiore? What does that mean?" Carley didn't take her eyes off the road. Stephen Wilton was coming for her. It was only a matter of time. He was at that party for a reason. He had a lead. He knew she was alive, and it was only a matter of time before he'd put handcuffs on her just like he'd put them on his beloved Paige and carted her off to jail. A woman didn't leave a man like Stephen Wilton without consequences. And if she did, she needed to make damn sure not to take his only daughter when she went. Well, it was too late for all that now.

"It means flower. You are a strong flower," Demitri said in that sexy Italian voice of his.

"Don't get comfortable in that bed," Carley warned him. The only reason he was still here was for all her tough talk, Carley didn't think she could protect herself from Stephen. There would be no sweet talkin' him. Not after what she did. She'd made him believe his only daughter was dead. Demitri was there because she wanted protection in case shit hit the fan tonight. She hated herself for that weakness. Though she did feel grateful he'd helped her escape.

Carley replayed the text she'd gotten back from Scott an hour after she left the party. She was still trying to decipher what it meant for her.

Scott: *Stephen is a US Marshal now. Assigned to the Kansas City area. He was coming by to wish me happy birthday and give his condolences for your death.*

Bullshit, Carley decided. He was coming to give Scott a warning. Stephen was coming for her, and state lines wouldn't hold him back from finding her. He now had jurisdiction everywhere. *Great*.

Had her life with Stephen really been so bad? So what if she'd been stuck in a loop of domestic hell. She'd had Anna fair and square. She'd had someone who loved her, actually loved her, who wasn't bad on the eyes and was a great lay.

In fact, it was the first thing she'd noticed tonight when she saw him for that half a second. Stephen looked good. He looked toned, muscular, and tan. He'd filled out that white button-down shirt and black suit jacket nicely. *Shit*, she admitted to herself. She actually missed him. But there was no going back. No room for regret. She'd made her choice.

"Who are you hiding from, Fiore?" Demitri propped himself up with a pillow and sat looking at her. His muscular chest and defined abs, like the rest of his body probably had zero percent body fat. He looked out the window in the direction she had been staring.

"Someone more dangerous than all of us put together," Carley sighed. To distract him from these questions, she stood in one cat-like movement, dropping her robe on the floor, and got in bed with him. His body warmed hers as she snuggled into him. It was all an act to deter any further conversation.

He rubbed her bare shoulder and traced his finger down the length of her arm. "Are you in danger? What have you done?"

"We're all in danger, Demitri. We don't play by the rules of normal, law-abiding citizens. Some people have the power to take away the only things we care about and leave us in jail cells."

"Ah," Demitri said as if something clicked in his brain. "It was that law man tonight at the party. He walked in, you looked up at him, and you were scared," Demitri said, piecing together Carley's reaction.

"I wasn't scared," Carley bristled and tried to move away from him, feeling annoyed. "How do you know he was an official, anyway?"

"Please, I can spot cops two states away. Two men walked in, and I saw instant fear in your eyes. Then you ran and pulled me with you. One of them, the tall one, had blond curly hair. Blond curly hair like your daughter. She looks a lot like him," Demitri was puzzling things out rather quickly. Almost like he already knew something.

Carley sat up and turned to look in Demitri's eyes, her own eyes flashing dangerous anger signals. "What the *hell* do you know about my daughter?"

"I've watched you from afar, Fiore. I know much about you."

"You *are* stalking me!" Carley's voice rose with anger and panic.

"Shh," Demitri put a gentle finger to her lips, attempting to silence her. "You are a strong, beautiful woman. You came out of nowhere. I am partnered with your uncle's family. It could cost me my life to align with the wrong woman. Consider it... admiration from afar."

"Damnit, Demitri, I want to like you but if you start putting your nose into my business, you'll need to leave."

"Okay, okay, calm down," Demitri pulled her back to him, closing the gap between them. "You belong right here. With me."

Carley let him kiss her, but she knew this was the last time she would invite him over. He knew too much too soon. He was not the sort of man she wanted to know her secrets. But tonight, she would enjoy herself with him one more time.

In the morning, she and Scott would come up with a plan. Hopefully, it would be a better plan than hers. Because every solution she came up with involved murdering Stephen Wilton and riding off into the sunset with his little girl.

Murdering Stephen Wilton was her only option.

59

CARLEY

FOUR AND A HALF MONTHS GONE

Just before dawn, Carley woke Demitri.

"Demitri, you need to leave," she whispered.

Demitri grunted with genuine confusion and squinted his eyes in the darkness.

"Get up. You need to go," Carley said louder with more authority.

"Why?" he asked sleepily as he tried to pull her close to him.

"I don't want anyone to know you were here," Carley hissed in a whisper.

"Ah, right," Demitri got up, half awake, and started putting on the clothes that were scattered all around the room. He came back to the bed to kiss Carley goodbye. She let him kiss her.

"Will I see you again?" he asked.

Carley shrugged and pulled the comforter tighter around her.

"Tonight? I will come see you tonight?" Demitri asked again.

"I have plans tonight, Demitri. I'll text you." Carley rolled over and pretended to go back to sleep, missing the way his eyes darkened in anger. She heard him slam the door a little too loudly on the way out. She immediately pulled up the cameras on her phone app to make sure he went out the front door. Then she threw back her comforter and started getting dressed. Carley hadn't slept all night. She couldn't rest for one minute. Not until she had a plan.

She texted Scott.

Carley: *Come over the minute you're up. We need to plan.*

Carley suddenly felt exhausted. She sat in a chair and closed her eyes for a few minutes before her phone woke her back up again.

Scott: *I can be at your house at 8a. Now quit texting me. Hungover and trying to sleep in…*

Carley smiled. Of course, just because she left the party early did not mean others hadn't enjoyed the whole night. She set her alarm for an hour and crawled into bed.

Carley's dreams were chaotic and full of fear. In them, someone was chasing her. The faster she ran, the faster the pursuer ran until she had no more strength left. She collapsed. When she looked up at the man looming over her, she felt confused. She had expected the man's eyes to be vibrant blue, but they weren't.

The man who was after her had dark brown eyes.

60

CARLEY

FOUR AND A HALF MONTHS GONE

"Maybe the answer here is to just come clean with Stephen," Scott suggested flippantly. He was drinking ginger ale and rubbing his temple. He was nursing a hangover and had already told Carley it was way too early for her freak out. "We have bigger problems than Stephen Wilton."

Carley sat back down huffily across from Scott. "What could be bigger? Stephen would happily cart me off to jail. He arrested his own baby mama before. He wouldn't hesitate to do the same with me."

"Maybe seduce him?" Scott threw out the idea.

"What? Is that your suggestion to everything? I'm not a piece of meat!"

Scott stared at her like she was crazy for a moment. "Who else have you seduced at my suggestion?"

"Demitri Abbott. You practically pushed me at him last night," the words popped out of Carley's mouth without thought or discretion.

Scott now looked horrified. "You're dating Demitri Abbott?"

Carley shrugged. "Not really. The word *dating* is optional."

"I didn't tell you to jump in bed with him." Scott shook his head. "I said be nicer to him because he's an important alliance. We need him to stay on our good side. I don't *fully* trust him."

"Now you tell me!" Carley threw up her hands.

"Not too long ago, it was *you* who warned *me* that he was stealing from me. He could have killed you when you stopped paying him what he was asking, you know. *Play nice* doesn't mean *sleep with him*."

"Noted," Carley said, ice flooding into her veins. Demitri would never kill her. Would he?

"This world is different than where you came from. You need to be careful and think things through. One wrong move can set off a chain of reactions that can end your life. Every move you make needs to be strategic." Scott took a long drink of his ginger ale. "I didn't think I needed to educate you on that."

"So we can't kill Stephen Wilton?" Carley was beginning to get the picture.

"God, no!" Scott leaned his head back and closed his eyes.

"Well, I'm not going to reveal my hiding spot, nor am I going to make nice with him and hand over his daughter," Carley slammed a hand on the table suddenly. "She doesn't belong to him. She's mine."

Scott nodded. "I believe you. So, here's my suggestion. We stay the course and stick to the plan. No one else knows you as 'Carley.' The only name Wilton will hear is Carla Milternett. Keep a low profile and don't do anything to be on his radar. In time, the trail will turn cold, and you'll be safe. You've changed your look and your hair color which might be why he didn't spot you last night. I supposed you could go a little blonder. 'Cause damn, that was a close one." Scott laughed a little with the shake of his head.

"Blonder than this?" Carley grabbed her ponytail and brushed through it. She had loved her brown hair and hated getting rid of all of it. Right now, she had a nice mix of brown with heavy blond highlights. Carley didn't want any more blond.

"Come on, you could match your daughter." Scott was still chuckling.

"It's a thought," Carley worried about this a little more. "I'll think about it."

As Scott left that morning, Carley couldn't help but feel that time was running out. She found Anna in her playroom that morning and plopped on the floor, picking up one of Anna's dolls. Playing princesses wasn't Carley's idea of fun. But she wasn't about to leave the house. And if time was running out, the one person she wanted to spend it with was Anna.

61

STEPHEN

FOUR AND A HALF MONTHS GONE

For all of his hard work and training over the past four and a half months, Stephen knew he should have been ready. Physically, he was in perfect condition to take on whatever, or whoever, challenged the law. Mentally, it was a different story altogether.

During that time, his thoughts had been consumed with plans of bringing his daughter home. He would admit the challenge of finding Carley was a close second in his list of motivators. Knowing Carley the way he did, it wasn't difficult for him to get an idea of where she was hiding. He knew Paige wasn't wrong. Find Carley, find Anna. But he couldn't figure out the connection to Demitri Abbott who had become first and foremost in his mind.

In retrospect, walking right through the front door to Scott Milternett's birthday party might not have been the best idea. Ironically, it hadn't even been his idea. Neither had his new position location been his choice. He was merely following fate around at this point and he had a strong feeling fate would lead Anna home.

He owed it to Paige to look into what she'd told him. He'd

already connected with Scott Milternett. He did not know anything about the Greenfield Village House or Carla Milternett when he'd first arrived. Now he knew that Carla Milternett lived *in* the Greenfield Village House. When he'd overheard she'd left with Demitri Abbott the other night, it had made her a more interesting person to Stephen.

So, he'd found the Greenfield Village House. He'd found a hidden place to park around the corner which had a view to her front bay window that had a sheer curtain over it. He ate his lunch in the car with binoculars and waited. He ate his dinner in that same spot in the car and waited. It seemed this Carla woman never left the house.

From what he could see, she had blond hair, she was thin, and she was tall. The curtains made the rest hazy. No matter, Stephen wasn't giving up so easily. She couldn't stay in her house forever. When she left, Stephen would be following her wherever she went. The problem was, she had not left her house all day.

No worries, he thought. *I have nowhere else to be this weekend.*

62

PAIGE

FOUR AND A HALF MONTHS GONE

"James?" I hissed, well aware it was likely sometime after midnight. I was jealous of the way he could sleep in this place. I felt like a zombie. My mind had not shut down once in the month I'd been attempting to sleep in this jail cell. My body hurt laying on this cot under me as well.

"Huh?" he gasped a little and stirred, trying to wake up. Finally, he opened his eyes. "What's wrong? Are you okay?"

"Yes, I just can't sleep. I keep thinking about the trial tomorrow. If it goes badly…"

"It won't," James said with confidence. "We didn't do it. They'll see. Have faith."

"It's just that, if it goes badly, this is the last time you and I will see each other alone."

James was silent, contemplating my words.

"I'm sorry I dragged you into this," I apologized. I had been thinking about the things I'd never done in life and all the things I never said.

"I chose to come. I chose to go with you. I could have said *no*. But I don't ever want to say *no* to you again. I'm with you

298

forever. Here," he put his hand through the bars and onto my heart.

"There's something else," I whispered. I could see his eyes on mine. "I think I might be pregnant."

"What?" James sat straight up. "It's a sign!"

"A sign?" I asked. I felt terrified.

"A sign that we're going to get out of here. We're going to get married and have a family. Complete when Anna comes home."

"James, you aren't obligated to marry me just because—"

"Stop!" he said sternly. "I never should have divorced you. I want to marry you and be with you forever. I guess now is as good a time as any… Paige Erin Mynart, will you marry me?"

"Yes," I sighed. *If we make it past this trial*, I thought still feeling worried about what tomorrow would bring.

63

PAIGE

FOUR AND A HALF MONTHS GONE

Twelve jurors sat in a box to the side of the room with front row seats to our murder trial. Sandra Stockman had brought us clothes.

To help you look respectable, she'd said.

James was wearing a crisp blue button-down dress shirt that matched his eyes. His tie had a matching pattern. He wore shiny dress shoes. My dress was conservative. It was a long white dress with a black belt and black high heels. I'd pulled my hair back into a low ponytail. Our look had the desired effect. Sandra wanted us to look wholesome.

I attempted to make eye contact and smile at each juror as they filed in and sat down. I knew my eyes were sad. Some looked compassionate. Others quickly looked away, I imagine, in an effort to stay neutral.

One girl looked to be my age. She locked eyes with me. She had kind eyes. She reluctantly broke my gaze when she sat down. In my gut, I thought she might also be a mom.

The last juror was an older woman and she reminded me of Ms. Darby. My heart squeezed as she looked back at me. I thought she must be a grandma. I might get a sympathy vote from her as well.

When the trial opened, I noticed Rick Boston seemed even harder and more aggressive than before. If his opening statement was any indication, he was not planning on losing this case.

"The defendants, James Friesen and Paige Mynart, were found hiding in the very room where the murder of Ralph Milternett took place." He paused to sweep a hand theatrically around the room where, once again, the photos of Ralph Milternett murdered in the basement were displayed in the courtroom from every angle.

"This gun was found on Paige Mynart." Rick picked up a plastic bag with my gun inside to submit it into evidence. "I intend to prove that Mr. Friesen and Ms. Mynart broke into the home of the deceased couple, William and Carolyn Abbott. I will show you how once they were there, they tortured and killed Ralph Milternett."

Sandra got up and immediately appealed to the jury for her opening statement. "Ladies and gentleman of the jury, remember that this couple is innocent until proven guilty. You'll have a chance to look closely at the evidence to determine if Paige Mynart and James Friesen actually committed the crime with which they are being charged. I will submit a police report that will show why the gun Paige carried was *not* the murder weapon." Sandra picked up the report to submit as evidence. "This report will also show that they did not fire the gun, nor did they have gunpowder residue, known as GSR, anywhere on them indicating that at no point were they near enough to the gun that was fired. You will hear their story and learn why they were there in the first place. And you will hear first-hand testimony to corroborate their story. By the end of this trial, I hope to show that Paige Mynart and James Friesen are victims of bad choices and poor timing, but they are not murderers. I appreciate your time and know that when all the evidence is presented to you, you will make the right choice, and justice will be served."

I noticed more than a few jurors sit up straighter. I saw some nod their head as though they were taking this very seriously. The rest looked bored and seemed hopeful it would all be over soon.

"The state calls Paige Mynart to the stands," Rick Boston announced.

My surprised eyes flew to Sandra. I thought she was the one who would call me up.

Sandra raised one eyebrow. "You can plead the fifth," she whispered as she nodded, encouraging me to go.

I shook my head *no*. I wanted to tell the truth. I stood on shaky legs and walked a few steps to the box with a chair where I swore an oath on a Bible and sat down.

"Ms. Mynart—is that the name you prefer? Or do you go by Deffer? I think there was some confusion with an incorrect passport one time…" Rick Boston sneered at me.

"Objection, Your Honor," Sandra called. "That's hardly relevant to this case."

"Fine," Rick Boston put up his hands. He went to his table and picked up a gun that was inside a plastic bag. "Ms. Mynart, is this your gun?"

My heart was racing inside me. I looked to Sandra who gave a curt little nod. I took a deep breath. I dare not lie under oath.

"Yes," I said. Out of the corner of my eye, I could see a juror lean forward.

"Did you break into the home of Carolyn and William Abbott?" he asked smugly.

"Yes," I answered.

"And did you carry this gun with you the night you broke into Carolyn and William Abbott's home?"

"Yes," I admitted again.

"I see, and where did you carry this gun?" he stroked his chin like he was puzzling over the secrets of the universe.

"On my hip holster."

Rick nodded and placed the gun back on the table. He turned back to me. "Where were you found when the cops showed up?" he asked.

"In a closet in the basement of William and Carolyn Abbott's home." I felt my face get hot and shame hit me hard. I wanted to cry. My eyes watered.

"The exact location where Ralph Milternett was murdered?" he exclaimed in mock horror and surprise. He was really pulling out the theatrics.

I didn't want to nod but the expectant pause made me feel obligated.

"So, mere minutes after a man is murdered in this very basement…" Rick paused and walked to a picture, pointing at the gruesome photo of Ralph and used his hand to draw a circle around the perimeter of the room, "the police find you and your boyfriend in the closet?"

I nodded.

"No further questions, your honor."

Then Sandra was standing in front of me. "Paige are you okay?" she asked.

I nodded but felt confused. Of course I wasn't okay.

"Paige, can you tell the court why you broke into the Abbott home?" Sandra asked.

I remembered to only tell the story we'd rehearsed. Sandra had reminded us not to make accusations even though we'd seen Demitri kill Ralph. I remembered all too well. We were the only ones on trial. "My daughter, Anna, went missing over four months ago. She had been kidnapped by someone we knew and thought we trusted. Then the authorities found the kidnapper's car which she had driven over the edge of a mountain. At that point, my daughter had been presumed dead." I took a shuddered breath reliving the moment and tears began to fall. I had been trying so hard to be strong, but I could not control my emotions when it came to Anna.

"Just breathe, Paige. Tell us what happened next?" Sandra encouraged me gently.

I wiped my tears. "When the DNA came back, it wasn't my daughter's body in that car. And it wasn't her kidnapper either. It was Carolyn and William Abbott."

A collective and surprised gasp sounded from the jurors and a few people sitting around the courthouse.

"The local police kept telling us they were collaborating with the Gayena Police Department, but they had no jurisdiction in Kansas. So, we decided to go investigate on our own just in case Anna was being held at the home of the deceased couple who were found dead in the car. It was a long shot. I was just desperate."

"Your daughter has been missing for four months?" Sandra asked for the benefit of the jury.

"Four and a half, maybe five months now…" It was hard to speak over the lump in my throat.

"That's a long time for a mother to be without her daughter. I personally can't imagine how many hours of waiting and worrying and praying you might have spent just hoping that someone will find your daughter and bring her home," Sandra said with more sympathy than I'd ever heard in her voice before.

The tears started again. I nodded. "Yeah."

"How did that make you feel?" she asked.

"Hopeless, helpless, afraid," my voice broke and I was crying now.

"Afraid of what?" Sandra asked.

"I'll never see Anna again," I whispered.

"I'm sorry, I didn't hear you, can you repeat that for the court?"

"I'm afraid I'll never see my daughter, Anna, again," I sobbed and then worked to get it under control.

"So when you had the chance—a lead, you might say—you took the opportunity to follow it where the police department could not go?"

"Objection, Your Honor," I jumped a little at Rick Boston's thundering voice. "Leading the witness."

"Sustained."

"Okay," Sandra acknowledged. "What happened when you heard the news about William and Carolyn Abbott?"

"I felt so frustrated. Like the police weren't getting anywhere. I thought I would go look for her myself."

"Which is what a good mom would do." Sandra turned to the jury. "Who wouldn't go find their child and bring her home? How old is Anna, Paige?"

"She'll be three in a month," I said.

"Tell us what happened when you found the Abbott's home?" Sandra asked.

"We broke in." I wiped my tears.

"We, as in you and James Friesen?" Sandra pointed to James.

I nodded again.

"Why did you break in?" she asked.

"I don't know exactly. I thought maybe we'd find Anna in there. We didn't know why William and Carolyn were in the same car where my daughter was last seen. We just knew there had to be a connection. So, we went inside to try to find Anna or a clue that would get us closer to her."

"And then?" Sandra asked.

"Then Demitri Abbott came home."

"You knew it was Demitri?" Sandra's voice was sharp. She had told us Demitri was not on trial, and we needed to keep it about ourselves.

"Not until later. We heard someone coming so we hid in the closet. We were afraid we'd get caught."

"Indeed," Sandra said as she walked back to the table. She pulled out the police report. "Can you read this for the court, Paige?"

"Neither Paige Mynart, nor James Friesen had gunpowder residue on their hands after they were arrested and checked. Neither did the gloves they wore on their hands nor the clothes they were wearing, which indicates they were in the closet at the time the murder occurred. The gun, while registered to Paige Mynart, is not the weapon that was used to kill the murder victim. Her gun clip was full, indicating no bullets were fired. The bullets fired did not match the bullets loaded in Ms. Mynart's Glock 43x. A ballistics expert noted the striation of the bullets, which indicated a different gun altogether was used as the murder weapon."

"Thank you," Sandra said. She put the report down, then turned back to me. "Paige, did you kill Ralph Milternett?"

"No. But I am guilty," I said suddenly.

"I'm sorry?" Sandra turned to me sharply in surprise. We hadn't rehearsed this. Her eyes flashed angry warnings at me.

"I'm guilty of breaking and entering. I'm guilty of investigating my daughter's murder without the authority of a badge." I looked at the jury to appeal to them. They would determine the outcome of my life. Tears streamed down my cheeks again. "I'm guilty of being a mother who was at her wits end. If any of you are parents, you know how far you would go to save your children. When your kids are in danger, you aren't thinking about what's legal and what's not. You just react. You shut down your brain and use your instinct. I still haven't found my daughter, but now I can say with certainty that she wasn't being held in that house. That makes all of this worth it."

"That will be all, Paige." Sandra dismissed me coldly and walked back to sit by James.

It was Rick Boston's turn to stand. "No further witnesses, your honor."

The judge turned to Sandra. "Defense calls James Friesen to the stand."

James' story mirrored mine.

"James," Sandra asked. "Did you make a phone call when you were in the closet that night?"

"Yes, I did," James said.

"Who did you call?" she asked.

"I called nine-one-one," he stated.

Sandra turned to the jurors. "I pulled the records from the nine-one-one call to see what number it came from, and it was, in fact, a phone number from Canada. Further investigation concluded the nine-one-one call did *not* come from Demitri Abbott at all but from my client, James Friesen. If James and Paige were guilty of murder, why would he have called nine-one-one?"

Rick Boston got up to cross examine. "That's quite a story," he challenged James. "It didn't occur to you that breaking and entering was illegal?"

James shrugged.

"Where do you fit into this? Why were you with Paige Mynart?"

"I love her and Anna, and I supported her decision to do whatever it took to find Anna."

"Whatever it took? Even murder?" Rick Boston leered at him.

"Objection." Sandra stood to her feet.

"Sustained."

Before Rick could ask another question, I saw Lieutenant Higgins walk into the courtroom. My heart lifted. Surely, he could help us out here.

James was dismissed.

Rick had no other witnesses.

The judge looked at Sandra. "Do you have any further witnesses, Ms. Stockman?"

"Yes, your honor. Defense calls Lieutenant Roger Higgins to the stand."

Lieutenant Higgins looked sharp in his black suit. He swore his oath on the Bible and sat down.

"Lieutenant Higgins, do you know this couple?" Sandra pointed to James and me.

"Yes, ma'am, I do." He nodded.

"What is the nature of your relationship?"

"Strictly professional. Ms. Mynart here has had a run of bad luck, from the death of her mom years ago to the recent disappearance of her child, all of which I've had the unfortunate experience of investigating."

"I see. Have you successfully solved these cases for her each and every time?"

"No, ma'am, I'm afraid not. We did eventually solve the case with her mom, but it took near two years. We're still in the middle of the investigation into the disappearance of her daughter, Anna."

"I see, and how long has that been going on?" Sandra asked.

"Her daughter disappeared in November, so it's been around four months." He seemed to be doing math in his head.

"So, it's accurate to say Paige Mynart is frustrated with the investigation?"

"Objection!" Rick shouted. "Leading the witness."

"Sustained. Please rephrase the question, Ms. Stockman," the judge ordered.

"Lieutenant Higgins, what was Ms. Mynart's state of mind when you last talked to her?"

"She was determined to find her daughter," he stated. "She wasn't going to let anything stand in her way."

"Did she tell you she was going to attempt to find her?" Sandra asked.

"Yes, though I advised her not to. I told her to leave the investigation up to us. But she went anyway."

"Why didn't you try to stop her?" Sandra asked.

"Couldn't," he stated. "We can't stop citizens from doing anything unless it's illegal."

"And looking into the disappearance of her daughter is not illegal?"

"No, ma'am." He shook his head emphatically.

"Did she tell you her plan?" Sandra challenged him.

Now Lieutenant Higgins looked sheepish. "Yeah, she was keeping me posted."

"What did she say the last time she talked to you?"

"She had some theories on what had happened the night the car with the Abbotts drove off the road. She was telling us so we could look into them. I asked her to stay put but she said they were going to go to Kansas to look further into the couple. She thought they might be connected to her daughter somehow."

"I see. Did she tell you she planned to break into the Abbot's home to search for her daughter?"

"No, ma'am, she did not," Lieutenant Higgins shot me a glance and I felt properly ashamed.

"Nothing further, your honor," Sandra said as she walked briskly back to her seat.

Rick Boston stepped up. "Tell me, Lieutenant Higgins, are you in the habit of giving permission to civilians to do your job for you?"

"I—"

"Objection, witness clearly stated he did not give permission," Sandra interrupted.

"Sustained," the judge answered.

"Is it your habit to get on the stands and vouch for criminal behavior?" Rick Boston tried again.

"Objection, your honor. My witness does not have to answer that."

"Your honor, I was merely trying to make the point that this witness appears to live by a double standard—"

"Unless you have any other questions, Mr. Boston, I suggest you have a seat. The character of this witness is not in question."

Rick Boston shot an angry glare at Sandra and stalked back to his seat.

The judge dismissed Lieutenant Higgins.

After listening to the closing remarks, the judge dismissed the jury to deliberate.

"Court is in recess, pending an answer from the jury." She banged her gavel.

"That went so fast!" I said, feeling surprised. "Don't most trials take a few days?"

Sandra shook her head, her lips tight. She looked worried and distracted as she answered. "Not in trials where there's a lack of sufficient evidence."

"Now what?" I asked.

"Now, we wait," Sandra said.

64

PAIGE

FOUR AND A HALF MONTHS GONE

"Don't ever improvise like that again without warning me somehow," Sandra fumed for the tenth time as we sat and waited for the jury to come back. She seemed to get more nervous the longer the jury deliberated.

I nodded absently. I held James' hand tightly. I'd been to jail once. I'd heard prison was worse. If they found us guilty, all of my searching for Anna would be pointless. I would never see her or James again. What's more, James would spend his life behind bars as well.

"We can always appeal," Sandra said.

"Please stop. You're making me so nervous," I whispered, wishing she would stop talking. Before she could snipe back, the jury came back in a single file line and sat back in their rows. It had taken less than an hour. Was that good news or bad news?

"All rise," I heard the judge say.

We stood.

"Have you reached a verdict?" the judge asked.

"We did, Your Honor," the spokesperson said.

The judge nodded at her.

"We the jury find Paige Mynart and James Friesen not guilty for the murder in the first degree of Ralph Milternett. We do find them guilty of breaking and entering." She promptly sat down.

I exhaled the breath I'd been holding and felt relief flood through me.

The judge spoke next. "I agree with the jury and find Paige Mynart and James Friesen not guilty of the murder of Ralph Milternett. I *do* find them guilty of breaking and entering as well. Defendants will pay a fine of one thousand dollars each. Court is dismissed."

I let out the breath I had been holding and laughed happily. James laughed with me. Sandra looked relieved but only for a minute. She waited until Rick Boston huffed out of the courtroom.

She then lowered her voice and looked us squarely in the eyes. "Don't think for one minute this is over. If what you told me is correct about Demitri Abbot, you might be in danger. He saw your faces. You need to go to the police and tell them everything you know."

"And have them put me in protection again?" I shuddered. "No, thanks! Not to mention, the police seemed pretty chummy with Demitri Abbott when they showed up. I couldn't help but think after what had just happened, this police department would never give me any credit. Thank you though, Sandra! For everything!" I put my hand out to shake hers.

"Just doing my job," she said curtly but her smile was unmistakable.

"I mean it." I reiterated. If Sandra were an approachable, huggable person, I might have thrown my arms around her. This was the second time she'd gotten me out of a murder charge.

Thanks to Sandra Stockman and Roger Higgins, we weren't going to prison for murder. But she was right, no thanks to this case, Demitri Abbott now knew us by name. He knew what we looked like. And he knew we knew he'd killed Ralph and his parents. We might just be sitting targets when we got home.

65

PAIGE

FIVE MONTHS GONE

James woke me up with breakfast in bed. I'd never had breakfast in bed before. Dawn had just crept in through the pretty, light-blue curtains, showing the first rays of morning. I snuggled into my matching blue comforter as I fought the sleepiness that weighed heavily on me. But the tantalizing smell of bacon won over more sleep when my stomach growled, betraying me and waking me up.

Since James had reappeared in my life, we'd been living in the master bedroom. We'd made new memories there. We'd bought matching dark oak wood furniture that created a warm, comfortable feeling in the room.

After the ordeal we'd gone through in Kansas, I thought I might never have a normal breakfast again. I felt grateful every day that we'd gotten out of the murder charges. I'd learned my lesson the hard way about investigating without a badge.

That was a week ago. Since then, we'd gotten a security system for the house. After the first few days of looking over my shoulder and jumping at shadows, I started to believe that Demitri Abbott was not coming for us. To him, James and I must just be a small, inconsequential detail. But we knew who he was. I carried my gun everywhere and I had James get one too. He'd also started going with me to the gun range.

Now, I smiled sleepily at James. He climbed in bed with me and watched me eat. When I was done, he moved the plates to the nightstand.

"Paige, I think it's time to talk about what you've been avoiding," James announced.

"What's that?" I asked, staring at him without comprehension. All my energy had been directed at finding Anna. Then it had taken all my energy to go back to work and just function in a normal capacity while I waited. I had not quite restarted my online classes.

"The pregnancy," James said.

I nodded.

"I've been watching you, monitoring your stress levels and your condition, the dissociative fugue. Before Kansas, I had researched and read more about it. It's been hard to tell, but there have been times when I don't think you're all there."

"Yeah…"

"There's something else," James seemed to be tiptoeing around something.

"Okay," I invited.

"You don't seem excited about the pregnancy," James blurted out the obvious fact.

"You're right," I admitted. "It should be the happiest news I could hope for. But I feel terrified."

"Why?" James asked.

"James, I couldn't keep my first child safe. What makes you think I can keep this baby safe? I kept thinking if I could find Anna and bring her home, I might deserve this second chance."

James' eyes welled up with tears. "You have me now, Paige. We can do this together. Life happens and sometimes it sucks but it's not a predictor of what's to come. You just do the best you can on any given day. It'll be okay. And when you're afraid, connect with God."

I smiled with tears in my eyes. Maybe he was right.

"I think she's a girl," James predicted. "Anna is going to have a little sister. I believe we're going to get Anna back. We just need to leave her in God's hands for now. In the meantime, maybe we can set up a doctor's appointment and start thinking about this. This addition to our little family."

I liked the sound of that. Maybe, just maybe, in the midst of all this chaos, and the pain of waiting, I could find happiness in the future. Maybe my higher power was giving me the gift of a restart. I was almost too afraid to hope.

Maybe I wasn't as bad as I once believed. Bad people don't deserve happiness. Right? I was feeling a little happier every day but there would be an Anna-sized hole in my heart until the day she came home.

Any happiness I felt in the meantime was miraculous. I wanted to grab onto it and bottle it for tougher days I still felt sure were ahead.

66

CARLEY
FIVE MONTHS GONE

Carley bolted awake from a deep sleep in the middle of the night. She peered into the black night, wondering what had woken her. What was that loud noise? Carley squinted, trying to peer into the darkness, trying to make sense of why her brain was on high alert. She reached a hand over to the other side of the bed, feeling for Demitri. He had been staying over more regularly in the last couple weeks. She debated asking him to go check things out.

His side of the bed was empty. The covers had been thrown back and he was not there. Nor was he in this room. Another loud thump sounded downstairs. Was she being robbed?

Carley sat up, wide awake now. She saw a little body standing in the doorway and jumped a little. Anna stood mute, shaking in fear. Carley swung her legs over the side of the bed. Anna came running to her. Carley folded her into her arms.

An alert sounded on Carley's phone. She looked at it to see red words that said *Alarm Alert* inside a yellow triangle box. *Odd*, Carley thought, *I've never had an alarm alert on my phone before.*

She clicked on it. Apparently, the alarm on the safe wasn't

the only hidden camera in the house after all. She shouldn't be annoyed. She knew there were cameras all over the house. She knew she had installed an app on her phone and could look at them at any given point in the day. She'd just never needed to before. Most days she forgot they were there.

The view from the camera came alive on her phone. She gasped loudly. Someone was in her study. The angle of the camera showed her computer. That someone had found her password and the computer screen was lit up in the darkness, showing the general ledger Carley kept. But something more terrifying caught her eye.

There was movement in the corner of the room. At first, Carley thought the movement came from a crouching animal. Then the animal sprang up and moved in jerky, almost feral movements. The animal stood to its full height and growled. At least, it started as a growl and became a chilling screech of anger. He moved like a trapped, injured creature. Only, he wasn't trapped. He was free.

He put his hands against the wall. Then he pulled his right hand back and punched the wall with all his power. His fist went through the wall and when he pulled it back, his hand was bleeding. It was then that Carley noticed there were multiple holes in the wall.

The animal turned and Carley could see him on the camera. It looked like Demitri Abbott, only there was something very off about the way he held his body and how he moved. His right shoulder hung lower than his left shoulder and his arm hung there limply like something had been dislocated. There should have been pain on his face. There wasn't, just a look of firm determination.

His eyes were the scariest of all. His pupils seemed to take over his whole eye, swallowing the brown shade they normally were. His eyes looked pure black, and he looked—evil.

"Where is it?" he yelled loudly. He ran over to the computer on Carley's desk and flung it to the ground. It hit the floor with a loud crash.

Anna clung to Carley, her little body shaking.

"It's okay, baby," Carley whispered as she put her finger to her lips. "Be very quiet."

Carley grabbed a t-shirt she had draped over a chair and put it on over the sports bra she'd slept in. She was wearing pajama bottoms, thankfully. She quickly slipped her feet in flipflops. She picked Anna up and started moving quickly. She soundlessly ran down the back staircase that led to the garage where Carley kept her SUV. She opened the garage door, got into the SUV, and locked the door. She hoisted Anna into the back, giving her bottom a little boost between the front seats.

"Buckle yourself in, baby," Carley requested. "I know you know how."

"Like this?" Anna asked. She latched the buckle.

"Yes, just like that."

Carley backed out of the driveway with the lights off. Regardless, she knew Demitri would see her. She figured she had bought herself some time though. The problem was, she had no clue where to go next.

Carley looked up toward her bedroom, which faced the driveway she was backing out of. A light illuminated the window frame. She could see Demitri's face glaring out at her, watching her as she backed the car out. He must have run up the front stairs. They'd left just in time. She shivered at how close they'd come to being the subject of his anger. He slammed his fist against the window, then he was gone.

"Go, go, go!" Carley said quickly. She was on the street now and she pushed the gas pedal harder.

"Who you talking to, mommy?" Anna asked.

"Myself," Carley said. It was only a matter of time before Demitri made it to his own car and chased her.

"Siri," Carley said loudly. Her phone automatically connected to the car when she got in. "Call Scott Milternett."

Anna didn't question this because she was familiar with Siri and the way the phone would go through contacts, find the person, and call them hands free. The phone started ringing. It was the fifth ring before Scott's groggy voice answered.

"Hello?" he mumbled.

"Scott! Thank God! I've got a situation here," Carley said in an elevated tone. Panic was evident in the tremor in her words.

"What's going on?" Scott asked.

Carley only hesitated a moment. She hated to scare Anna, but she didn't have time to waste. "An alarm alert went off on my phone that showed me a live feed of Demitri Abbott tearing up the study downstairs in my house. He was clearly looking for something. Maybe he was looking for the safe?"

"Really?" Now Scott sounded more alert. "Hang on."

"Scott, whatever you're doing right now needs to wait. I got Anna out of the house and I'm driving aimlessly around town. What should I do?" Carley asked breathlessly. She couldn't see Demitri's car, but she knew it was back there. Somewhere close behind. It was only a matter of time before he found her.

"Don't come here. In fact, you can't go to anyone's home who you know," Scott responded. "If he comes after you, it's because he's desperate and couldn't find what he was looking for. I'm going to text you the name and directions for a motel. The owner is a friend who will ask no questions and have a key waiting for you at the desk by the time you get there. Go there now and I'll meet you. Is he right behind you?"

Carley looked in the mirrors and chanced a glance behind her. "I don't see him, but he might be minutes behind me."

"Okay, get onto the highway heading east and then follow the directions. There, I sent them."

Carley heard her phone ping. "I got them. Hurry, Scott. I don't have a gun on me or any way to protect us."

"Let me make the phone call to the motel, then I'm on my way."

Carley exited onto the highway and headed east. She hit the gas. Her and Anna's safety depended on them getting to that motel before Demitri Abbott.

Carley was unaware that a sleek, black BMW turned on the highway ten minutes after she did. She had no way to know that her new boyfriend had put a tracker on her phone so he would know where she was at all times.

67

STEPHEN

FIVE MONTHS GONE

Stephen Wilton was sleeping in his car when his phone rang. It was where he fell asleep most nights, not that any of his Marshal coworkers knew. He'd inquired about Carla Milternett and no one had heard of her. It was like she'd come out of nowhere.

Stephen knew where she'd come from. Only, his plan to follow her when she left her house wasn't working. He'd camped out for the past four nights and Carla never left.

Stephen squinted in the dark and blinked sleepily. His phone rang again. It was an unknown number, one of those star sixty-seven numbers. It was untraceable. Stephen noted the time before he answered. It was after midnight.

"Stephen Wilton?" a man's voice broke through the sleepy fog in his brain.

"Yes?" Stephen answered.

"It's Scott Milternett—"

"How did you get my number?" Stephen howled in outrage.

"There's no time for that. I make it my business to have all your numbers in my phone. There's trouble and I need your help."

"Why would you call me, not the deputy director?" Stephen asked. He really didn't want to blow this new job opportunity.

"Listen to me," Scott hissed, his voice was sounding desperate now. "My niece is in trouble. Demitri Abbott is pursuing her as we speak. He's dangerous, volatile. I can't stop him."

"Why would I stop a domestic dispute?" Stephen asked. He'd taken out his binoculars and could see that a light was on in an upstairs room where he assumed a bedroom might be. It wasn't on when he'd fallen asleep. Stephen was feeling more alert now.

"Because my niece is Carley, not Carla!" Scott was talking fast now. He was twisting his words.

Stephen felt like he'd been punched in the gut. The air seemed to woosh out of his stomach. He'd suspected as much. He was even following that hunch, wasn't he? So why did this confirmation take him by such surprise? He knew the answer. Because he'd been wrong before. Stephen had let his emotions get in the way and cloud his judgement.

"Stephen are you there? Do you understand me? You need to get there before Demitri does. I sent her to a motel. I have friends there, but she won't be safe long. I'm sending you the address."

"Does Carley have Anna?" Stephen asked.

Now Scott was silent.

"Answer me," Stephen yelled. "Does Carley have my daughter?"

"Yes."

It was all Stephen needed to hear. His phone lit up with a text of the address. Stephen turned on his car and buckled his seatbelt as he drove out of the neighborhood. He cursed the fact that he didn't have a siren on his car. He did the next best thing. He turned on his flashers and hit the gas as he got onto the highway.

Next, he called his deputy director who answered the phone sounding just as groggy as Stephen felt.

"Sir, I need to tell you I'm in pursuit of two people in a domestic dispute—"

"You're not a cop anymore, Wilton. Hand it over to the police," Rob sounded irritated.

"Please, hear me out. It's Scott Milternett's niece and Demitri Abbott is pursuing her. Scott says it's bad and I believe him. I'm requesting back up."

"Okay, where to?" he asked.

Stephen rattled off the address, told him to hurry, and hung up the phone. He had no idea what he was walking into, and he didn't have time to explain the connection to his daughter.

"Please, please," Stephen said a prayer aloud to the God Paige kept mentioning. "Please let my daughter be alive when I get there."

68

CARLEY

FIVE MONTHS GONE

Carley threw the car in park in front of the motel office. She jumped out and then unbuckled Anna. An older woman walked up to her with a key.

"Are you Carla?" she asked in a rough voice.

"Yes," Carley turned. She grabbed Anna out of the car seat. The woman handed Carley a key to a motel room on the second floor.

"It's round back. You need to hurry. In fact, I'd park my car back there if I were you. We'll stall him, tell him you aren't here, whatever we need to do."

"Thank you!" Carley snatched the room key. She jumped back in the car with Anna on her lap. She didn't have time for seatbelts. It was just around the corner. Anna clung to Carley, burying her face in Carley's shoulder.

Carley parked her car. She threw her car door open. She picked up Anna with her as she got out of the car. She barely remembered to shut her car door. She took the stairs two at a time.

Carley was out of breath when she finally opened the motel room. She shut the door behind her, locked it, and leaned against it. She wondered if Demitri was close behind her. She bolted the door and knelt in front of Anna. Anna was shaking. Her face was white with fear.

Carley noticed her own hands shaking as she reached out to take Anna's little shoulders in her hands. She attempted a fake smile but failed.

"Anna Banana, we're going to play hide and seek. You are the best hider in the whole world. Remember? Remember you're a ninja?"

Anna nodded with big, scared eyes.

"Okay, you're going to hide and no matter what you hear, don't come out for nothin,' okay? Even if you get scared or you want to help me. The only way to win is to not come out. You can't make a sound. No matter what. Promise me?" Carley was trying to keep her voice quiet. She couldn't control the wobble she heard.

Anna nodded again.

"Promise. Say it!" Carley commanded.

"I promise," Anna started to cry.

"No, no, none of that," Carley tilted her head up and looked into Anna's eyes. "Ninjas are brave. Ninjas don't cry."

"Okay, mommy."

Carley started looking around the room. It was a tiny room with not a lot to choose from. She threw open the door to a cedar wardrobe. It seemed like such an obvious place. But maybe if she covered Anna up.

Carley could hear sudden footsteps. It sounded like they were running.

Carley lifted Anna into the wardrobe. She picked up a blanket and an extra pillow with one hand. Anna curled up into a little ball.

"Lay down, baby, hurry!" she whispered. She covered her up with the blanket.

Something loud and hard slammed against the door. Anna whimpered.

Carley put a finger to her mouth. She put the blanket over Anna's head. Anna's face peeked out just enough to breathe. Carley shut the wardrobe door.

The door to the motel room flew open violently. Demitri Abbott was standing in the door, a gun pointed into the room. Carley froze in fear.

Carley gasped. "How did you—"

"I put a tracker on your phone," he snarled with pride in his eyes. "It was easy to close the distance. And anyone will talk with a gun to their head, even your loyal friend at the front desk. Took two seconds to for her to spit out your room number." From the way he burst through the door, Carley would have guessed he'd kicked the door having put his whole-body weight behind it.

That wasn't what scared Carley the most. It was Demitri's appearance. His dark hair was wild. His muscles were swollen like he'd just had a good workout. His veins were bulging in his arms. But his eyes were truly terrifying. He looked at her with those black, enlarged pupils like he didn't know her.

He paused only a minute before he was in the room. He caught Carley quickly under her chin and against her throat. He lifted her up off the ground. He pinned her to the wall that was a few feet behind her.

Carley couldn't breathe. All air seemed to have left her. He was cutting off her air supply.

"Where's the safe?" Demitri yelled at her.

Carley's feet were off the ground. She weakly tried hitting his hand. It did no good. She was starting to see stars. "I can't," she desperately tried to croak out but couldn't answer his question.

"I can't hear you!" Demitri screamed in her face.

Carley felt her eyes roll back in her head and she saw only black for a half a second.

Demitri released her. She fell straight from that height to the floor. Her bottom instantly stung from the impact. She gasped deeply for air. Then Demitri was in her face again.

"Where's the safe, Carla?" he slapped her across the face.

"I dunno," Carley tried to focus on his word but really, she thought she might pass out.

Demitri pulled out a gun. He pressed it into Carley's gut. Carley groaned. He had it pressed right up into her stomach.

"The safe, Carla. The safe in the study. Where at in the study?" Now Demitri hissed the words. His head tilted in a sharp, hawkish movement.

He took her silence as refusal. But really, Carley was having a hard time breathing again.

"If you don't tell me, I'll find your daughter and kill her." He smiled. His smile curled up into a sneer. "She might even be in this room."

Carley panicked, feeling sure he was about to start looking.

"There's a fake wooden panel that looks like the wall behind my computer desk. The wall rolls away and the safe is inside." Carley took solace in knowing he wouldn't have the numbers to the safe.

"Clever, girl," he said. "There, was that so hard?"

Sirens sounded in the distance.

"That's my cue to leave," Demitri said. With the gun still pressed firmly to Carley's stomach, Demitri pulled the trigger. He ran from the room, not even bothering to close the door.

Pain radiated from the center of Carley's body and slowly traveled to every limb, up her neck, and to her brain which began to shut down. She closed her eyes. She would just rest a minute. The excruciating pain that radiated through her began to numb her from the inside out. She felt ice cold and the feeling spread from the middle of her body to her veins. She lay unable to move, so great was the pain.

Then she heard a familiar voice. She tried hard to open her eyes. How long had she been out?

"Carley?" It was Stephen Wilton. His voice sounded far away. "Carley, hold on! We're gonna get you to a hospital. Just hold on. We need an EMT in here."

Who was Stephen talking to?

She felt sudden pressure on her abdomen. She heard Stephen curse. She felt so very sleepy. But something important rolled around her head. It was a thought. It was eluding her. Then with a burst of clarity, she breathed her last words.

"I'm sorry. Tell Paige… I'm sorry."

Then Carley died.

69

STEPHEN

FIVE MONTHS GONE

Stephen was sobbing. He could hear his grief come out first as a gasp, then as a sob. Carley wasn't breathing. Her pulse was gone. Dark blood was pouring out of her body. The bullet had gone straight through her, damaging a vital organ in a way that was unfixable. Not everyone was as lucky as he had been and had the ability to survive a major gunshot wound.

Stephen wrapped Carley in his arms and clung to her.

"Nooo…" he cried.

"Sir?" someone tapped him on the shoulder.

Stephen looked up and focused on the EMT worker through his tears. "She's gone," he told her.

"Sir, you need to step back and let us examine her," the woman insisted.

Before Stephen could answer, he heard his deputy director's voice in the room somewhere.

Someone had found a light which flooded into the room. Stephen looked up to see a room of four people looking at him in question.

He gently released Carley and got up off the floor. He

backed away, unaware of what he must look like with Carley's blood staining his shirt.

"Stephen Wilton?" Deputy director, Rob, said his name sharply and with question in his tone.

Before he could answer, Stephen heard a small voice.

"Daddy?"

The room went silent.

The wardrobe door swung open and a little girl with curly, frizzy blond hair peeked at them from under a blanket.

"Anna!" Stephen covered the distance between him and his daughter in less than three steps. He pulled Anna out of the wardrobe and clung to her. She threw her arms around him and squeezed tightly.

"Anna, I'm here. Daddy's here," Stephen whispered. "I'm never going to let anyone take you away again. Are you okay?"

Anna's whole body shook. Stephen quickly walked out of the room so she couldn't see Carley.

Rob followed Stephen out. "You wanna tell me what the hell is going on, Wilton?" he asked sharply.

Anna started to cry.

Stephen shot him a dirty look.

Rob looked apologetic.

"This is my daughter, Anna. She's been missing for five months."

70

PAIGE

FIVE MONTHS GONE

It was a beautiful spring day in April. The sun, which had been radiant and warm all day now cast an orange glow across the freshly cut green grass. James had a gazebo delivered earlier so we could have the wedding in our back yard.

As I opened the back door and stepped out, the wedding guests stood. Non-traditional music began to play from a music app. The song was nostalgic and the lyrics sang about coming home. It said everything I'd been feeling in my heart since James had walked back in my life for the second time via a fateful trip to the grocery store.

There was a white runner from the backdoor straight down the aisle of my little cabin home to the gazebo James had bought. Someone, most likely James, had thrown down rose petals on the runner. Molly was standing next to James.

I paused at the top of the step to see a small handful of people sitting on folding chairs in the backyard on either side of the white runner that formed an aisle down the middle of the backyard. I waited a good minute there on the back porch before I descended the steps.

I could see James' parents, Mike and Mona Friesen, standing

on the groom's side. Stephen's parents, Bruce and Linda Wilton, stood on the bride's side. Amy, my friend from recovery group, along with her new husband, stood smiling expectantly at me. Brandi Burnett was standing next to Sandra Stockman. They must have come together. Three people from my vet office stood together on the back row.

Stephen Wilton was not in attendance. While I'd expected that, I did feel disappointed. Though we weren't meant to be together, I still felt we were meant to be in each other's lives.

I could not have asked for better weather. It was my favorite time of day, the four o'clock golden hour. The guests glowed with natural lighting. As beautiful as it was, I knew the photographer I'd hired would fail to capture it as I remembered it. No picture could do that natural lighting justice. I felt thankful to the God who I was beginning to discover. He was the God of nature who had painted a colorful sunset in the sky for me on my wedding day. In front of the beautiful cedar-stained gazebo stood the pastor James and I had hired. We had counseled with him for the past month. Beside the pastor stood James.

James looked dashing in his black modern-cut suit with his red tie. His black curls had grown out a bit and almost came to the top of his ears. It looked the way it did when I first met him. His blue eyes sparkled in the remaining light of day. Then I realized, they weren't sparkling. They were misted with tears. James was crying. I knew what he saw as he stood there looking at me.

I had found a wedding gown that fit snuggly around my chest but fell loosely over my waist, which was already starting to expand. It flowed to my ankles where I had chosen to wear ballet slippers, knowing how dangerous high heels might be for me. My hair fell in loose curls down my back. My makeup was exactly the way my friend, Mina, from Canada, had taught me to wear it. It was the way I wore it when I first met James.

I took careful steps down the stairs and onto the white

runner. I held a bouquet of red roses James had gifted me. I had no one to walk me down the aisle. I was oddly at peace with that. I felt it signified I was strong and independent enough to make choices for myself.

After what seemed like an eternity of walking slowly and making grateful eye contact with all my guests, I was beside James. I placed the roses in a vase that was sitting on a bench in the gazebo. James took my hands in his and gazed into my eyes.

"Beautiful," he whispered.

My heart felt warm and full of love.

The ceremony was over quick. I barely acknowledged the pastor's words until it came time for the important part.

"I do," said James.

"I do," I said.

"You may now kiss the bride—"

Only, James didn't kiss me. He stood staring dumbstruck as a collective gasp rose from the small crowd. First, I noticed that no one was looking at us anymore. Then I noticed they were looking at something behind me. I turned and everything began to move in slow motion.

Stephen Wilton was walking into the backyard holding the hand of a beautiful, blond, curly-haired, blue-eyed angel of a child who resembled the picture of the little girl I had not seen in person for over two years.

"Anna," I breathed. My feet were moving, then they were running, then I was kneeling on the ground, oblivious to the grass stains that instantly formed on my dress.

Anna took a few steps behind her dad's legs and shyly peeked out.

"Are you my mama?" she asked.

I nodded. Tears streamed down my face. Could this be real?

"Dear God, beautiful little girl, I've missed you so much!" I said as I held my hands out.

Anna took a step around her dad hesitantly.

"It's okay, Anna," I heard Stephen say from somewhere overhead.

It was so hard to be patient and wait for her to come to me. I wanted to crush her in my arms, run away with her, and never let her go again. Finally, she took a few more steps and stopped in front of me.

"Can I hug you?" I asked.

Anna paused and then nodded. It was all the invitation I needed. I folded her into my arms and gently rocked back and forth with her. She was stiff at first but eventually, Anna hugged me back.

Suddenly, James was beside me, kneeling down.

"Hi, princess," he said with tears streaming down his face.

It didn't occur to me that this attention might overwhelm Anna or that it might be too much too fast. I did notice Anna was quiet and looking rather shy. I chose a distraction. I felt happy the wedding was small and intimate.

"Okay, everyone, who wants cake?" I asked in a loud, cheerful voice. James did not leave Anna's side. He scooped Anna up and Anna put her arms around his neck.

I walked to the small table set up to the side of the ceremony and found myself beside James.

"You two are picking up where you left off," I smiled, feeling emotional to see them together again.

"Well, I doubt she remembers me," James said. "I just have one of those super trustworthy faces."

"Oh, is that it?" I laughed. "Anna, do you like cake?"

She shyly snuggled her head into James' neck but nodded.

The crowd had gathered to watch as I fed cake to both James and Anna. With cake all served up and on our plates, I looked around to see that everyone was eating and talking.

That's when I saw Stephen leaving the party. He couldn't leave yet. I had so many questions.

"Stephen?" I jogged up to him when he paused walking. "What happened? Where did you find her? Is Carley in jail?"

"I want to answer those questions in depth, and I will, but right now doesn't seem like the best time. Not to mention, I'm exhausted, it's been a long night, and I really need some sleep. Yes, Carley had Anna. Demitri Abbott killed Carley. So no, she won't be going to jail."

"You found Anna last night? Why didn't you tell me the minute you found her?" I tried to keep my tone neutral, but I felt surprised.

"It happened late last night. Past one in the morning. I took her straight to the hospital and they kept her all-night running tests. I texted you when we got home. We crashed for a few hours. I had to notify the authorities and cancel the Amber Alert. Then we came here."

"Oh!" I didn't even know where my phone was right now. I hadn't seen it all day which is how I'd missed that. I had been busy with the last-minute decorations and details that seemed to fall through. It wasn't Stephen's fault I didn't know sooner. It was mine. "I'm just glad she's here. Won't you come have a piece of cake? Say *hi* to your parents?"

"I don't know, Paige. I've still got a bad guy out there to catch."

"Please, it would mean a lot to have you here," I reached for his hand.

Reluctantly, Stephen accepted and walked over with me to James and Anna.

James stuck out a free hand. "There's the hero of the hour! You did it, man! You found her."

Stephen accepted James' hand and smiled. It was a sad smile. It was then that I saw how puffy Stephen's face looked. I knew in that moment, he had watched Carley, a woman he had once loved, die. He had most likely experienced those emotions of loss over her for a second time.

Stephen hugged his parents for a quick *hello*, but I could tell his energy was waning.

"Thank you, Stephen. Thank you for bringing our girl home," I said.

Stephen's eyes softened and he leaned forward to hug me. Then he kissed me on the cheek. "You look beautiful, Paige. Enjoy your special day. You deserve to be happy. I'm going to grab some sleep."

I nodded.

Stephen turned to Anna. "I'll be back tomorrow. You be good for your mama?"

"Okay," Anna agreed.

Then I watched him walk away. Stephen deserved to be happy too. Someday, I knew, he'd find his perfect match.

I brought my attention back to the party. Anna was now sitting on a chair beside her grandmother, Linda Wilton, and swinging her legs while she ate her cake. I found James and sat down beside him. I meshed his fingers together with mine, admiring the beautiful wedding ring he had put on my finger. Together, we watched Anna. She was really here. Anna was home.

James pointed upward.

"She's God's gift," I said. "The perfect ending to a perfect day."

Then James kissed the bride.

THE END

If you liked *Dawn That Breaks*, check out book 5 in the series—WHAT COMES AFTER DAWN.

PROLOGUE
Mina

The mangled dead body lay on a cold, steel slab at the morgue. She knew the temperature could not be higher than a frigid forty degrees Fahrenheit. She was wrapped in a long black peacoat, so she didn't feel the cold. The dimly lit room was sterile and held the vibe of a hospital room, save the lifeless corpse that lay in front of her. Morgues didn't bother her. She had always been able to view a body without emotion. Until today.

A single light bulb in the middle of the room flickered.

"Creepy," she acknowledged while looking up, but not even that creeped her out. She turned her attention back to the reason she was in the morgue.

He was uncovered. She could see that his right kneecap was grotesquely swollen and misplaced. The lower half of the leg was bent and twisted up next to his body at an unnatural angle. At first, she viewed him in the same emotionless, clinical way she had viewed other bodies in the past. As a former crime analyst, it had been necessary to assess a body here and there for clues others might have missed.

Several bones were broken to enable his leg to twist the way it did. His neck was positioned at an odd angle. One arm dangled lifelessly over the side of the table. She chose not to look at the back of his skull. His skull was the place where he'd received the most damage. His head had likely bounced off the pavement after impact. Bruises and swelling made his face almost impossible to identify. Almost.

But she'd know him anywhere. He was fit for his age. He

was an older man, but this had only made him more attractive to her. His arms showed muscle tone. His stomach was flat. His physical appearance never mattered to her much, though. All that mattered now was this was the body of her one true love.

Mina Martin, formerly a crime analyst at the Police Services of Winnipeg, now lovingly covered Ludwig Lacose's body with a sheet. No one should have to see him like that. No one should remember him this way.

She preferred to remember that final night of his life. The last night she'd spent with him. When he'd finally seen her. Seen her as a woman with all her love to give. All coldness melted away and the tears leaked from her eyes and down her face. She covered her mouth and screamed in silence. Some morticians had a habit of hovering. She was thankful this one— Morty, she had nicknamed him—had left her alone while she "examined the body."

Mina Martin no longer worked at the police services—far from it. But Morty didn't know that. Not yet. They'd kept Mina active and listed her as *on leave* in hopes that she would return. She no longer played for the good team. She was an outlaw, a fugitive from justice, who had chosen love only to align herself in life with a star-crossed lover.

The mission was doomed from the start. She wished she had calculated that possibility. If she could rewind time, she'd beg him not to go. Or better yet, to take her with him. She would've killed his murderer without a second glance. Then they would have ridden off into the sunset to live happily ever after, or some other cliché that didn't leave her lover dead at the end of the story.

Before she covered the face of her beloved, she leaned over and kissed his rigid blue lips. She heard a noise behind her. She straightened, quickly wiped her tears, and jammed a pair of oversized sunglasses on her face.

"He's really not breathing," she tried to joke lightly as they sometimes did in this business. Had they seen her kiss him? Her pulse sped at the thought. She turned slowly with a sad half-smile on her face. The mortician was standing with a middle-aged blond woman, who looked like she had once been pretty. Now she carried about thirty extra pounds around her mid-section, and her face sagged a little.

Mina stifled a gasp, not only at her poor timing with her morbid joke, but at the fact that his wife now stood in the room with her. With them. His wife was the third wheel.

She doesn't belong here with us, Mina thought protectively, fighting the urge to order her out of the room.

Summoning every ounce of professionalism she possessed, Mina put her shoulders back and walked forward. She paused in front of the wife. Mina spontaneously grabbed her hand. For one moment, Mina identified acutely with the wife's pain. As she looked into her eyes, Mina knew his wife did not know about her.

"Becky, I'm so sorry for your loss," Mina said quietly.

Becky Lacose stiffly nodded. Her face was white. Her eyes kept straying just beyond Mina. To Lacose. Mina released her hand and walked out the door.

His wife and the mortician were none the wiser. Mina had no right to be there. She had no claim to that man. No position of authority that would make anyone open the door and let her in. But they did. From that realization, an idea began to form.

She got into her car and stared at nothing in front of her for minutes. Then Mina lay her head on the steering wheel, remembering the night she'd learned of his death, and cried.

Had it really been twenty-four hours since Mina Martin laid sobbing on the cold tile floor in his kitchen? She had been too weak to get up and go to bed. She had been too tired to care. She had been too heartbroken to feel the cold floor under her. She had been painfully aware she was utterly alone. Again.

One minute, she'd been looking around for a bottle of

champagne to celebrate a victory and the impending return of her lover.

The next minute, Mina had been crushed by the news of his death. The news that had come as a text from a former coworker who thought Mina would celebrate the death of that *vile serial killer*, Ludwig Lacose. He—her love—was dead. Murdered. Pushed violently. He'd plummeted out of a five-story window. *Paige* had murdered him. Paige had changed everything from the day she'd started working at the police services.

Nothing could have saved him. No one, not even Mina, could have kept him alive despite her advanced tech skills, her creative problem solving, and her newly kindled love for him. He'd been on a suicide mission from the beginning. No one could have kept him safe. Least of all Mina. She understood that now. The mission was doomed to fail from the beginning. All because Paige had stepped in to ruin their lives.

Doom, doom, doom, Mina had droned on to herself while lying on that floor, her tears momentarily subsiding. She had made a small salt-water puddle on the floor next to her head. When she'd been with him, she'd had purpose. Her life had held meaning. In such a short time, he had become her everything. Now that he was dead, she wanted to die along with him.

She could die. Or she could kill his murderer. It was all her fault. That nasty little traitor had betrayed them all and changed the course of Mina's life forever. Paige Mynart had taken the one person who had been precious to Mina. Because of Paige, Mina's love was dead.

What do I do now? Mina had whimpered aloud as she looked up at the ceiling. It was his ceiling in his apartment, which was his secret lair, nestled in a forgotten corner of an apartment building.

The rest of Lacose's team was dead too. Every one of them had been killed on that mission. The darkness of night surrounded the silence that echoed in her ears.

Get up, a male voice had finally answered. The voice was as clear as the last time he'd spoken to Mina. *Finish the plan.*

Darling? Mina had sat up suddenly, her heart fluttering with hope. She'd peered into the night. She couldn't see him, but she felt his presence as if he were standing in the room with her.

You are my clever minx, and this floor is beneath you, he'd said in a strong, commanding voice.

Mina had giggled. *Of course the floor is beneath me! Who's clever now?*

Go to bed, Mina, he'd said. *You have a long day of planning ahead of you.*

I do? Mina was on her feet now. She peered into the black apartment. Though she still couldn't see him, she had obeyed him. She'd gotten up. But she hadn't gone to her own room, she'd gone to his. She lay down in his big, warm bed and remembered the last time they were together. She could almost feel his strong arms around her.

There, as she fell asleep in his bed, she knew she would move forward with a new emotion in place of sadness in order to function. Anger. Anger would be her new companion. Anger would help Mina come up with a new plan and a new purpose.

Now, sitting in her car, she lifted her head, wiped her eyes, and turned the car key in the ignition. It would be a very long time before Mina would recover from the pain and heart-wrenching grief over losing him. But she'd mourn later. Right now, she needed to focus.

After all, it was only a matter of time before someone Paige treasured fell into her petite hands. Mina would be there to scoop up the object of Paige's love and destroy him the way Paige had destroyed Mina's lover. All Mina had to do was wait for an opportunity. Or create one.

REVIEW REQUEST

If you enjoyed this book, I would be extremely grateful if you would leave a brief review on the store site where you purchased your book or on Goodreads. Your review helps fellow readers know what to expect when they read this book.

~ Addison Michael

ALSO BY ADDISON MICHAEL

A Mynart Mystery Thriller series is ghostly suspense with psychological elements. Tap the links to buy these books today!

Book 1 - *What Comes Before Dawn* - A tragic death too close to home. A young woman seeking answers. But will the truth prove fatal?

Book 2 - *Dawn That Brings Death* - Two men are dead at the Mynart Murder House. Paige, a newly single mom, is hiding in Canada. Will she be able to keep her daughter safe when a new enemy emerges?

Book 3 - *Truth That Dawns* - When Paige's secrets are exposed, she must face the consequences including a serial killer looking for revenge. He'll stop at nothing. Will Paige live to see her daughter again?

Book 5 - *What Comes After Dawn* - Soon-to-be father James is on his way to a business meeting when he's kidnapped with no way out. James soon realizes he's being used as a pawn in a game of revenge that may cost him his life.

The Other AJ Hartford - A phantom on a train. A mysterious kidnapping long ago. Can she connect the dots before all her futures disappear forever? If you like good-hearted heroines, ghostly phenomena, and nail-biting high stakes, then you'll love Addison Michael's mind-blowing adventure. Tap the link to buy the book today!

Join the Addison Michael Newsletter and receive the FREE story *How it Began*. Plus, receive alerts for new releases, FREE and ON SALE books, and what's new.

ABOUT THE AUTHOR

Addison Michael writes riveting, character-driven stories heavy in suspense with a focus on the intriguing motivations that make a person a murderer.

Addison grew up in a home where rules were not meant to be broken. As such, she was the "goodest" of the "goody two shoes" around. Being the oldest of six siblings forced Addison to lead by example. Her golden reputation solidified well into her thirties.

But every good girl needs to have an outlet. Behind every smile and sweet comment, there is a dark side waiting to emerge. Addison Michael found the outlet for her dark side writing thrillers. She has an uncanny ability to step outside herself and create believable characters who navigate unbelievable circumstances involving murder, mystery, secrets, and suspense.

Made in United States
Orlando, FL
07 March 2024

44496659R00192